Dedication

Dedicated to the bright lights I know; may you all continue to shine in the darkness.

Chapter One

ONE OF THE worst days in Sarah Goldman's life to this point started out well.

It was her responsibility as vice chair for the Hollowville Hanukkah festival to attend some of the closed-door meetings of the village Board of Trustees. Usually it was a mere formality—sharing updates, getting good bits of information. And that's how it began. She was able to tell the board how some village business owners had signed up to advertise in the Hanukkah festival journal, and get a few more commitments.

Except the trustee who had joined the board in a snap election held in the strangest fashion raised his flannel-clad arm, fingers as pale as ice waving back and forth.

"The Chair recognizes Trustee Gregory Webster."

"Thank you, Mister Chair, and Miss Goldman. You know," the trustee had said, "this Hanukkah stuff is wonderful, but I'm feeling like we need a change. If we want to include the whole village, even the whole community, we need to turn this into a 'holiday' festival next year. And invite Santa Claus."

And despite all of the enthusiasm the board of trustees had expressed only seconds before, Hanukkah suddenly became an afterthought, lost in the excitement of plans and thoughts for next year.

It had taken every bit of restraint Sarah had not to scream about how taking away a celebration wasn't inclusive, not to mention that turning Hollowville's festival into a carbon cookie-cutter copy of every single 'holiday' celebration that existed wasn't going to make people want to come to Hollowville.

Because Sarah knew how that went. In that context, the word 'holiday' wasn't generic. It didn't refer to Diwali or Eid, and it didn't refer to any of the other religious holidays celebrated during December. It especially didn't refer to Hanukkah. In that context, with the added Santa Claus, 'holiday' meant Christmas.

But nobody would listen to her.

So she sat, held her breath, and waited until the meeting with the board of trustees was over before trying to talk to the mayor. Mayor Erlichman had known her since she was little. He had been her father's friend on the school board.

"So what's going on?" he'd asked, white skin showing hints of red as he furrowed his brow.

She'd decided to be blunt. "What can we do, on the festival committee, to make sure that the festival remains Hanukkah-centric?"

The mayor sighed, and the expression on his face wasn't pretty.

"It's all about the numbers," he said, rubbing his beard with his palm. "You need to make this huge. We need to be on the map for these people to believe that Hanukkah is and should be our focus."

She nodded. "In other words, our campaign needs to be 'Hollowville is Hanukkah.'"

The smile that brightened the mayor's face was answer enough. "That would help. As well as the profit coming in to justify the expense."

And with what amounted to her marching orders in hand, she'd left the meeting and headed to the park between the library and the bookstore. She sat on a bench in the middle of the park, and tried to figure out what to do. How to turn their small town Hanukkah festival into something bigger. Better. More.

It would, she decided, take a miracle.

BUT SHE DIDN'T find it at the festival committee meeting that night. Upon passing the information she'd learned on to the rest of the committee, one of the committee members, Judith Goldberger, wondered, "Why not make it a 'holiday' festival?"

Holiday.

That word again.

She tried to breathe and bank the fire that wanted to erupt from her ears.

The festival had been born from a small temple bazaar ten years before. It eclipsed the small temple's space after three years, continuing to grow like a miracle out of the famous Hanukkah story for seven years until it filled the whole central area of the town.

And yet.

Through all of that time, it stayed true to its origins, even as more of the town residents participated.

Those who celebrated Hanukkah shared their customs with the ones who didn't. Children sang Hanukkah songs, merchants sold silly Hanukkah sweaters, people raced in dreidel costumes across the open ice, and they shared joy along with crispy latkes and sweet soofganiyot.

Hollowville needed a Hanukkah festival. Because it wasn't just a festival. It was a sign of acceptance, of support in difficult times.

And she was going to do her best to make sure it had one. "I—"

Chana Levitan, the committee chair, put up her hand, exasperation clear in her eyes, her normally olive skin pale with anger. As the committee came to silence, Sarah held her breath.

"This isn't a holiday festival," Chana proclaimed in her best chair-of-the-committee voice.

"But," Judith continued, "we owe it to the community to—"

"We owe our gratitude to the community for letting us

use more of the town proper to stage the festival, for sure. But we are *not* putting on a holiday festival," Chana continued. "We're putting on a Hanukkah festival."

"But we're not making enough money as a Hanukkah festival," said Jack Lewis, a city finance guy and also a new member of the committee, his nose pink with either alcohol or frustration. She couldn't tell which. "We need to cut our losses and let other people do this."

"What kind of advertising have we been doing?" Sarah wondered. "Where's our social media? Where is our outreach? Newspapers? Where's our webpage? Why haven't we been doing anything to tell people about us?"

There was silence.

"Good point, Sarah," Chana said, smiling as she opened a file on her tablet and started to page through it. "Looking at last year's attendance records, we discovered that we'd started to get traffic from outside Hollowville. Tiny little local newspapers, a few patches and things. And the *Empire Daily*?"

Yep. She made a note to ask her best friend Anna, who was an assistant curator at a museum in Manhattan, for a list of the journalists and critics she trusted. If they weren't capable of covering the festival, they'd know someone who would be.

"But that was it," Chana said, finishing her answer. "Yet the bottom line is that Hanukkah is our identity," Chana's eyes rested on the members of the committee. "It's our past, it's our future, and it's definitely our present."

"So," Sarah said. "That's where we start. We have an identity. We use that to create a cohesive and clear social media and advertising campaign. We also need to create a press kit, send releases out."

"We also don't have a logo," Shelly Averman, a long-time committee member, pointed out. "I used to be in advertising and I can absolutely help with the releases and things. Shake a few of my old contacts. Not so good at the social media. But what I do remember," the older woman continued, tapping a white finger against the table in front of her, "is that we need a logo and a slogan."

"Slogan is obvious," Jack Lewis said with a smile.

Sarah nodded. She'd even said it to the mayor. But they needed to say it out loud. "Hollowville is Hanukkah."

And suddenly there were cheers in the room.

"Still no logo," Judith Goldberger pointed out, pink lips pursed in distaste on her pale face.

"I should think that's obvious too," Sarah added. "A menorah, of course. And we need a large one to light in the middle of town."

"So we're finding someone to design a logo," Shelly Averman said, "and we also need a sculptor for the menorah."

"But," Chana said excitedly, "we have a direction and a slogan, someone to create press releases, and we're going to do our best to pull off a miracle."

Chapter Two

THE MUSEUM HER best friend worked at was in SoHo, the part of Manhattan that confused her the most, and so Sarah found herself staring at her phone for directions as she walked along the streets. The invitation had come soon after she'd told her best friend about the meeting with the board of trustees, and the sudden need for both a logo and a sculpture.

"It's been a while since you've been able to visit me here," Anna Cohen said, full of disapproval as they embraced just outside the building.

"I'm so sorry." Sarah stuffed her hands in the pockets of her sweater, trying to do something that didn't scream she was embarrassed. "Things have been wild, both at work and with the festival, and I just don't know what to do with myself," she confessed.

"Well," Anna said, a smile highlighting the olive undertones in her skin, "I'm glad you're here and I also think I might be able to help you."

"How?"

"First of all you need some girl time."

Which was right.

"Second," her best friend continued, "one of my colleagues put this exhibit together and I think it might help you."

Not needing any further preamble, she followed her friend into the museum.

They stopped briefly at the desk, Anna flashing her badge and getting a sticker for Sarah to place on her cardigan.

But instead of paying attention to what Anna was doing, Sarah found herself staring at the illuminated manuscript just beyond the entrance.

"Maybe this might give you some ideas for a logo?"

Sarah laughed. "Inspired by history is good, but I'm not sure any of the writing in the manuscript will work in a logo. Inspiration is totally fine though." But she stared nonetheless, looking at the different types of lettering the illuminated manuscript on the wall showcased.

Soon after, she felt a tap on her shoulder. "Ready to go?"

Sarah nodded. "To the other exhibits, for sure."

Anna grinned. "Excellent. Because there's one you definitely need to see..."

She knew Anna well enough to trust her judgment. They headed up the stairs to the second floor, passing old photos and a description of Jewish history in New York.

As they headed deeper into the museum, they stopped in front of a glass door. There was...something in there.

"Go," Anna said, staring at her phone, her nose scrunched up in a way Sarah recognized. "It's in there. I have to take care of something."

And knowing her friend was at work, and still had responsibilities, she followed instructions, opening the door and stepping into a multicolored garden of metal.

ISAAC LIEBERMAN SAW her out of the corner of his eye. Rather, he heard the excited exhalation after the click of footsteps against the tile floor.

That's when he turned; she was shorter than he was, though it didn't take much considering his height. She had pink undertones in her pale skin with a few random freckles on her arms, and intense brown hair which looked as if it had been flattened within an inch of its life.

But her smile?

That was something he'd like to draw.

"Like what you see?" he asked.

"Yes," she said, as if she couldn't get any more excitement in the word. She turned, and he watched the pink blush shade her face. "I mean…"

He smiled, gesturing to the sculptures. "I love the technique. It's so abstract…"

"It reminds me of menorahs," she said, the words rolling off her tongue and making her seem even more excited.

"There's something about these pieces that make me think of Hanukkah and menorahs."

He laughed. "They're bright, sure, and I can see the outline of the shape in the metal." He gestured toward one of the pieces and the way the sculptor had soldered flowers and hearts on it. "I don't think I'd put all of those bits on a menorah though. I think a menorah needs to be the focus of something, not a frame for other things."

He could see skepticism in those green eyes of hers. "So you don't like it?"

He shook his head. "I do, actually. I like it as it is, as a canvas, as a whole piece. As an example of technique. As a sculpture. But not as a menorah."

He liked watching her take in the information, the way her skepticism turned to understanding. "I see," she finally said. "So you're the basic menorah type? Small, window, candles?"

He laughed. "Well, yeah, especially when you're with your family, celebrating Hanukkah the way it should be celebrated. Easier to see that small menorah that way."

She smiled briefly before the laugh erupted from her mouth, altering the lines of her face and making her eyes sparkle. "Well then," she said, shaking her head. "I see that despite how handsome you are, there's no hope for you."

"No hope for me?"

She nodded. "Yep. You're a Hanukkah snob."

"SO YOU CALLED him a Hanukkah snob, didn't ask his name, and didn't get his information?"

Sarah nodded and took a drink of her soda. The Colombian restaurant was supposed to be fantastic and her favorite food was on the menu. Dinner was going to be perfect as long as her best friend managed to get through the meal without raking her over the coals about the conversation she had with the hot guy and his weird opinions. "Yep. That's about it."

Anna stared at her. "I can't believe you."

"What do you mean?"

"You find a dude you arguably think is hot, you're with him in a sculpture gallery, you guys are having a good conversation, you don't like one thing he says and so you call him a snob and then leave?"

"I thought we went over that part already. We don't have to go over it again, Anna."

"Yes, we do. Because you need to get your head out of the soofganiyot-laced fantasy world you're in and come back to reality."

"I don't know what you mean."

"Life sucks for everybody. We have good parts and bad parts and we deal with it, but we all need to move on. Just because your last relationship…"

"And the one before that and the one before that and the

one before that. Did I tell you the one about the guy who showed up in just a Christmas stocking?"

Anna rolled her eyes, and Sarah found herself reaching up to rub hers. She wasn't going to start crying again over bad dates and horrible choices.

"You did," her friend said, exasperated, "and all of the disastrous bad dates you've been on have turned into bricks in a wall you've built around yourself. You need to stop hiding, Sarah."

"I'm not hiding," she informed her best friend. "I'm working at the bookstore, and the library, and doing the festival this year."

"Armor, Sarah. All of it, armor. But you have to open yourself up to something…to love or even friendship."

"Oh come on, like you should be lecturing me."

There was something painful in Anna's eyes.

"You okay?" Sarah asked.

"I'm fine. Just thinking about things. The most important thing is that you can't close the door on love or dating because it's not comfortable. Promise me you'll try."

Trying was possible. If circumstances were right, she'd try. And so she nodded her head and took her friend's outstretched hand. "I'll try."

Anna nodded. "Good. Now we order."

Chapter Three

ON TUESDAY, SARAH found herself back on the park bench that separated the library and the bookstore. She had five minutes to breathe, and enjoying nature and a coffee on a spring day was her lunch break of choice.

Day jobs and work events and a festival dilemma she still couldn't solve were going to end her life before she reached her next decade. And watching the Hanukkah parody of a Christmas song yet again didn't help.

"Well, hello, Sarah. Enjoying this wonderful spring afternoon?"

She looked up to see a familiar face. Elsa Lieberman ran Hollowville Hebrew Centers' sisterhood, and Sarah had known the older woman since she was in kindergarten. "Hi, Mrs. Lieberman," she said, trying to put a cheerful note in her voice.

"What? What is wrong, *mamaleh*?"

Once Elsa Lieberman's little girl, always Elsa Lieberman's little girl. "Trying to solve a problem."

"What kind of problem?" Mrs. L. asked. "What have those *fakakta* trustees done now? As if it wasn't enough that they're stopping the festival. The nerve of them. Do you know we're going to picket city hall?"

Wait. "What?!"

"So the sisterhood has decided, as part of our *tikkun olam* program, that we're going to stand up for the festival in Hollowville. They're calling in an expert to teach the history of social activism and then we're going to protest as a final exam. So many people have forgotten our history and so we have to learn it again."

All she could hear was *protest for the festival.* And that was the last thing she needed. "I don't think we have to go that far, Mrs. L…"

"Oh we're not protesting tomorrow, *mamaleh*," she said, gazing over the rims of her bright pink tortoiseshell glasses, which did a great job in highlighting the pink undertones in the beige of her skin. "We're protesting later in the year. We still have to find our educator. But what would help you now?"

"So we've decided that the town needs a menorah. A large one. A menorah big enough to fit in the town square."

"I love this," the older woman gushed, her eyes sparkling. Mrs. Lieberman's smile warmed Sarah's heart. "So bright during the dark months of winter. And yes. It's perfect. We can place it in the center of the town, next to the tree. Make it beautiful and bring it out each year. It's a beautiful idea."

"I'm so glad you think so. I've been somewhat concerned."

"Why would you be concerned?" Mrs. Lieberman wondered. "If you want to have a public celebration of Hanukkah, you need a menorah big enough for everybody to see. Frankly I'm surprised you've waited so long to see about procuring one."

"It's just been a difficult process," she admitted.

"Why? You've just started?"

Mrs. Lieberman's reply was quick, tight. Which meant Sarah had to start from the beginning. "Well you don't really need that long to figure out the problem."

"And what might that be?"

"Nobody sells large enough menorahs, which means in order to get one, we need a sculptor. Preferably one who works with a non-flammable medium. Metal is the ideal."

Mrs. L. sat comfortably, arms folded on her lap. Unchanged and practically unmoved. "And? What's the problem?"

"No sculptor we spoke to would take us on, or if they did take the commission, they won't do exactly what we want."

"Why not? That's a *shandeh*."

Shame is the least of what it is.

But she sighed, again, and tried to be more specific. "Yeah. At our quoted price, we were mostly offered snowflakes, lights, and latkes. The few sculptors who said they'd figure out a menorah ended up quoting us a price way out of our price range. So now I have no idea what to do. And I feel like I've let the committee down, the town down, and the festival is going to end because I didn't find a menorah."

Mrs. Lieberman waved a hand in her face. "That's your problem?"

Sarah nodded. "Yes, Mrs. Lieberman. Pretty insurmountable obstacle—not having a sculptor—wouldn't you say?"

The look in Mrs. L's eyes sent her right back to kindergarten. What had Sarah missed in her description of the situation?

"I don't see a problem," Mrs. Lieberman repeated.

She raised an eyebrow but tried to modulate her voice. She needed to be respectful, but it was hard. "With all due respect, which is a great deal, and with love, Mrs. Lieberman, it is. Unless you can manifest a metal sculptor out of nowhere, we're in trouble."

Mrs. Lieberman smiled.

The words were stuck, settled behind an impenetrable wall. Especially in the face of the older woman's calm, placid smile. What was hiding in her expression?

"Umm..."

"Not out of nowhere," Mrs. Lieberman finally said, "but out of my family tree."

"What? I mean..."

"My grandson Isaac—you know, my son Moshe and his wife Clara? Their son who lives like an artist in Brooklyn?"

Small town Jewish geography never failed. Ever. Someone in Hollowville always knew someone. Except it was never easy to digest the information, no matter how implausible. "Your grandson is a metal sculptor?"

Mrs. Lieberman beamed. "He is. So many commissions, so many awards, my *tateleh*. Let me talk to him and see if he can help. Because he's such a *mensch*, I think he will."

Would it be this easy to fix? But even if her Brooklyn sculptor grandson wasn't the solution, Mrs. Lieberman would deserve a medal for even asking. "Thank you, thank you, thank you."

"This is what we do for *mishpacha*," Mrs. Lieberman replied, reaching out to cup her cheek, patting her jaw with gentle fingers. "Let me feel him out, okay?"

That was an easy request to agree to. "Anything," she said. "Let me know what I can do to help you."

"Nothing," Mrs. Lieberman replied. "Just relax, *mamaleh*, and I'll let you know."

Which was both the easiest and the hardest thing to do. But for the sake of her sanity, and the festival, she'd try.

Manhattan

ONLY FOR FAMILY, but most specifically for his *bubbe*, would Isaac Lieberman brave the midweek, midtown rush hour. But *Bubbe* had wanted to try a tiny restaurant not far from Grand Central she'd heard about from friends in Hollowville. So, Isaac left his Brooklyn loft, held his breath, braced himself and stepped onto an already full-to-bursting Manhattan-bound express subway train and rode it all the way to Grand Central.

People got on and off, but Isaac found himself standing in a corner, holding on to the walls of the train for dear life. He felt like little more than a sardine as he tried his best to make himself as small as he possibly could.

He followed the wave of people off the train once the subway arrived at his stop, up the stairs and up to the grand hall of the station. His *bubbe* was already waiting near the clock at the center—their chosen meeting place—directions printed on a sheet of paper in her hand because her phone had the battery size of a flea.

When they arrived at the restaurant, appropriately named Abe's Kitchen, they were bowled over by the smell. Why had he doubted his grandmother's food intuition?

"This is delicious," Isaac proclaimed not for the first time as he took a bite of one of the matzah balls floating in the middle of his fragrant chicken soup.

"It is," she said approvingly as she sipped her soup. "Not like mine, of course."

He shook his head almost instantly. "Nope. Definitely not like yours. Yours is better—different, but better."

"Good answer, *tateleh*," she replied. "So, how are you?"

He sat back against the cushioned bench. "Fine," he replied. "Working on a few pieces for the show in June, but otherwise trying to wind down for the year."

"Isn't that early?" Concern filled his grandmother's face.

"It is," he answered. "But I'm trying to make sure I can enjoy the rest of the year. Especially Hanukkah with you. I don't want to have any work hanging over my head, so I have to start wrapping things up now."

"A good reason, yes?" She smiled, and he could see the thoughts running through her expression. "You didn't do this last year, though?"

"I didn't," he replied. "I guess because Mom and Dad's black-tie, formal, fancy, three-hundred-guest gala isn't exactly my idea of how I wanted to spend Hanukkah."

He laughed as his *bubbe* snorted. "Yes, it was nobody's idea of how to do anything. I get it."

"So," he said, bringing the conversation back to where he wanted it to go, "this year I gave myself some leeway, you know?"

"Yes, yes, *tateleh*. You want to spend Hanukkah with family, latkes sizzling on an open flame, snow in the air, sing Hanukkah songs, yes?"

He laughed, as the Hanukah parody video of a Christmas song that he'd watched earlier that morning spun through his mind. "And maybe see, for real, if dreidels can spin upside down." He paused, grinning at his bubbe. "You saw the video too?"

"Of course I saw the video," she said, laughing. "It was funny. But you, *tateleh*, let's get back to you. You think you can find this Hanukkah you dream of in Hollowville?"

"I'm not sure. What I do know is that I can find something close to it with you. In your house."

"But you know"—the excitement in *Bubbe's* eyes made him a little bit nervous—"the residents of Hollowville? We have a tradition of our own."

Nope. Nope. Nope. He didn't like where this was going, not at all. He hadn't liked the idea of commercializing the holiday when his agent had dangled offers to design special *holiday* pieces for big box stores, and he *definitely* didn't like this version of it. Even when it related to a thing *Bubbe* loved.

Which meant his answer had to be firm but gentle. He didn't want to hurt someone he loved so much, but he didn't want to create hopes only to dash them later. "*Bubbe*," he said, "I love you. But I really don't like the festival."

"*Tateleh*, you've said this before," she replied, "and I love you. But you've never said why you don't like the festival. Tell me why."

He sighed. Reasons upon reasons. So many reasons, but he needed to express one she would believe. "I don't want to turn the simple joys of Hanukkah, of candles, lights, and *mitzvot*, into something much bigger and much less festive than it should be. We're celebrating the resilience of our community, not fighting a war fueled by applesauce and sour cream."

"You know, *tateleh*," she continued, seemingly oblivious,

"our festival is a *mitzvah*. It's a way of giving back to the town and a way of sharing the joy of Hanukkah with the larger community. We no longer live in isolation. We're part of the larger world, and it would be a shame to not share with our neighbors and friends." She paused, and he could see the mischief in her eyes. "Even if they do dip their latkes in sour cream."

And as the dinner and conversation continued, one thought ran through his mind: What could he do for his *bubbe* and the town she lived in that didn't involve the festival?

Chapter Four

A FEW WEEKS later, Sarah had a playlist filled with Hanukkah songs and a plan. Shelly Averman and her publicity crew were sending out press releases to anybody and everybody, even without a logo, and Shelly had even convinced her niece to create a website and work the social media for the festival.

There were moments Sarah wanted to celebrate, and there were others where she was bombarded by nightmares of an angry Mayor Erlichman shutting the festival down despite everything they did.

But now, on a train to the city, she couldn't think about any of it. She had to be clear and confident—the strong planner and representative of Hollowville she could be. Because she was heading to an art show to meet the mysterious Isaac Lieberman.

Isaac was, in fact, as good as his *bubbe* had advertised; Mrs. L had even gone to the trouble of setting up a private meeting, but when pressed on the matter of whether her grandson would be interested in making a sculpture for the festival, Mrs. Lieberman had only said, "You need to ask him."

Which wasn't exactly encouraging, but here Sarah was anyway. Thankfully, she hadn't been in one of the train's designated quiet cars when her phone buzzed with a call from Anna.

"I think you're nuts going by yourself," said her bestie, her voice clear on the other end. "It's really not hard for me to send someone to join you."

"It's an art show." Not that she didn't like talking to Anna; it was the fact that she was repeating herself. There were texts, emails, and now this call. Sarah settled further into her seat and adjusted the phone in her hand. "I'll be fine."

The sigh was expected; why else would they be having this conversation for the third time if Anna wasn't exasperated?

"If I weren't staying late doing last-minute copyright checks on images for my boss's latest exhibition, I'd join you and drag my friend Matt along. He's obssed with sculpture and."

"Again," she said, smelling a setup a mile away, "it's an art show. I don't need cavalry, educated or otherwise. Besides, staying late could allow you to talk with your boss about your exhibit idea."

"I mean yeah, I can, but she's not entertaining that conversation until after this Gilded Age exhibit is prepped and ready to go. So doing the permissions check is good for that. But you're doing it again."

"What am I doing, exactly, aside from worrying about my friend?"

"Changing the topic back to Hanukkah festival preparation, or anything that has nothing to do with your social or emotional life the second someone else brings it up?"

Now it was her turn to sigh. "Oh, come on, Anna. Really?"

"Yes. Using Hanukkah as a way to separate yourself from the rest of the world was understandable for a few years, but now? Now that the festival is going to end…"

"Don't say that. It's not. It's going to be amazing. Hollowville is going to show that schmucky trustee that Hanukkah matters to us."

"Look," Anna said. "I love Hanukkah too. I think it's bright and gorgeous and beautiful and yes, it is important to represent the holiday these days, but…not in a way that keeps you from living your life. Hanukkah can't be your life."

But who would she be without Hanukkah, without the festival?

She'd only been involved in the planning for a year herself; the years before were spent helping her father as he planned, so it probably wouldn't be too hard to fill the space the festival would leave in her life. Maybe organize a book club, sign on to a few dating apps?

Where the guys would tell her she wasn't worth their time, or too boring, or ignore her, or cheat on her once they found someone more to their liking.

"Sarah? You there?"

"Sorry," she said staring out at the window, pulled back to reality and the directions that would take her to the meeting. "Anyway," she said, "I'll come over afterward and tell you the whole story, okay?"

There was a long pause, and Sarah tried not to hear the soft sound of her friend blowing her nose in the background. "Sure. That would be great. See you later…I'm losing you."

"Love you," she said, hoping her words would be the last thing her friend heard before the tunnel ended the call.

AS SHE GOT off the subway, Sarah used her phone to figure out where she was in SoHo, the part of Manhattan that confused her most. The area was gorgeous if she didn't actually have to be somewhere but horrible and weird when she was going somewhere specific. Thankfully, the gallery in question wasn't supposed to be far from the subway station where she'd chosen to exit.

But heat had come early to the city, and she didn't want to be completely parched and dehydrated when she walked into this meeting. So she stopped and grabbed a bottle of iced tea at the first bodega she saw. As she waved goodbye to the cashier, Sarah opened her bottle, turned toward the door, and smacked into someone, spilling all of it over…

Oh my God.

He was…

She didn't have the words or the mental capacity to process.

"Menorah lady?"

She blinked, looking way up into a pair of brown eyes, warm like melted chocolate…

"What?"

A little farther down were full lips that had molded into a smile.

"You're the lady who had all the opinions on menorahs at the museum," he clarified.

And, yes, the floppy dark hair, the tall slim build and that bright smile against that cool pale skin looked familiar. "Oh! Right." She stopped, not wanting to call him what she'd accused him of before. "I'm so sorry about—you know."

It was lame, of course, but there were a lot of things she wanted to apologize for.

"It's fine," he said. And then he gestured at the shirt he was wearing, the un-tucked, white dress shirt…with a huge brown spot on it. "Didn't want to wear this anyway, so you saved me that."

"I can pay for your dry cleaning…"

"It's okay, but I do have to go." He paused. "Are you headed somewhere? Can I walk you?"

"Actually," she said, suddenly feeling completely weird-for so many reasons, "I do have to go. I have an appointment and I'm going to be late."

The smile he gave her in return warmed her all the way to the tips of her toes. Which despite how hot it was outside, was not a bad thing in the least. "I'll make sure you get wherever you're going. That is..." He bit his lip and she melted then and there.

"That is, what?"

"If you want me to?"

She desperately needed to go and she didn't want to be late. She wasn't far from the gallery, and if he was offering, she would gladly accept. "Yes. I do want you to. Thank you. I appreciate it."

"Not a problem. So where are you going?"

She pulled her phone from her purse and looked up the address yet again. "The Vincent Gallery. On 26th between 10th and 11th."

"Oh. Right." He looked up at her again, and she wondered what he saw, or more importantly, what he was looking for. "What do you have to be there for?"

She'd worn the only pair of heels she owned, trading comfort for style, which meant she was already reaching the end of her ability to stand on the concrete sidewalk without pain. "I'm meeting someone there."

The corner of his mouth quirked up. "Strangely enough, so am I."

ISAAC WONDERED WHAT she was doing there. He desperately hoped she wasn't the person his *bubbe* had sent from Hollowville; he probably wouldn't be that lucky considering whoever she was meeting was at the gallery where his show was opening.

But she was adorable, a damsel in distress, and he couldn't help himself. "Do you know anything about this person? Is this a blind date?"

And where did that come from? Why did those words exit from his mouth like that?

She shook her head. "Nothing like that. A fact-finding mission."

He raised an eyebrow, and despite all thoughts to the contrary, he was intrigued. "Fact-finding about what? Do you mind telling me?"

If there was a word better than smile, he'd use it to describe the expression on her face. But there wasn't. "Finding out if someone would do something for a committee I'm on."

Oh no.

Danger. Danger.

He should stop, then and there, not forage any further knowing he wouldn't like the answer at the end of the quest. But he shouldn't deceive her anymore.

"I'm going to be late," she said.

He nodded, chewing on a thought. "I don't want you to be late so let's go."

Thoughts ran through his head as he led her down the sidewalk, offering his arm. She was going to murder him once she realized who he was.

"Listen," he said. "I need to tell you something."

She bit her lip. Was she nervous? "Can it wait?"

"Can I tell you that this meeting is going to go both better and worse than you think it will?"

"How do you know?"

He smiled, and then realized that they were at the door to the gallery. "Because," he said, making sure to force the words out before someone came to retrieve him, or broke the news of his identity to her before he had a chance to. "I have a strong suspicion that you're meeting with me."

"Wait…what?"

He carefully held out his hand, trying his best to dampen the force of his revelation, though he could already tell she was annoyed. "I'm Isaac Lieberman."

"So," she said, and bit her lip. "I guess you already know that I'm Sarah Goldman?"

"I do. And I'm excited to chat with you and to show you my sculptures, but I have to go." He looked hesitantly at the door. "You're going to be okay for a few minutes while I go and glad-hand some investors and critics?"

He watched her straighten her shoulders, visibly pull herself together. "I think so."

Once again he offered his hand, and was surprised that she took it.

But all the same he yanked open the door with his free hand and stepped through, making sure she followed him. He didn't let go of her hand until he'd made sure she was settled on the couch.

"Be right back," he said.

She nodded as he ran off to grab a bottle of water from the little fridge they'd prepared for the evening.

"This is my three p.m.," he said to the receptionist. "Make sure she's comfortable until I come down, okay?"

"Yes, Mr. Lieberman."

He nodded, then headed back to the couch, handing over the bottle of water. "Take this, and ask the receptionist, Matilda, for anything you might need, okay?"

"Thank you," she said.

But the sound of her voice wasn't encouraging. And as much as he wanted to spend time to try and fix that, he couldn't. So he took her at her word and headed upstairs to the people who expected him.

SHE'D SPILLED ICED tea all over Isaac.

She'd also called him a Hanukkah snob, but that was earlier and probably not worth thinking about. At least he wasn't thinking about it.

Or was he?

All she knew is that she was in pain, drinking a bottle of water he'd gotten her as she sat on a couch at the front of the gallery, probably looking more bedraggled than she should. She was also luxuriating in air conditioning in a way she usually didn't.

Apparently up was down and down was up.

"You don't have to wait for him here," said the young woman behind the reception desk, formality and politeness mixing and dripping off of her words in a way that turned them into a specific order. "You can go back through the front part of the gallery. He's got some great pieces in there."

She pulled herself together as much as she could and stood, testing her feet on the floor of the gallery. Her feet a little better after the break, short as it was, and she started to walk, heading into the gallery itself. Wood floors, wide windows, lights meant to shine attention on the sculptures placed around the interior. The metal seemed to flow, substance turned into lava or liquid on the various displays. Isaac Lieberman was good.

"It's one of my favorites, too."

She turned to see a pair of dark brown eyes, bright at first and then darker with recognition. He was breathtaking. He wore a white shirt with thin straps that barely covered the breadth of his shoulders with the black pants now, his cheekbones clearer with the smile.

She could hardly think, much less speak.

"Hi," she managed.

"How are you feeling?"

"Better, thank you. Your shirt…I'm so sorry."

He shrugged, and she couldn't take her eyes off the way his shoulders moved. "I'm not. Didn't want to wear long sleeves. You gave me an excuse."

"I'll still pay for your dry cleaning."

"No. Not necessary."

He seemed pretty adamant so she smiled. "Fair enough."

He bit his lip, and she wondered if he thought they were at as much of an impasse as she did. Neither wanting to actually broach the reason they were supposed to meet, probably because once she mentioned what she was doing there, this strange interlude would be over.

And that would be sad.

"I hope my grandmother's well?"

She nodded, glad for an entrée that was neutral. "Elsa's wonderful. She's such an amazing lady."

"Glad to hear that. She likes you, you know."

"I feel special," which was probably the dumbest thing in the world to say but those were the only words she had.

"Me too." He took a deep breath. "Can I show you the rest of the floor?"

"See why you're such a critic in the first place?" And maybe steal a little more time before she left, disappointed.

"I'd love that."

And so she let him take her hand, and walk her across

the gallery floor.

HE LOVED TO listen to her voice, loved how she pointed out the way he'd worked the metal.

"So this is why you had such opinions on menorahs."

And that was when he came back down to earth. "I made my first one when I was young," he said. "The one that sits on my *bubbe's* windowsill, if you've ever seen it."

"How old were you?"

"I was at camp, maybe twelve? Thirteen? I came back from that camp and my parents started paying for lessons."

"So you started with a menorah." She paused. "What changed?"

"What do you mean?"

"Like, have you lost the desire to celebrate Hanukkah, like it was something you did when you were a kid?"

"Why would you think that?"

He watched her formulate the question before she spoke it. "Elsa didn't think you were interested in the festival, so I thought maybe it was because you thought the holiday was childish."

He put his hand up. "Stop right there. My feelings about the festival aren't related at all to any…things I had when I was a kid or as an adult. I just have always felt that Hanukkah was something you celebrated at home, with your family. Not in the middle of a town square."

That was when the air came out of the room, the current that had been tightening and sparking between them suddenly loosened and went out.

"So…you're not interested in making a menorah for the festival."

He wasn't. His feelings for her notwithstanding, he was in no way interested in making a menorah for Hollowville's festival. "I'm sorry."

But he wasn't done talking, because he missed that connection. "I don't like crowds, and I don't…well, I don't often speak to people who aren't critics or who aren't financially capable of acquiring my work."

"You mean you don't often randomly speak to people?"

He laughed, and he loved the fact she asked. "Not when I don't have to," he replied wryly. "But my grandmother didn't just send you to meet me because she thought you'd like my stuff."

"Well, Mrs. Lieberman thought you'd be a good person to ask about making a menorah for the festival." She stopped speaking as if to hold herself together. "You know they're shutting it down."

That's why his *bubbe* said so much at dinner, why she sent…Sarah. Because she'd thought he wouldn't be immune to the heart she had in her eyes. "I didn't. I'm so sorry."

She lifted her hands, rubbing her upper arms as if to warm herself. "It's fine, really. Things change. Life changes.

More people need things, and traditions fall away and, before you know it, ten years of a festival means nothing in the face of the ever-increasing need to make red and green as ubiquitous as red, white, and blue."

He wanted to pull her into his arms, but he couldn't. He wished he could give her a different answer, but he absolutely did not want to, no matter how much the hurt in her eyes knocked him for a loop. "I'm sorry. I really appreciate the fact you came all the way down here."

"It wasn't a big deal. Hollowville isn't far from here by train."

But it could be oceans away. "I'm sorry I couldn't give you a better answer."

"So am I," she said. "So am I."

And then before he did anything he regretted, he heard voices getting closer.

"You have to go," she said, a sad smile making him hurt. "And so do I. Good luck tonight."

And then she headed to the door, opened it, and walked out of his life, leaving him no time to think about the sense of loss because he and his art were on display.

Chapter Five

Hollowville

MONDAY MEANT BACK to work and not rehashing everything that had happened over the weekend, not the way Isaac had turned her down and definitely not the way she'd gone through wine afterwards with Anna.

Monday work also meant coffee, which meant a trip into the Caf and Nosh.

Best coffee in Hollowville.

Especially considering how many people were waiting outside, whether to have breakfast or to get a latte.

Small town charm, small town monopoly.

She shook her head and smiled.

"Well, hello, Sarah."

The sound of that voice was both grating and officious, if it could be both at the same time.

"Trustee Webster," she said, half out of obligation and half rote. If she didn't, there would be consequences—small town and all. "Good morning."

He pursed his lips and removed a handkerchief from his pocket. "I'm quite sure it is," he said. "I just haven't made up my own mind." He blotted his forehead with the handkerchief before putting it back in his pocket.

"Haven't seen enough of the day, huh?"

"I have not. My train upstate was canceled, so I can't make it in to work today. I'm teleworking, and I am just not in the mood to stay home."

"I see," she said.

And then out of nowhere, as if he'd flipped a switch, he was beaming, his pale eyes almost twinkling. "Oh. I saw this lovely article about something called 'holiday trees' over the weekend, which look fantastic. I sent an email to Pete Fitzgerald, over at the Fitzgerald Tree Farm; you've heard of it, I assume?"

"I have," she said. "They make wonderful contributions to the fall harvest fair in town. Beautiful sukkahs and a few other things. Their apple pie is to die for."

"SU-cah, oh! You mean those fall festival houses, hmm?" He smiled. "Great, great, great. I wonder if we can get an Easter bunny in town..."

Sarah bit her lip politely as he continued to speak.

"Anyway, he's totally up for donating one of his Norway spruces, and I think we can get a decorator to put on some holly and some draydeli doohickeys and maybe a donut?"

First she had to figure out what the trustee wanted. Then when she realized the man actually wanted to put dreidels, soofganiyot and holly on a Christmas tree, her brain stopped completely.

Which…no.

"I think," she said, adopting her best professional phone voice, "that might clash with the atmosphere of the rest of the festival, and there might not be space because we're getting a menorah."

"A little candle thing? But think of how amazing a symbol it would be if we had them both, kinda standing together, with the star at the top of the tree towering over the…"

"A large menorah," she replied, even though her voice was starting to shake. "A large menorah with a pretty big candle span, so we probably shouldn't have flammable things like trees nearby."

Trustee Webster nodded as they walked into the Caf and Nosh. "Hopefully, the candle thing will bring people into the festival. Needs to make money, not burn it, you know. Enjoy your coffee."

And as he ended the conversation, Sarah wanted to cry. She settled for a soofganiyot latte. "Iced vanilla latte, raspberry syrup, whipped cream," she said. Sugar and caffeine would make her feel better even when she felt like her world was ending.

Brooklyn

ISAAC LET HIMSELF sleep in. A rare luxury after a successful show, but this was the best way to reward himself for creative endeavors. He'd been on his toes for months, preparing for this, and now that it was over, he had only a few things left to organize before December and the beginning of Hanukkah.

And so, he got up and stretched, heading toward his big, open windows, only to discover the sun was high in the sky and Brooklyn was awake and in full blast. He checked the clock on the wall; it was after noon. He rubbed his face and picked up his phone from the charger.

Conveniently enough, the second it hit his palm was the second it buzzed. He was tempted to ignore it. But he could never ignore a call from his *bubbe.*

"*Bubbe,*" he said, smiling despite how tired he still was. "How are you?"

"I'm disappointed in you."

He sighed, sat against the kitchen chair. "I love you too, *Bubbe,*" he said. "What did I do?"

"You turned down the festival. I'm disappointed."

"I told you I don't like the festival, and I even told you why over a bowl of matzah ball soup." Which, at the time, he'd hoped was akin to swearing some kind of sacred oath. Apparently, it wasn't.

"But that's different, *tateleh.*"

Of course it was. For some reason he couldn't fathom, this festival meant something to his grandmother. And his feelings about it hurt her enough to mention it to him.

"How?"

"Chana, you know, from the Caf and Nosh, called me this morning. Sarah was such a wreck when she came in, and Chana…"

Sarah.

His heart stopped. He'd been off his game at the beginning of the show because her words kept running around in his head.

"*Tateleh*, are you there?"

He'd missed something important. "I'm sorry, *Bubbe*, I'm…"

"Distracted, yes. Of course you are. Your show. It was great?"

He nodded. "It was wonderful, thank you. I wish… I want you to be able to see one of my shows."

"Of course I will, *tateleh*. At some point soon, you'll do a show in Hollowville and I'll be there. But I have a more important question for you, which is what did you think of Sarah?"

What did he think about her?

That was a question.

He liked her honesty, from the moment she'd pegged him as a Hanukkah snob, and he'd appreciated how she'd loved his art.

There was also some kind of pull between them, and he wanted to explore that in a way that didn't involve the festival. He wanted to see her, and spend hours talking to her, take her to more sculpture gardens and show her what inspired him. And maybe kiss her. Maybe introduce her to his friends…

But he wasn't going to say any of that to his grandmother. Instead, he hedged. "She's nice?"

"Isn't she?"

"Yeah."

"You know," *Bubbe* began, making him think there was a story coming. "Her father used to run the committee. Now that she's on it, they named her vice chair, and basically that committee is making her do all the work."

Ouch. "That's horrible," he said.

"It is." His grandmother paused. "And she wants to leave her legacy even though the town is threatening to take away the festival—"

"Take away the festival?"

"Some *fakakta* trustee wants to make it Christmas. So they're taking advantage of her and the committee. Making them do twice as much, work twice as hard because the board of trustees is being silly."

Making red and green ubiquitous as red, white, and blue.

He had to do something to help that didn't involve him actually sculpting a huge, basic menorah. "There must be young sculptors chomping at the bit to help out a community, hmm?"

"No, *tateleh*, there aren't." She sighed, a vehicle for her disappointment. "Hollowville is a small town; people know each other. People care about each other. People do things for each other."

So what could he do for his *bubbe*? How could he make her smile without making his skin crawl? Because that was important, not the festival. Her.

His love for his *bubbe* was the reason why he wanted to spend Hanukkah with her in the first place. They were family, and building relationships didn't happen only on holidays, no matter what those holidays were.

"So what can I do for you that isn't the festival?"

"Let me think. You can visit me this weekend."

She capitulated way too quickly for his comfort, but all the same, she'd offered him an alternative he was more than happy to take her up on. "Absolutely. I'd love to," he replied.

"Good. Good, *tateleh*. In fact…"

What did she have in mind? What was she planning? A preview for the festival she'd just have to bring him to? Or something else?

"Yes?"

"How about you come Friday morning? A gallery just opened in town, and I love it so far." She paused. "It would be lovely if you met the owner."

If only everything his *bubbe* wanted was as easy to deliver. Doing a show where she was as much the center of attention as he was excited him. Heck, she was a large part of the reason he was sculpting in the first place; it was way overdue for her to get some kind of public credit.

"Okay," he said. "I'll meet her, then come to you till Sunday. Okay?"

"Perfect, *tateleh*." The joy in her voice was a symphony to his ears. "Let me give you the number of the gallery."

As he wrote down the number on the closest piece of scrap paper, anticipation roared in his blood. At minimum he'd offer to do a small show of more sentimental pieces; if he liked the owner, thought she was good at what she did, he'd even do more outreach depending on what he thought the small town and the gallery could handle. It would be a great deal different from anything else he'd ever done. And he couldn't wait to start.

Chapter Six

ON FRIDAY MORNING Isaac was packed and on his way to Grand Central. The idea of being on a super crowded Manhattan-bound subway early in the morning made him nauseous. So he'd ordered a car through one of the rideshare apps. The extra bit he paid was worth it for air conditioning that didn't make him feel like he was in the middle of a blizzard and the comfortable seat he got all to himself.

Luckily, most people who took commuter trains on a Friday morning were heading into the city and not out of it. Which meant that even though he knew the station was going to be crowded, the train to Hollowville wouldn't be.

As he stepped into the station, tourists were staring up at the famous ceiling, and commuters were scurrying between the tracks like ants freed from the bottom of a rock. He took a deep breath, braced himself and forged ahead.

Visions of moments on *Bubbe's* patio with a cool drink in the summer breeze filled his mind as he purchased his ticket at one of the multiple machines dotted across the stone and marble terminal.

Ticket acquired, he looked up at the screens to figure out where his track was. Local train should get in just about eleven-thirty, giving him a nice, long, slow ride up the Hudson, and more than enough time to enjoy the weather as well as research and organize before his two-fifteen appointment.

Perfect.

Once he found the track listing, he headed along the passage, shoes sliding against the marble flooring, following the numbers posted along the walls.

Finally, he reached into his bag for his all-important bottle of orange juice. He'd finished most of his breakfast, but not the juice. Now, it was his reward for making it to the train without incident.

He continued to walk in the general direction of the track while taking long swallows of the beverage, only to bump into someone. All he saw were orange dots as the liquid spilled all over the white parts of a sundress, as opposed to the flowers. The dark green, magenta and orange bits stood out against the white background, but now heightened the fact that the background was no longer white.

"I'm so—"

Hazel eyes met his in…amusement?

Wait. Was there a smile?

Then he paused and focused. She was cute, familiar.

It isn't a big deal. Hollowville isn't very far by train.

Sarah.

"I'm so sorry," he began.

"I'd be angry," she said, "but considering what I did to you the last time we saw each other, I'll just call it a tie."

He laughed. Oh, he laughed. He couldn't help himself. "I wish your solution could be as easy as mine was."

She shook her head, eyes bright. "Not really, Orange Juice."

"Still," he said. "I'll absolutely pay for your dry cleaning."

"No worries, Mr. Orange. It'll come out in the wash." And then she paused. "So what brings you to Grand Central?"

"Going to Hollowville. Got an appointment."

"Hold that thought," Sarah said abruptly.

He wondered what had happened, what she was thinking. But before he could ask, she reached out a hand.

"Follow me or you'll miss the train."

He took her hand with his free one and let her take him to where he needed to go.

He'd follow her anywhere.

Where the hell did that come from?

He didn't know, didn't care, just followed her past the people standing and talking in the great hall, past the people standing just beyond the train, waiting for another one. He let her guide him along the train, stopping and turning as they entered through a doorway slightly taller than he was.

She didn't stop when they got on; they walked past sets of two and three seats, facing different directions.

"Do you get train sick if you're going the wrong direction?"

He had a whole bunch of issues, but that wasn't one of them. "Stop where you feel lucky," he said. "But thank you for asking."

She nodded as they stopped in front of a seat prepared for three people.

There were a few scattered others on the train; some were eating fragrant bagels, others drinking hot beverages that smelled like coffee. Others stared at the window, used their phones, or typed on laptops.

"It's not crowded," she noted, "but we probably shouldn't be too greedy because it's an express."

"Greedy?"

She nodded, gesturing across the car. Two-seaters, half full, four-seaters ready to be filled, and three-seaters like theirs, filled the space up and down the car. The light scent of someone's day-old perfume filled the car, warring with the air conditioning.

Right.

She didn't want them to take more seats than they could reasonably expect to fill. Which was fine. But still. "I take it you do this often?"

"Don't you?"

Easy question to ask, harder one to answer. He'd give her the truth because she deserved it. Complicated as it was. "I probably should know more about this than I do," he admitted. "I take the train to visit *Bubbe*, but not as often as I could, and definitely not as often as you do."

"Fair enough." Her smile made him want to...

Join her? Smile as well? No matter what, it made him feel better. Much better.

It was definitely going to be a good ride.

SARAH SPENT A lot of time on trains; the rides were usually the same. She sat by herself, listening to music or reading or following social media. No talking to anybody, even people she brought with her. It was as if she traveled in a bubble and didn't get out of it until she got to the station. Wherever it was.

This time was different. There was a space between her and Isaac, but she wanted to close it. She wanted to sit closer. She actually wanted to *talk to him.*

What the heck was wrong with her?

"This is gorgeous," he said.

Which was why she let him have the window seat, and why her choice of seat had been near a window. The view was, in fact, gorgeous.

"It's the Hudson," she said matter-of-factly, as if it were obvious.

He laughed, and she was starting to like the sound of that laugh. "Living here gives you so much; this view is just unbelievable."

"Inspiring, huh?"

He settled back in his seat, his long frame more relaxed in the smaller space than it should be, the distance between them made shorter the more comfortable he got. "It is."

She watched as he reached up, covering his mouth and a yawn with the back of his hand. "You can close your eyes if you want. I'll wake you when we get there."

And as if all he needed was her permission, he closed his eyes, and soon after, his breathing evened out and he was sleeping.

She turned to stare out the window, letting her mind race. She had to start setting up for work events at both the bookstore and the library as well as type up a progress report for the town board. The list went on and on…

Except all she wanted to think about was how adorable he looked when he was sleeping, his long lashes dark against his pale cheeks. He looked like he hadn't slept properly in a long time. She wondered what he'd been doing to get himself that exhausted.

As the train shuddered to a stop, she panicked then realized they were a stop away. Which brought her to a whole new set of troubles. How was she supposed to wake him?

This wasn't a fairy tale, not yet at least, so she sighed, braced herself, and tapped him on the shoulder. Carefully.

He sat up instantly, his eyes gorgeous, wide, and bright. "Wh…what's—?"

"We're almost in Hollowville," she said. "Which means you need to get ready to get off."

He nodded, slowly, looking at her with eyes that pulled her in like tractor beams.

And then the train shuddered to a halt.

"Come on," she said, grabbing at his shirt. "If you don't move, we'll miss the stop, and the next one isn't for a while."

She didn't stop to see whether he listened; she just bolted off the train, hoping he'd follow suit. "Nice, isn't it?"

Because he was with her, this time, unlike any other time she'd gotten off the train at the Hollowville station, she looked around the old brick and stone station house, the view of the riverfront, the bridge, and the new developments. Hollowville was a mix of old and new, of tradition and modernity, of small town and a bit of city. "Best of both worlds," she said.

He nodded, as if he was trying to take the village in in one panoramic glance. "It's just far enough away from the city, and yet it's so close."

She was trying not to stare, so she forced herself into a nod and a subject change. "Is Mrs. Lieberman picking you up at the station?"

It took a minute for recognition to make its way across his face. "No," he said. "I've got a meeting and she's got a bit of a busy day, so I told her I'd take care of my business and then head up to her place."

Right. He'd said he'd had a meeting and then he fell

asleep on the train before they had a chance to explore it further. "Who's the meeting with?" Ugh. That might have stepped over the line just a bit. "I'm sorry. I'm being nosy."

He shook his head and reached into his pocket, pulling out his phone. "No, it's fine. I think her name is Molly Concannon. She owns a gallery in town, right?"

"Yeah." She grinned at him. "Molly is *the* gallery owner in town."

"*Bubbe* likes her," he replied, as if that were the character reference he needed. "But is Hollowville big enough to have more than one gallery?"

"I don't think so." The idea of multiple galleries dotting the small town business district stole her words in a fit of giggles that she barely managed to suppress. "I mean, we have fifty million antique shops, possibly about the same number of nail places. The gallery's been in town more than a year, so we consider that a victory at this point."

"Town still likes its antiques, hmm?"

"It likes its traditions, and it likes to share in the mythology, even though it doesn't take a central role in it, like other towns do," she replied. That was the best way to describe Hollowville in a way that didn't require a member of the historical society or a local guidebook.

She looked at her watch. "Speaking of tradition, today's a late day for me so I don't have to be at the bookstore till two, which means I have some time to kill. What time's your meeting?"

"About two-fifteen, so I also have a bit of time to kill. Much more than I expected, actually."

"What did you mean?"

"We took the express," he admitted. "I was going to take the local, which means I have loads more time than I planned for."

They'd left Grand Central just after ten a.m. and it wasn't even eleven. Which meant she got him to Hollowville at minimum a half hour earlier than he'd expected. She felt terrible. "Oh my God, I'm sorry."

The smile on his face warmed her heart. "I'm not. Gives me more time to take in the scenery. Usually I'm here with *Bubbe*, getting her perspective on things."

She was about to say something, but she was stopped by the myriad of emotions she saw running across his face: joy, wonder and…nerves?

What reason did he have to be nervous?

"How 'bout I buy you lunch or coffee or something so maybe we could…kill time together?"

That's why he was nervous.

She had to love this; it was mandatory. Especially considering she wanted nothing more than to spend some more time with him. "I like this idea," she said. "Any particular food you're craving? Any place you've seen you've wanted to try?"

"My *bubbe* keeps talking about this one place, but she never takes me there. The Caf and Nosh I think it's called?"

Truth to tell, walking into the Caf and Nosh with Elsa Lieberman's grandson the sculptor seemed like the worst decision she could possibly make. Anybody on the festival committee who might be at the Caf and Nosh at that time would not have a problem expressing their displeasure at his decision to not make a menorah for the festival, unless it was any of the people who were interested in seeing the tree Trustee Webster was going to supply instead of a menorah.

It would be tense and nerve-racking. And yet, it felt like the best mistake she'd ever heard of.

"Sounds good," she said, and despite every instinct telling her not to, she was genuinely looking forward to it.

Chapter Seven

HOLLOWVILLE WAS GORGEOUS.

Usually, Isaac was driving through Hollowville with *Bubbe* so he was paying attention to her, soaking up every word she had to say like it was the most important thing in the world. But this drive was different; he was in Sarah's small car, crammed in like a pretzel, nervous that if he moved the wrong way, or said the wrong thing, the tension between them would explode in the worst way possible.

Whatever that tension was.

So he forced himself to stare out the window.

Instead of being a bad decision, he found the view fascinating. So many different elements went into the town: greenery mixed with stone and brick; old mixed with new, in a way that echoed the design of the station house. It seemed symbolic in a way, maybe putting forward the idea that small towns like this one were more complex than anybody gave them credit for.

He'd definitely have to think about that as he got to know the town a bit better. Which was going to be interesting. Especially considering the way people were watching him as he stopped in front of the drugstore, waiting for Sarah to emerge with a stain-removing stick. He felt like he'd stepped out of his apartment in his little corner of Brooklyn for the first time in weeks. Except in a wider space, and maybe with fewer people.

Yet the scrutiny, as it was, felt the same. People didn't know how to react, so he met their gazes with his most open and pleasant expression.

"Yessss!"

He turned, seeing Sarah emerging, her brown ringlets blowing in the breeze. "Found it?"

"Yep. They had the extra-strength stuff and"—she gestured excitedly at her dress—"it worked!"

He looked closer, now seeing the flowers and the colors that accented her hazel eyes on the white fabric as they were intended to be seen; she wore a work of art. But instead of saying that, he said, "I don't see any orange."

"The stuff I bought worked so well I don't have to go home and change before eating!"

"Because that would have turned into a disaster?"

"Pretty much." She gestured widely. "Would have at least been the talk of the town."

He nodded as they walked down the town's main street. And out of the corner of his eye, he noticed the level of scrutiny increasing as if they'd been dropped into the center of a drama and given starring roles without their knowledge.

"It's okay," she said, as if she knew what he was thinking. "This is Hollowville."

"And if nothing else," he replied, "Hollowville is a small town, following the traditional small town playbook, used in small towns all over the country and the world."

"Yeah. Pretty much. The unknown quantity, walking down the central street with a beloved local to the town's favorite restaurant."

"Story practically writes itself," he replied. "Add in the fact that the unknown is related to one of the town's most beloved denizens..."

"And the restaurant is owned by, well..."

She didn't seem to want to finish the sentence for some reason. But that was okay. He could just as easily finish it for her. "Let me guess. The restaurant is owned by one of the other beloved denizens, who is bothered by the unknown quantity's most recent principled stand."

"How'd you guess?"

"Relax," he said, desperately trying not to reach out and put his arm around her. "I'm not surprised. Small town, everybody knows everybody, and bad news travels fast. This was also my choice, so any difficulties or tension are my fault."

"I promise, despite what you might think, you don't have anything to worry about."

He bit his lip. "Not everybody's as nice as you've been when I say no, so thank you."

"I'm sorry," she said.

He could see sympathy in her eyes, maybe anger there too.

"You're in the middle of a town full of gossips," she continued. "They're harmless—mostly."

He nodded, the stories his grandmother had told him over the years percolating through his mind. "*Bubbe's* been like a shield. I mean, her reputation."

Sarah nodded, waving to the people passing by, greeting them as they smiled in her direction. "Yeah. Nobody wants to cross Elsa Lieberman."

"Not anybody with a lick of sense."

"But you?" she said, smiling. "You're fair game."

He raised an eyebrow. "Because?"

"As far as they're concerned," she replied, "you turned the town down, you turned *them* down, and your reasons are irrelevant."

"I hope they, and you, realize I turned down the festival for reasons unrelated to you or the town."

"Like I said…" She shrugged. "It doesn't matter, even if you make the art gallery the most successful gallery on the east coast by curating all of Molly's shows for the rest of your natural life. They have the potential of seeing you as the one who's responsible for the end of the Hanukkah festival."

"I see," he said, because what else could he say? "So…what are you doing with me?" He waited for her answer, his breath stuck in his lungs.

"I seem to have a soft spot for the underdog," she replied, the look in her eyes starting his heart again. "And I think it's a crime that you haven't been inside the Caf and Nosh."

She pointed to the glass door. "Let's go in," she said.

He smiled and pushed open the door, finding himself in another world. It was air-conditioned and the smell of baked goods made his mouth water. The walls of the café were off-white tile with deep blue mats on the floor. There were stars on the crown molding if you looked closely enough, and a white marble counter space with a clear glass counter.

"Like an old-school deli," he said, the first words he could think of.

"They make egg creams here, homemade ice cream, breads and baked goods." And then as someone waved them over to one of the open tables, three people dropped their menus to stare at them. "You get the gossip and observers for free."

He shook his head as he sat down. "You did warn me, so it's fine. As long as they don't confront me with baby pictures and words about how I'm breaking my *bubbe's* heart along with their observing."

"You'd be equally as lucky to escape without the invitation to make a star, for a Christmas tree, you know, if you're not careful."

"Still commercial public observance, still no. Besides," he took a look at the menu, "there are so many artists who celebrate Christmas, ask them to build large stars for Christmas trees."

"Holiday trees," interjected an unfamiliar voice that made him squirm in his seat. "They'd be holiday trees, Miss Goldman."

A dude, shorter than he was, attempted to loom over the table. Behind weird, thick-framed glasses with extremely thin lenses, beady blue eyes stared back at them. A beard, which looked as if it had been trimmed with artisanal scissors, dotted a very pointed face. "Sorry, Mr. . . ."

"Lieberman," Isaac said. "Isaac Lieberman."

"Oh, very nice to meet you. Very nice to meet you, Mr. Lieberman. I'm Trustee Webster. Newly elected to this proud town's government. Recent transplant. But yes," the dude sighed. "It is unfortunate that Hollowville doesn't have a good celebration for the winter, you know. Like the other small towns across this country. And I'm aiming to change that."

"With . . . trees?"

Webster nodded. "Yep. Very important to a winter holiday celebration. You can't have a winter holiday celebration without a tree, and lights and a star up at the top. You know."

"Mr. Webster," said another voice. It was tight, a bit of an Israeli accent. He tried to figure out where the voice was coming from, only to look up and a woman with short dark hair and flashing eyes barreling toward their table. "The next time you interrupt a patron's lunch before they've had a chance to order will be your last. You will let Sarah and Elsa's grandson have their lunch and then if they wish, they can continue their conversation about your *fakakta* nonsense on the sidewalk. But that's only if they wish, and frankly, I don't wish."

"But, Mrs. Levitan, really."

"No. This is my restaurant, and according to your town code, which my husband recently okayed as the town counsel, you cannot peddle anything—goods or politics—in *private* restaurants."

"And I suppose if they were speaking of other candle-related things, you'd be okay with it?"

"The key word is *they*, Trustee Webster," the woman said. "I didn't interfere in a private conversation. And if patrons wish to have a conversation about why the Hanukkah festival needs a menorah, they are welcome to. Here or at our regularly scheduled festival committee meeting, taking place soon at the Hollowville Hebrew Center."

"And if your patrons wish to discuss the reason why Hollowville needs a holiday festival and a tree to go with it, they can contact me."

And as the trustee left the Caf and Nosh, Isaac could only stare.

SARAH WANTED TO curl up into a corner or leave. "I'm

sorry...this was a horrible idea," she managed. "I'm sorry you had to..."

And suddenly Isaac's hand was on hers. "It was my idea, and you warned me. You told me this was a possibility. And yet I said yes."

"I could have stopped it. I could have insisted or burgers or sushi or something else entirely, like empanadas and quipes, or falafel instead. I could have thought more."

"Not when my heart was set on either matzah brei, or challah French toast. Wouldn't have worked."

How he could think about the menu when the situation was this tense was another thing. She couldn't do it. "I..."

"Say you'll split something with me," he continued. "You pick. I'll have either. It doesn't matter."

"But..."

"Look. I'm not going to make the menorah. I won't make his Christmas star, and I definitely won't call it a holiday star. But what I will do, right here and right now, is buy you lunch because every single decision you make in this town shouldn't have to be about the festival, no matter how important it is."

"It is important," she managed. "It is so very important. Because so many towns across the country, so many people have a festival like the one Webster wants. And people get forgotten. Traditions get forgotten. Communities get ignored. We're fighting for space; we're fighting for recognition. First it's the tree, then it's red and green, then it's carolers, and then *oops.*"

"And I'm not saying it isn't," he interjected. "But what I am saying is that you need to take a moment to enjoy your lunch, the way we were going to before Webster showed up. It's hard to fight against the world when you have an empty stomach."

Which was true, as clichéd as his words were. And adorable in a way she was trying to ignore. And so she nodded. "Okay. I'll let you buy me matzah brei and share your challah French toast. Deal?"

He nodded, obviously pleased with himself. "Absolutely."

Resisting him in order to avoid bringing him back into her messy life was going to be almost impossible. But she was going to do her best. After the day was over.

Chapter Eight

"THERE'S SOMETHING I don't get," Sarah said as she took a huge bite of her matzah brei.

The intense way Isaac focused on her made her feel as if answering her questions was his most important obligation. "Tell me." He cut a slice of the French toast. "I'll be as clear as I can."

And that's when she got nervous. What if she went out of bounds? Too far? "Nah, it's okay."

He shook his head. "It's totally fine to ask me a question. And seriously, if I don't like it, I won't answer. Simple."

"Fair enough." She took a drink of her iced tea, swirled it around her mouth, and thought. "You and I are around the same age, right?"

He nodded. "I mean, I think so."

"So why haven't we met before now?"

He sighed, but her relief came from the light she saw in his eyes. "My mom never liked small towns. She wanted me to have a *good* upbringing, and by good, she meant in the city like she had."

"The less exposure to Hollowville the better, huh?"

"She had an idea of what she wanted," he said before taking a long swallow of his juice. "You see, Hollowville wasn't really a part of her vision, so she made sure the time I spent with *Bubbe* and Zayde wasn't here."

"So no hanging out in Hollowville during the summer?"

The sound of his laugh made her insides turn to jelly. "Lord, no. We spent a lot of time traveling during the summer. Brought *Bubbe* and Zayde with us." He took a bite of his bread. "To tons of places with *cultural import.*"

Ahh, yes. Those places.

She rolled her eyes. "Any place with a museum and potential to be mentioned in the arts sections of the *important papers*, huh?"

"You got it," he said. "When they complained about my chosen profession, I told them it was their fault for taking me on these trips."

She failed to hold back the laughter. "They must have been thrilled."

"All of my grandparents were so proud they couldn't gainsay it."

"And your *bubbe*?"

"She was thrilled," he said. "Without a question. Shoved me toward art school, made sure I didn't back down, dragged my Zayde to art shows in the city before he died, then came to a whole bunch of group shows early in my career."

"Has she ever been to a show in the city? Of yours?"

"She has." He paused. "But not for a long time. Which is why I hope my meeting with Molly Concannon at her gallery goes well."

"And I was just joking when I suggested that you were going to curate her shows for the rest of your natural life."

"I wouldn't go that far," he said. "I'm looking forward to meeting her, seeing what I can offer. Maybe a show. But mostly to give something to the community where my *bubbe* lives."

"For what it's worth," she said, "I really like her, mostly because her heart is in the right place."

"That's good to hear. What about her gallery? What kind of exhibitions has she had? I honestly haven't paid much attention to it, so I appreciate your insight."

"Well," she said, tapping her fingers on the table, "she's had different exhibitions, some very traditional, some not as traditional, and because she's very good at speaking to the locals, she's been pretty successful and she's gotten a really good foothold in the community."

"Thank you." He looked like he was about to say something more, but he stopped.

"You're welcome." She reached for her fork and speared the last piece of challah toast on her plate. "Amazing as usual."

He looked at his watch, then looked back up at her. "What time do you have to be at work again?"

"Two. Your meeting's at two-fifteen? Which means we

both have a bit more time on our hands. What were you thinking?"

"That I wouldn't mind stealing a bit more of your time," he said, before a huge grin spread across his face. "What do you think about dessert?"

She felt her lips curve to match his expression. "I thought you'd never ask."

She found herself wishing this lunchtime idyll wouldn't end. But she would savor dessert and conversation with a really hot guy for as long as she could.

ONCE THE LUNCH was over, Isaac swiped the bill out from under Sarah's hand. "My treat, remember," he said. "It's probably a pittance in the tray of gossip you're going to have to deal with after this lunch."

"You sure you want to do that?"

"There's going to be talk," he replied. "Right out of the small town playbook, but I kinda don't care."

He could hear the click of shoes crossing the tile floor. "What, you trying to sweet-talk the Hanukkah fairy into something?"

He looked up to meet a pair of unfamiliar eyes. "Um..."

The owner of the restaurant was once again standing by their table. Up closer, when she wasn't focused on removing the trustee, he was able to get a better look at her. Her dark hair was short, shot with gray, and landed above her ears. The way she held herself reminded him of veterans he knew, and yes, the accent was Israeli.

Ex-military.

He was out of his element on so many levels: small town intrigue, the sudden unease prickling the back of his neck, the realization he was stuck in the booth.

But he wasn't alone. He was with Sarah. And he turned slightly to catch her expression, searching for some degree of reassurance, just like she'd offered every other time he'd been confronted with evidence of the small town playbook. But instead of smiling, she was rolling her eyes, her sigh gustier than a tornado.

"Really, Chana?" she quipped.

"Well, of course," Chana, the owner and the committee chair, said. "I had to check to see if you two were okay after the run-in with the awful Mr. Webster."

"I think we're all right," Isaac said.

"I can't stand him."

Chana shook her head. "If I had my choice, I'd permanently ban that waste of humanity from the place, but I don't want to cause too much trouble."

"Sooner he's kicked off the board of trustees, the better," Sarah said, picking up her tea. "I cannot believe people in this town voted for him."

"Wait," Isaac said. "I don't know what's worse: the fact that he was elected or the fact that I thought he wasn't."

"Small towns," Chana said, shaking her head again. "There are the people we see and the people we don't see. Depends always on the lens you're looking through and the people who welcome you. The people we don't see? The ones who think there should be a *holiday festival* instead of the Hanukkah festival we've had for the last ten years? They want someone like Webster. They think he's wanting change, but he's wanting to make our town like every other small town people see and read about."

"Silencing the voices he doesn't like in exchange for the nostalgic towns he remembers," Sarah added. "Because Hollowville is a small town, but it's always respected people who live here no matter where their families are from or how they celebrate or who they love."

"Yes. The key is respecting those who live here. All of those people. Which begs the question," Chana paused, and he could feel her gaze on him as opposed to just seeing it. "Aside from bothering the fairy here, what are you doing in town?"

"Well," he said, "aside from seeing my *bubbe*, I'm going to the gallery."

"Yeah," Sarah interjected. "Don't you have to get there soon?"

"I think I do. I don't want to be too late. Don't want to make a bad impression."

"Clearly," Chana said. "Molly Concannon has a very discerning eye, or at least I thought she did."

"Which means I should probably go."

Sarah nodded. "You don't want to get on her bad side and I need to get to work, so I'll walk you out."

"I need to pay the check," he said, glad she'd offered to walk him out. He wanted to spend more time with her, not to mention he also had no idea where the gallery was. "You really don't have to if you have to talk more committee business."

"First of all," Chana said, looking back and forth between them. "You got pulled into the kind of town drama that makes people not want to come back, so no bill. And don't fight me on this. It's my restaurant, and I can say who pays a bill and who eats for free." And then a pause. "You did enjoy your lunch, yes?"

He nodded. "I loved all of it: the soofganiyot and the matzah brei and the challah French toast."

"Good. You need good fuel to meet Molly, and if you mess up this meeting because of me, Elsa will have my *tuchus* for dinner."

The burst of laughter came out of him before he could stop it, and once he had, the expression on the older woman's face was priceless: stony but almost amused despite a clear lack of desire to be. "Yep," he said finally, grinning in Sarah's direction, "you don't cross Elsa Lieberman."

And as they got up to head out of the restaurant, Isaac wanted to take Sarah's hand, but he didn't. The conversation with the trustee as well as the group that couldn't help but stare in their direction as they left the restaurant made it very clear that people were watching them.

"This was nice," she said as they reached the street.

"It was more than nice." He grinned. "You're heading to work now?"

There was reluctance in her nod. "Yeah. I have a bunch of things I need to do before I have to go to my parents' house for dinner."

"Yeah. Meeting, then *Bubbe's* house. I'm here all weekend, catching up with her, just so you know."

She laughed. "I've got a busy weekend, but you know, if I see you trying to abuse a bottle of orange juice..."

Laughter was apparently contagious. "I'll be careful. I promise. Also, really dumb question."

"What?"

"The gallery." He shoved his hands in the pockets of his pants. "Where is it?"

"Oh! That's right." She pointed down the street, past the pharmacy and the pretzel shop and the hair salon. "Head down to the end of the street, by the gift shop? Then make a left and you'll see the gallery on the left-hand side."

"And the store? The bookstore?"

"For...? Wait."

What was going through her head? What was she thinking?

"I am so sorry, because I am so completely dense."

"Why?"

She bit her lip before looking down at her sandals and then back up to meet his eyes. "So the store? Well the store is just beyond where you have to turn. It used to be the gourmet food store, but it works so much better as a bookstore. Which is probably TMI, but anyway, I'll just walk you down."

More time with her, which he liked the idea of very much. "Thank you."

"You're welcome."

That was when she held out her hand. Of course, he took it. It was small, warm, and so comfortable in his. Which was how they headed down the block. He was supposed to be paying attention to the landmarks, but all he could focus on was the way her hand felt against his.

"So here we are," she said suddenly as they stopped.

He looked around to see glitter and gold lettering on a purple sign. "Gift shop?"

She nodded. "Gift shop."

"Thank you. I hope you're not too late…"

"Not really," she said. "No worries either."

And then they stood there, hand in hand, staring at each other. He had no idea what to do, what he could do, what he could say that wouldn't step over any lines. "Till we meet again?"

"Which will probably happen sooner rather than later because Hollowville is a small town. At least," she said, "I hope it will, especially now you know where the bookstore is."

But she didn't let his hand go, didn't flex her hand in his.

Finally, she did let go. "I...hope I see you before you go. Now I really have to go."

"I do too. I hope I see you soon."

And as she turned to leave, he couldn't help but hope the small town romance playbook would be on his side this time.

Chapter Nine

THE STEPS SARAH took away from Isaac were some of the most difficult she'd ever taken. Connection, conversation, those were wonderful, but there had been something else that arose out of the time she'd spent with Isaac.

And God help her because she wanted more.

She found herself staring up at the *Tales from Hollowville* sign instead of watching him walk down the hill toward the gallery, forcing the emotions that swirled in her stomach to stay there.

That was when she went into work mode, pushing through the front door and putting on the mask; smiling and waving at everybody—the customers, the booksellers, and the managers as she walked in. Retail was hard, even though she didn't spend much time on the floor, but she wouldn't change her position for anything.

As she headed upstairs to her office she stared to think about the things she needed to do before she left work for the day: email, orders, and calendars sat high atop her list. She didn't have any work events in the final stage of planning, but there were a few in the earlier stages. Projections on how many people would attend, which meant how many books needed to be ordered; were they simply local interest or the sort that would turn a tiny little event into a standing room only affair?

Not to mention, paperwork waited for nobody, and though she'd known the store's owner for a long time, as a boss she wouldn't be very forgiving if anything fell through the cracks.

She'd just settled down at her desk, turned on her computer as she waited for her to-do list to come on screen, when there was a knock at the door.

"Come in."

The door opened to reveal the store's owner. Carol Thomas was smart, great to work with, and always had a smile for everybody. "Who's that guy you were with?"

"Hi, Carol," she said, forgetting for a moment how in tune Carol was with the town gossip despite the fact she pulled eight-hour shifts at her own store. "How are you doing? How's the store today?"

Carol smiled, bringing attention to the warm undertones in her black skin, but the look in her dark brown eyes made it clear she wasn't being fooled by the sudden change of subject. "Customers are good; life is amazing."

"That's great to hear. Any more events you want me to include in today's conversation with Dr. Hernandez at the library?"

"No," her boss replied, shaking her head. "Nothing off

the top of my head, other than telling Marylise I said hello. But stop trying to change the subject."

"Would it be me if I didn't?"

Carol laughed. "No. Not really. You wouldn't be you if you let your social life, whatever it was, derail your productivity. However..." her boss huffed out a breath "...I worry about you, Miss Hanukkah Fairy. You're doing so much for everybody else that you're not doing anything for yourself."

"Which would be fine if people like Trustee Webster weren't poking their noses in where they don't belong."

"First of all, Webster needs to learn where he's not wanted. He's already complained about the presence of some of the young adult titles, as being too sensitive to young eyes, because they give the wrong impressions about cities."

She rolled her eyes. "Let me guess. He asked where the Bibles were?"

"I told him," Carol said, grinning, "that he could find his Bibles in the religious section and that he needed to keep his nose out of the way I run my bookstore. Kids these days have so much more on their shoulders than my generation did, or even yours. They have to fight to gain the knowledge we were given freely, and then fight for a better tomorrow than the one my generation is giving them."

"You," Sarah said. "You were the best school librarian and confidante for me when I was a young, awkward, ridiculous girl and now you are the best bookstore owner Hollowville has ever seen."

"Why thank you," Carol replied. "But you're changing the subject again and I don't like it. Because people like Webster will always exist. It's up to us to deal with the garbage and find love. Now speaking of love, who is this guy?"

She laughed. Talking about Isaac was awkward, but if she was going to look for advice without judgment, Carol would be the best place to go. "He's Elsa Lieberman's grandson," Sarah began, slowly. "I'd asked him to do the sculpture for the fair, but he turned me down."

"And you're still talking to him?"

Leave it to Carol to put her finger on the real issue, or at least the issue that was confusing her enough to actually ask him about it earlier. "I know, right?"

Undeterred, Carol forged on. "So what happened? He turned you down flat, and then what?"

Not exactly. But how should she explain? How could she explain the complicated feelings that were threatening to explode out of her? At the most recent beginning was probably best. "Well," she began, "I was on the way back to Hollowville this morning—I was at Anna's last night."

"That's right. How is Anna?"

"Way too busy as usual. Trying to get on her boss's good side by staying late and doing every single little task her boss throws at her." Which was a hedge in itself, but it would do.

"She's gonna burn out like that."

And wasn't that the truth? "I keep telling her she needs

to finally present this idea for an exhibit she has to her boss, but according to Anna, there never is a good time."

"Like talking to a brick wall, huh?"

"Seriously." She shook her head, her friend's stubbornness a tangible image running through her head. "Anyway, I ended up dragging her to the signing I went to last night and stayed on her couch."

"Oh yeah." Carol grinned. "How did that signing go?"

"It was fine. There were things I want to incorporate into one of ours, and the author was lovely, and I honestly think this store needs more romance."

"You're not going to quit until romance fills fifty percent of the store, at least."

"Well," she said, "considering how much revenue the genre brings..."

Carol rolled her eyes. "I'll consider it, especially if you keep telling the story."

That was a bargain she'd gladly make, considering she'd already decided she wanted Carol's advice. "Fine, fine." She filled Carol in on the events of the morning, from bumping into Isaac to showing up at the Caf and &Nosh with him.

"He spilled orange juice on you, and you still wanted to take him to the C&N?"

"First of all, the orange juice wasn't that big a deal because I spilled iced tea on him the first time I met him. Second of all, the Caf and Nosh wasn't my idea; it was his. And I agreed because I wanted to spend time with him, but I totally made sure he knew what he was getting into before we sat down."

"When did you do that?!"

She blinked; there were a few things she'd mentioned that Carol could be referring to. "Do what?"

"Spill. The. Tea."

Right. That would be the incident Carol would want to know about. "The very first time I saw him, when I asked him if he wanted to do the sculpture for the festival."

Carol threw up her hands like a crossing guard at a red light, and the look on her face was confusion personified. "He turned you down and you still took him to the Caf and Nosh? And I'm not even talking about the mutual spilling fest you two have going on."

"The spilling wasn't deliberate. Neither was Webster's appearance."

"Oh dear Lord. He had the stones to show up there?"

Sarah proceeded to tell Carol the story, not to mention Isaac's reaction to seeing the Trustee, finishing with the way Chana practically kicked the trustee out of the restaurant.

"That must have been impressive." Carol paused. "Come to think of it, she left that part out of what she told me."

"Faulty wire in the small town gossip chain?"

"I think it's probably Chana editorializing, which the woman is wont to do as we know. Lord, I really wish Trustee Webster would head back to one of those small towns he thinks Hollowville is, and leave us alone. Not to mention our

Hanukkah festival. Speaking of which, are you going to convince the sculptor to do the festival?"

"I'm not sure how," Sarah admitted. "There are the beginnings of something between us and I don't want to lose that. But at the same time, we need a menorah. We need a symbol to last even if the festival doesn't."

Carol put a hand on top of hers and patted it. "Don't think like that. First of all, the festival will survive. Nobody in Hollowville, no matter what holiday they may celebrate in the winter, wants to give up that festival. We like learning about other cultures and faiths and sharing in the diverse traditions of everybody who lives here. No matter what that waspy Webster says."

"Webster isn't the only one who believes that, though."

"You think you have to tell me that?" Carol rolled her eyes. "You know as well as I do that those people have been around for years, trying to center themselves where they shouldn't, making their priorities the most important. But here? In Hollowville? We just have a reputation of not letting them be the loudest voices in the room, hmm."

Which was true. "You're right. I'm sorry."

"And," Carol said, "as long as you're admitting I'm right, let me run something by you."

She was slightly wary, but nodded. She'd wanted Carol's advice and she was going to get it. "Okay. I'm listening."

"So here's the thing. No matter how many people say otherwise, the five boroughs of New York City are basically like a huge small town. Blocks and neighborhoods, where people know *all* of your business, and way too many of the people who live there have connections to the surrounding counties and towns. *We* all know that. So running into someone, especially on a local—"

"Express."

"Okay. Running into someone you might know on an express train to Hollowville isn't quite the random, unexpected thing people make it out to be. But the fact that you did only a few days after he turned you down? That could mean something."

"Are you trying to tell me that Isaac organized a meeting with Molly Concannon at the gallery the day after he turned me down?"

"Is that why he's here?"

Yet another thing that Chana had left out of the conversation she'd had with Carol. Very interesting. "Yeah. That and to see his *bubbe*."

"Well for what it's worth, I don't quite remember the last visit he had with his *bubbe* in Hollowville. I know she took him to some restaurant in the city…Abe's Diner? She and a friend from HHC were here a few weeks ago talking about it."

She paused. "So it was special that he's here?"

Carol smiled. "Yep. Who knows. Maybe that boy's realizing his grandma's not getting any younger and deciding that he wants to see her more. I don't know. But whatever it is, something's afoot."

Which was all well and good, but something else was nagging at her. "What else did Chana say?"

"The mysteries of Chana," Carol replied and shook her head. "She must have rushed to some kind of judgment after seeing you and Isaac together. Especially when he said what he said about what Webster wanted."

"What kind of judgment? About us or him or…?"

"About what you're doing with him, which I informed her was none of her business."

Sarah laughed. She'd known Chana for a while, and being told to mind her own business wasn't exactly something the woman would take well to. "And how did that go?"

"I told her that if anybody has the right to complain about your potential friends or romantic partners, it would be your parents, and then possibly me because I've known you longer. And that she should mind her own business because you, Sarah Goldman, are in fact a grown woman."

"So let me guess," Sarah found herself saying. "You have opinions that you'd like to share?"

"I adore you, Sarah, like a daughter, like the student I got to know during my librarianship. So I am in favor of you spreading your wings. Stepping out of your comfort zone, doing things that make you feel special, not just the things you think you should."

Carol's words made her heart pound against her chest.

"If hanging out with this dude is one of them," the older

woman continued, "I say go for it. No matter what anybody—Chana, your parents, the committee—might say. Whether they think you're wasting your time because as of now he's not going to make the menorah, whether they think you're making a mistake because he's a city boy or an artist or whatever made up dumb reason they feel they need to offer, ignore them. All of them."

"But what if I don't know what I'm doing with him?"

"It doesn't have to make sense, Sarah. You don't have to know what you're doing with him. All you have to do is enjoy it."

And she could do that. She didn't have to question her growing feelings for Isaac as being related to anything else she was doing. She could take him for herself and not share him with the rest of the town. She wondered how long that would last.

AFTER A LONG day of ups and downs, highs and lows, and things that he still was pondering over, Isaac was in a cab, pulling up to the space where his father grew up and where his grandmother still lived. He could see the small, slightly rolling lawn, the bright maple color she'd recently had put on the front of the house. It was fresh, clear, and beautiful. And in so many ways, it was home.

His hands shook in anticipation as he tipped the driver

and got out of the car, breathing in the air. Here, Isaac wasn't a random dude from the city, with questionable intent and even more questionable motives. Here, he was family.

He tested the front door handle and found it was open. He stepped through and took a deep breath. He was *home*.

"*Bubbe*?"

She didn't answer, but she knew he was coming. The unlocked door made that clear. As did the familiar smells of a special meal. Sweet cinnamon kugel, fresh-baked challah, accompanied by the persistent sizzle of chicken baking in the oven. His stomach practically leapt with joy. She'd made his favorite Friday night dinner.

He walked into the kitchen, searching for signs of her aside from the beautiful array of pots, napkins, and silverware that decorated the table. But she was nowhere to be found.

"*Bubbe*?"

"Ahh," she shouted from across the house. "Be there in a minute, *tateleh*. Pour yourself a drink and I'll be right in."

He grinned as he put his bag down and headed to the refrigerator. Iced tea, just as *Bubbe* had made for years, in a glass pitcher ready to be poured into one of her glasses. He grabbed one, and headed to the table.

"*Tateleh*," she said as she came into the kitchen, her shoes clicking against the kitchen tile. She let him put his glass on the table before giving him a hug. "How are you?"

"Good, *Bubbe*," he said. Because he was. "I'm really good."

"Glad to hear, and I am even happier to see you. How was your day?"

He wasn't sure he had an answer for that question, so he settled with the answer he figured she was looking for. "Molly Concannon is a treasure."

"Oh, I'm so glad to hear it." His *bubbe* beamed. "I hoped you'd like her."

"I do. I love how she presents her knowledge of art to the town, like modern art should be an integral part of a town that loves its history."

"That's wonderful. So?"

And here was the kicker. "I told her," he began slowly, setting the mood, "that not only was I willing to do a show for her, but also that I'd give her a sculpture outright to exhibit and sell as she chooses, on the condition that the proceeds, if any, go to funding arts in the Hollows school district and the libraries, as well as any developing sculptor series who needs it."

"Oh, *tateleh*, that's amazing." She gave him a quick hug before pouring herself a glass of tea. "She's smart, and I knew the two of you would connect. I didn't expect you'd give her all of that, but it's so good of you to do so. It's going to bring her some business, if not sales."

"And," he smiled, "I told her if she sold it, I'd give her another one." He paused. "I also gave her the option of having a semi-regular show, depending on how the first one does and your presence in town."

"You," *Bubbe* said as she ruffled his hair, "are a *mensch*."

The highest compliment she could give, and this time, he felt almost worthy of it. "I try. I don't always succeed, but I try."

Her answering smile meant the world. "So. Dinner?"

He nodded. "Dinner."

It was comforting to watch his *bubbe* remove the food from the stove, the oven, and the fridge. "This smells wonderful."

She cupped his cheek. "For you, love." And then she smiled as she sat down. "And for me. I deserve this time with my grandson, eating good food."

They said the blessings, cut the challah, and began to eat.

"So, what's going on with you and Sarah Goldman?"

What was going on with Sarah?

He savored the bite of kugel on his tongue as long as he could before answering, but of course his *bubbe* beat him to the point.

"Listen, *tateleh*. I've gotten calls from Chana, Carol—Sarah's boss at the bookstore—and at least one other person telling me they saw you with her and giving me their opinions on the subject. So, I'd very much like to hear what you think is going on before I tell all three of them to keep their noses out of my *tateleh's* business."

He shook his head, took a drink of his tea. "What did

they say, exactly?"

"The usual. Which is to say that Sarah was with my grandson, in the middle of the Caf and Nosh, sharing lunch even though he didn't want anything to do with the Hanukkah festival. He tried to pay, but Chana was insulted so she gave them a free lunch."

Insulted was new. But okay.

"And the other? Carol?"

"Carol heard from Chana, saw Sarah staring at someone through the window before she came in to work with a perpetual smile on her face, and said Chana needs to stop and that you need to keep doing what you're doing because you're making Sarah smile."

He found himself smiling as he grabbed a piece of challah. "I'm being her friend," he replied. "Spending time with her because I like her. And also, for the record, I think Chana must have been insulted because our lunch was interrupted by a hipster council dude."

"That *putz*," his bubbe said as she rolled her eyes. "No wonder she was insulted; your lunch was interrupted by a piece of garbage spewing his filth. That one deserves a knuckle sandwich."

He wanted to laugh at the image of his beloved *bubbe* punching anybody, but he knew all too well that she was capable of anything she could do to protect the people she cared about. But then he had the opportunity to ask a real question. "What's…his issue?"

"People like him," his *bubbe* began, "are part of the reason your mother doesn't like small towns, *tateleh*."

He raised an eyebrow. "What do you mean?"

"Well he's used to towns that are like him, where people all celebrate the same holidays, eat the same foods, worship at the same place, on the same day and in the same way. But he's come to Hollowville and realized we're not like that. And, really, haven't ever been like that."

"So instead of embracing Hollowville's inclusivity, he's trying to erase it?"

"You got it right on the nose, *tateleh*. And target one is the Hanukkah festival."

And then he asked the most important question on his mind. "Does he have a chance?"

That was when his *bubbe* looked a little uncertain. "I love Robert Goldman. He was a great temple president, but he had his ways about things, and the Hanukkah festival was one of them. If they can fix it this year, they can make the kind of money that it was projected to make for local businesses. And money is the thing that will help a town like Hollowville justify supporting a festival like this one, as opposed to something as red and green as the other area festivals."

"And if they can't?"

She shrugged. "Then no more Hanukkah festival, and we get a tree and lights in the square, and red and green and carols and things. Figgy pudding too."

"Because that's really what Trustee Webster wants."

Bubbe nodded, took a sip of her tea. "Red and green now, some eggs in the springtime, maybe a bunny. No sukkahs in the fall festival—the list goes on and on. Maybe some ashes and fish for variety, but that's it. Hollowville becomes like every other small town people talk about. And proves your mother right."

Proves your mother right.

He didn't want to dwell on that. There were other, more important things to dwell on.

"And Sarah?"

"What about Sarah? What are you asking me, really?"

He wasn't sure. Not at all. "I guess, is there any advice? Anything you can say?"

"First, *tateleh*, you're a man, responsible for yourself and your own choices. What I care about," she said, "is that you be mindful of those who are going to be impacted by your choices."

"Do you mean the gossip?"

His *bubbe* took a sip from the wineglass next to her glass of tea before she spoke again. "That girl, that woman, really, has had *tsoris* in love. She's had trouble moving past bad relationships, so the gossip is only the half of it. It's her too."

He nodded. "I will be careful, and be smart. And be clear."

"Clear, *tateleh*. Be very clear. She and you both deserve that." She paused, grinning. "That and someone who's going to eat as much food as I can cook over this weekend."

"I'm looking forward to exceeding all of your expectations."

"I'm glad to hear that."

But what would he do about Sarah? He'd adored spending time with her. Was there anything else? Was that enough for now?

It had to be enough.

SARAH BARELY MANAGED to make it through the day. There were three new fiction events to organize, paperwork to send to Dr. Hernandez at the library on a possible paired nonfiction event for October, as well as next-stage work on a few other events. By the time five p.m. rolled around, the relatively short nature of this shorter day surprised even her. She left the office, shut down her computer, helped close up the store (they closed early on Fridays, of course) and said goodbye to everybody before heading to her car.

Traffic wasn't that bad, thankfully, and within a sane amount of time, she headed toward the hill that separated Hollowville's central business district from her parents' house. Friday night dinner with her parents was a tradition, one she looked forward to each week. Her mother was an amazing cook, and she loved to talk with her parents.

As she pulled into the driveway of the house she grew up

in, she couldn't help but focus on the pathway to the backyard where she spent hours as a child, running in the grass, climbing trees and taking in the fresh air. She spent so many hours there, her parents thought she was going to be a botanist.

But books were her first love; and her favorite hours were spent inside the house, under a blanket in front of the fireplace reading as many books as she could get her hands on. And that meant she had to get inside; not the front door, of course, where deliveries and guests who didn't know better came to knock and ring the deficient doorbell.

No. People who mattered, those who were loved, went to the side door. The side door that led directly into the kitchen, the family's focal point. And as she did every Friday, her mother was standing in front of the stove, putting together a meal that would be the highlight of her culinary week.

"Hi, Mom," Sarah said, slightly overwhelmed by the smells of kasha varnishkes and baked potatoes and roast beef and the tang of the salad dressing. "Oh wow."

"Go wash up," her father said as he breezed by, kissing her on the cheek. "We're about ready to start."

"Okay." She headed inside, past her mother, and into the bathroom to wash her hands and take a few moments before dinner, dropping her things in her old bed-turned-guest-room.

When she returned, the table was set, napkins folded,

and dinner spread out like a masterpiece. There was roast beef, baked potatoes, the barley and bowtie pasta mixture already dished onto her plate, and fresh-baked challah on the cutting board at the center of the table.

They said the blessings, cut the challah, and she dug right into the food. It was perfect.

"I hear you had coffee with someone at the C&N this afternoon," her mother casually said as she passed the salad dressing. "Anybody in particular?"

Just like that, the perfect mirage shattered into a thousand pieces. It was family after all, and family was never perfect, just loved. "Just a friend," she said, the phrasing almost a reflex, the words she'd repeated multiple times to multiple people in a way she still hadn't gotten used to and probably wouldn't. "And," she said, "it wasn't coffee. It was brunch."

Her mother laughed as her father passed her the challah. Sarah could see herself in the golden warmth of her father's beige skin, in the freckles that dotted her mother's whiter skin. She took another slice of challah and sighed.

"Brunch with the metal sculptor who'd turned you down is interesting news."

Her parents were pretty good about not interfering in her life; they advised, they loved, but they didn't push. Usually. "Dad," she said, the challah suddenly going sour in her mouth. "Please. This isn't… I'm not…"

Her father raised an eyebrow and turned to her mother. "Interesting," he said.

"It's boring, not interesting," Sarah replied, grinning at them both. "What's interesting is how both of you are doing and, failing that, I'm fascinated by how wonderful this meal tastes. There's so much of it."

"You have a wonderful appetite," her mother interjected as Sarah was getting her fourth helping. "I'd like to think it was my cooking."

"It is," she replied. "Enough home cooking to keep me sated on salads, takeout, and easy-to-make things for another week."

"Also," her father said, "a very clear procrastination technique."

She pointed at her father's plate. It was as full as hers was, if not more so. "Which you're also engaging in."

"I just like your mother's cooking," her father replied. "Touché, nonetheless."

But this was Friday night, with a good meal on the table and happiness. There were more important words to be said. "I love you. I love you both."

"Better when it comes with a brilliant home-cooked meal," her mother quipped.

Sarah shook her head. "Unconditionally. Even when you want to be yet another player in the game of town gossip."

"I was at HHC, picking up a book," her father said, by way of an explanation she neither needed nor wanted. "Minding my own business, of course."

"Of course." She rolled her eyes. "And let me guess, someone told you that I was in the C&N with Elsa Lieberman's grandson."

"Yes," her father said. "That and you two were ambushed by Webster. I can't believe he's causing that much trouble."

She raised an eyebrow. "Why are you surprised, exactly?"

"Because I never thought that there would be people in Hollowville who didn't understand the tradition of the festival, of why we have it." Her father shook his head. "That it's really..." He paused. "It's the idea of us losing institutional town memory. I can't believe I didn't think something like this would happen."

She sighed. "Times change, and sometimes not for the better. So we're doing what we can, reminding this town and the outside world how important it is to remember what and why Hollowville is the way it is. And why Trustee Webster and those like him are wrong about our traditions."

"Traditions like love and happiness?"

Her mother was so predictable.

"Love, yes," she said. "But also happiness, inclusivity, and mutual respect for all faiths and all people who celebrate holidays in December, not just one."

"Speaking of love," her mother continued, "because we need to talk about that, do you have plans to see him again?"

She shook her head. "I walked him to his meeting and then I went to work, where I was for the rest of the day. Satisfied?"

Even as they nodded their heads and changed the subject, she would eat her socks instead of this gorgeous meal if this was the end of their line of questioning.

Chapter Ten

HE HADN'T MEANT to stop by the bookstore.

Liar.

He had. He'd meant to stop by, see if she was there and then leave. So why was crossing the threshold so hard?

It was gorgeous outside, so standing randomly on a Hollowville street wouldn't be that weird of a thing. One of the few times the traditional stereotype of being an artist might help him?

"She's not here, you know."

He looked up into the dark brown eyes of an older woman. Her graying hair was cut short and framed her face.

"Um…"

"Carol Thomas, proprietress of *Tales from Hollowville.* Friend of"—she waved her hand—"anybody who matters in this town. You are, I think, looking for Sarah?"

He shoved his hands in the pockets of his jeans and nodded. "Hoping I'd catch her here. I guess not?"

"She's here often," Ms. Thomas agreed. "Not now though."

"So I should come back?"

"I'd love to see you come back here," she said. "Maybe buy a book or two. But finding Sarah? Now I think she's having an impromptu meeting at the Caf and Nosh. She muttered something about a website and drinks and bolted."

"Do you know what time she'll be back?"

"I'm only her boss," Ms. Thomas said, winking, "not her keeper. You know, you can go find her now that I told you where she is."

He thought about the idea, and whether he wanted to interrupt Sarah's meeting. "I'm leaving, going back to Brooklyn soon."

"Leaving that grandma of yours already, hmm?"

The weekend was over, and he needed to get back to his own space. "Weekend's over," he said, after parsing his words. "But I do have time to get a latte before I go to the train."

"Good decision. Keep making good decisions, Isaac." Ms. Thomas paused. "You look just like the pictures your grandma's been showing me. She's proud of you."

"Thanks, Ms. Thomas," he said. "I very much appreciate the compliment and the information." And with a grateful wave, headed down the street to the Caf and Nosh.

SARAH TOOK A deep drink of her soofganiyot latte and nodded. Batya Averman, Shelly's niece, had time off from her actual job at the Historical Society of the Hollows and finally had time to refresh the awful festival website.

"So without a central logo, this is the best I can do." Batya said, focusing on the screen in front of her as she put her dark brown hair in yet another bun. The bright blue glasses she wore matched the inkstain on her cheek, and brought out the olive undertones of her pale skin.

"You don't have a logo?"

Anna. Of course. Sarah rolled her eyes at her best friend's question. "Not really. We have the general typeface and the…you're helping with the press releases, and gave a list of contacts who might be interested in covering the festival. How did you not know we didn't have a logo?"

"Because I'm helping my boss organize an exhibit, and then trying to put together a proposal for something I might want to talk to my boss about, taking care of all of my other responsibilities at the museum, as well as vetting your list of reporter/critics. I can barely see straight."

"You have a point there," Sarah confirmed. "I guess."

"You guess what?" Anna took a piece of her hamentaschen and shoved it in her mouth. "I think if my friend spent more time searching for an artist and less time flirting with the sculptor who turned us down, she'd have an easier time getting a logo."

"We are not flirting. We're…having fun."

"I need to hear this," Batya interrupted. "Because someone needs to have fun."

"First of all, there's nothing to tell," Sarah said, fighting her impulse to crawl under the table. "And second of all, Anna, where is the 'us' coming from?"

"I'm your best friend," Anna pointed out. "If there is a thing you're doing that's taking a lot of your time, making me judge your priorities, then it is never a 'you' but an 'us.' Second of all, you are blushing, which means that something is going on that you need to tell me about."

In the silence that followed, where Sarah tried to figure out what to say, the bell rang against the front door of the restaurant. It was clear and loud, and it felt as if the entire Sunday brunch crowd had turned to see who'd arrived.

Of course it was Isaac. He filled the doorframe, looking adorable and hesitant and entirely too unsure of his welcome.

"Would you like a table for yourself," Chana said, filling the silence Sarah wanted to occupy, "or would you like to join a party that's already here?"

"Uh," she heard him say. "Can I get a soofganiyot latte and then decide?"

"Of course you can," Chana replied.

And that's when Sarah walked towards him, though she didn't remember getting up from the table. "Hi," she said. "I'm glad you stopped by."

"Carol told me where you were. I hope I'm not intruding?"

"Not really, but," she bit her lip, "we're working on festival stuff. Website and all."

"I see." Disappointment in his tones.

There would be in hers too if she could manage to say something smart. "Later?"

"I'd like to, but I have to get back to Brooklyn. Need to take an inventory and start the process of negotiating what the show could be like."

"You figured out the show? Oh that's wonderful."

He nodded. "I figured out there could be a show. So thank you."

"For what?"

He smiled and she tried not to faint.

"For reassuring me that having an art show in Hollowville was something I wanted to do."

"I'm so glad," she managed as Chana passed a soofganiyot latte across the counter. "I'm glad to hear it."

He reached into his pocket and pulled out what looked like a wallet. She watched his hands fumble within it, emerging with a white card. "Here," he said.

Her fingers brushed his as she took the card from him. "What's this?"

"Number, email et cetera. I have to go now, but maybe you could call or email when you can?"

She nodded. "Yes. I would love that."

"Me too." He swiped his credit card with a flick his wrist.

"Till next time?" she said, forcing the words out of her

mouth.

"Yes." He turned to Chana. "Thanks for the latte."

"*B'tay avon,*" she replied. "Good appetite and good day, Isaac."

And it was the hardest thing to watch him leave, bag she'd not seen slung across his back. But she did. And then she forced herself back to look at the masterpiece Batya had created. She had work to do, after all.

HIS TRAIN WAS late; that's what the overhead clock said. Which meant he'd be waiting at the Hollowville train station longer than he'd expected, the train he'd have to take without Sarah. A train he'd be taking away from her and his bubbe.

But there was a to do list a mile long waiting for his attention. So he was headed home.

"Mr. Lieberman!"

He turned; people were starting to learn who he was already in this town. He wasn't sure what he felt about that.

The person in question was an older man, wearing a suit jacket. "I'm Jack Lewis. Member HHC. Big fan of your sculptures."

He smiled. "Thank you."

"Saw your show at the Vincent, not the last one but the one before. Great stuff. You know," Lewis said, "you do good, strong, minimalist stuff."

"Thank you," he said, "I'm inspired by the metal itself. The sculpture comes out of the substance, not always the other way around."

Lewis nodded in the way of people who genuinely enjoyed art, the kind of people he liked talking to about his sculpting. "You're not doing the menorah."

"No," he said. "I don't do commercial celebrations of any holiday, whether I celebrate it or not."

"So you think a tree's better?"

"That's not what I said," he replied, trying to keep calm as the man seemed to close the distance between them. "I just don't..."

"You know," Lewis continued, his hands fisting, one covering the other before the man put them in his pockets, "the festival committee still don't have a logo, which means the website's good, but it's not great. Which means the press releases are not the way they should be. Which means we can't get our message across the way we need to. Which means..."

Isaac bit his lip, stepped back, and looked at the schedule. "What, Mr. Lewis?" he asked, putting verbal distance between them, hiding behind the mask of professionalism. "What?"

"Which means if we don't have a menorah, the festival will fail." Back and forth the hands came in and out of the pockets.

Isaac stepped back again. He nodded. Breathed again.

"Rest of the committee are trying to sweet-talk this thing, make it look good, like some kind of Hanukkah harmony thing. But not me." Lewis shook his head. "Because I'm a numbers guy. Live and die by the numbers. And, friend, I can see where those numbers come from. And in the end? If this festival fails? If we don't have a sculpture, well…"

"This is the train to Grand Central."

Isaac had never before in his life been so happy to hear the sounds associated with an arriving train. "Okay," he said as he turned and walked the few steps that separated him from Hollowville, and from Mr. Lewis.

"Just remember," Lewis said as the doors of the train closed.

His heart pounded as the train pulled away, and as he found the closest seat, he stared out the window at the river going by. Far away from the platform and farther away from Hollowville.

Chapter Eleven

Late August

ISAAC EMAILED HIS agent as soon as he got the photos back from Molly Concannon. She'd given him a concept he could work with, and he'd approved the design of the space she'd given him. It had taken a bit of time to organize it, but it was done. There would be a show.

Finally.

He didn't think he'd have to wait long for a reply, so he organized a few things and started to make his breakfast. Sure enough, just as he'd poured a glass of orange juice, his phone buzzed with a FaceTime call.

He opened the call to see his agent. Dark circles under his green eyes, even his freckles looked pale against his normally pinkish pale skin, "So," Sean said without preamble, "what's up?"

"I want you to draw up a contract for a show at the gallery I sent you. Address is there too."

There wasn't a pause; Sean was supposed to set up the shows and organize things. "Standard agreement?"

"Few additions to the basic agreement."

"I'm listening."

"First, maybe tiny bit less on the commission and profit sharing. More on the gallery's side than mine."

"Are you sure?"

Sean sounded dubious; Isaac figured he hadn't read the address. "Check the name of the gallery," he replied. "Maybe that will put things into perspective."

There was a long pause and a very deep breath. "You're doing a show in Hollowville?"

From dubious to outright incredulous in thirty seconds, but Isaac didn't care. "Yep."

"Why exactly are you doing this show? There?"

"Well," he grinned, "doing a different type of show is always good every once in a while, especially if it's something that's going to test my skills in a way I don't usually get to."

"That's the answer you give the papers and the critics when they wonder why the heck you're doing a show in Westchester."

"To them I'd also say that the community is finally growing its cultural scene. So I figured I'd give them something to look forward to, and possibly a tent pole exhibit to help it along."

"That's great. But what's the real story? What's the story you're telling yourself?"

He smiled. "My grandmother. I want to do a show where she's the center of attention as much as my art is. Which is the very least she deserves for her support of me and my choices and my career."

"Sounds like you're contemplating something larger than a show."

"I have most of everything I want here," he said, reading in between the lines. He wasn't moving to Hollowville for one gallery and his *bubbe*. "Plus, spending time with my *bubbe* doesn't mean giving up anything."

"What's the other thing?"

"The other..." He paused, then realized he'd asked Sean for something else to go in the contract. "I want that 'I don't want people to influence my decision' clause in the contract."

"What do you mean? Where is this coming from?"

"I was asked to do a charity commission," he began. Which wasn't exactly what the festival sculpture was, but it was the best way to describe it. "And the people who asked me to do it, some of them don't have the best boundaries, and if I'm going to do this show, I don't want to deal with that."

He still shuddered when he thought of how close he'd come to disaster, back on the train station platform; whether it was a punch or fear or something.

"Makes sense." Sean paused, and he wondered what his agent was thinking. "Though I gotta tell you, charity commissions are pretty good. Especially during the holidays."

That song and dance again. "They are. I'm still not going to do this one," he said. "I'm just navigating a bunch of factors in order to do the gallery show. That should be enough."

Sean snorted. "Yes. Though that's going to go over well..."

"What?"

"You're effectively banning people who asked you to do a charity commission from a show that's taking place in a small town your grandmother lives in. Not going to judge, but I think it's a mistake."

He sighed. All he could see was the train platform and the doors that separated him from the angry man in the suit jacket. "I can't."

Sean nodded on the screen. "I get your reasons, but you have to deal with the consequences."

"I know," he replied. "And I will."

"Good. I'll write it up and send it to you ASAP."

All business again. Now he was ready for the show. Now he could look forward to it. "Thank you." Because the most important thing about this was letting his *bubbe* share in his accomplishments, no matter what he had to do to make that happen.

Hollowville

FIVE IN-STORE EVENTS, four second-stage events, three partner events.

Next, she'd be looking for turtle doves, tablets, partridges, and who knows what else. But the life of an events and orders coordinator was never smooth.

"Good news," Carol said as she entered the office.

"Tell me," she said grinning and taking a long sip of her soofganiyot latte. "What's going on?"

"Dr. Leonard Abraham wants to do an event in Hollowville!"

"That's fantastic." Dr. Abraham was a well-respected author and historian; his books routinely hit the best seller list, and his most recent title was about local history. "Did the representative say which title?"

Carol shook her head. "Actually, no. She didn't. She did say that Dr. Abraham somehow got a press release. About a festival, and he wanted to sign here and see about it. So we talked, and I think we picked a date that was clear."

"Wait. He called here because of a press release?"

Had Shelly's press release and Batya's website actually worked? Was there hope for the festival?

"Yep." Carol sat down in the chair across from her desk. "The press release came from Hollowville, and believe you me I tried to pin down what he liked about it or the town, but I couldn't, so there we were. Anyway, this is the only bookstore here in town, so he called us."

"That's wonderful news."

"There is also *not* so wonderful news."

She bit her lip. "Okay?"

"So apparently…"

Suddenly, the speaker in the office crackled. "Sarah, you have a call on line one; Sarah, line one."

"You're probably going to want to take that and I'm going to want to listen," Carol said, suddenly solemn.

She shrugged and picked up the phone on the desk as Carol stood and closed the door before returning to her seat. "Hello, Tales from Hollowville, Sarah Goldman speaking."

"Sarah, it's Chana. And hello, Carol, because I know you're listening."

"Hi, Chana."

Something worrisome was going on. Chana did not call during the middle of the day for any reason. "What's up?"

"I've accepted Jack Lewis's resignation from the committee," Chana said without preamble. "Jack told me that he'd confronted Isaac, and I confirmed with Elsa…"

Images crossed her mind, of fists flying and concern and…

"Confronted?!" she asked. She needed details, wanted to know what had happened so that she could do something. "As in what confronted? Were there fisticuffs? Were there…?"

"There weren't actually fisticuffs," Chana replied. "There were words, and Lewis said he might have been a bit more intimidating than he should. Elsa said, from what she could get from Isaac…"

"Told his *bubbe* under duress, I think," Carol interrupted. "If he had his way, that boy would have forgotten the entire incident. At least until he put some kind of clause in that contract of his, banning the committee from any shows at Molly's gallery when he's there."

Sarah didn't know what to feel: upset for him, angry at whatever Jack Lewis had done to make Isaac feel it was necessary, angry at what the town board of trustees might do when they heard about the incident, unsure in general. Didn't know how to react.

Banned. From his show.

"So we…I'm…banned."

"Anybody on the committee," Chana replied. "And if we want to get technical, anybody currently working on the festival this year is also specifically banned from the show on the first night. The preview night."

"When he's here. In Hollowville, unveiling the show for his *bubbe*, for Elsa."

"Yes, Sarah," Carol said. "You're among the people banned from the show that night."

And now she understood why Carol had wanted to listen in on the conversation. Why it had mattered.

Why did it hurt so much?

"Now we've scheduled the Leonard Abraham signing the day after…"

"Same day I'm having the cavalcade, so people can go directly from the signing to the cavalcade."

The Cavalcade of Latkes was a town event that heralded

both the beginning of Hanukkah and the Caf and Nosh's corresponding Hanukkah menu with tons of latkes of different styles and components. The proceeds of the event went to a charity of Chana's choice. "Wow," she said. "But that's going to be a really busy weekend. You'll need me in the store."

"Nope."

Sarah blinked "What? I mean..."

Carol shook her head. "We'll start planning now. You'll get as much as you need to do done before the end of business the Friday before the signing. If there's any last-minute details you won't be able to take care of, you'll leave me a list, and I'll call you if there's any trouble."

"You do so much," Chana said. "We'll take over the final stuff, so when you come in at eleven on the Sunday to supervise the last-minute details at the library, everything will be ready for you."

And that was the real reason they wanted to take the call together. Because they knew she'd be hurting. "So you'll take over as much prep as I need?"

"We'll find a way," Carol said. "Yes. I mean, Dr. Abraham is a big-ticket event, but your mental health is more important. So, myself, Dr. Rodriguez at the library, and Chana will make sure we get this done."

She was so lucky she knew these women, so lucky she worked with them, and so lucky she lived in a town where people knew her all too well.

And she was also lucky that she had friends who lived in a city just close enough she could visit easily, and far enough away where she didn't have to be anywhere near the guy who didn't want her anywhere near him.

Brooklyn

ISAAC WAS EXHAUSTED and hungry to boot. He'd just gotten back from the shop, having done preliminary work on some of the pieces he was bringing to Hollowville, when his phone buzzed. "Hi, *Bubbe*," he replied. "Miss me already?"

"*Tateleh*," she replied.

There was censure in her tone, and he didn't like it. "Yes?"

"I'm disappointed in you."

Yep. Censure, upset—a tone that stopped his breath. "What? What did I do? How can I fix it?"

"You were right in banning committee members from the preview night, but you forgot something."

"Something?" He got nervous. "A local town conflict? A meeting? A fall tradition?"

"No. Not something. Someone."

And then he knew.

Sarah.

Sarah, the cute girl he'd dragged into the town's central restaurant, Sarah who'd stood by him as he dealt with the trustee, who'd smiled at him and showed him where he needed to go.

Sarah who made his heart stop, who'd smiled at him and called him a Hanukkah snob when she first met him, who'd split matzah brei with him.

Sarah was the vice chair of the committee.

He knew he'd banned the vice chair of the committee, checked off a list of people.

He just didn't think of what that meant.

Until now.

"Yes," he said, the words painful on his tongue. "I banned her from the preview night. I banned the committee and she's on the committee, and I screwed up."

"You did, *tateleh.*"

"I didn't think. I didn't."

"And you hurt her. You hurt her because you didn't think of what you were doing."

And that's what hurt the most.

"I know." There was no pause, no thought. He was owning this. "How can I fix this without making it worse?"

"Flowers?"

He shook his head. She didn't seem the type who'd appreciate flowers…

He had a connection to a jewelry designer. Maybe she'd help him out with a special delivery.

"Does she have pierced ears?"

Bubbe laughed. "I think so. But why are you asking me?"

"Because you see her more often?" Which was completely lame, but it worked better than *I was trying not to stare at her.*

"Okay." She paused. "So where are you sending this special delivery of yours, whatever it's going to be?"

There was only one answer. "The bookstore. *Tales from Hollowville*—that's the name?"

"That's the name," *Bubbe* said, approval in her tones. "Give her a card with your phone number or email address inside of it."

And again, from the sound of his *bubbe's* voice, he could tell he'd made the right decision. He was definitely glad for small miracles. "Will do."

Hopefully, he'd be able to begin the process of fixing the mistake he'd made in a moment of thoughtlessness with a simple gesture that showed he cared.

Hollowville

SARAH CAME INTO the store for a bit on Saturday, stopping short when she saw the envelope atop her desk. She picked it up, saw her name, and on the corner, in very careful handwriting was Isaac's name and address.

She stared at it, ran a finger across the front. She didn't know what to feel about Isaac or how even to react to this. She looked up at Anna who'd come into the store with her on the way to meet Batya for coffee. "I don't know why he would be sending me anything."

"You don't?"

"No. I mean...we haven't talked and he banned me from his show, so..."

"My thought," Anna said, "is that this might have to do with the latter. Maybe some kind of apology gift."

"Really?"

Anna shrugged. "Open it." She paused. "Unless you think it's dangerous?"

"No. I just don't know what it could be."

"Only one way to find out."

Which was true. So, Sarah opened the envelope to find a card and a box. The card, in simple slashing handwriting, read, "Please accept my apology and my friendship." And his email address. Interesting, she thought.

The box itself was small, the size of her palm. She opened it to find a tiny envelope that unsealed at the top. After she removed the thick tape covering the opening, she saw silver hooks attached to what looked like bottles.

Small bottles: one orange and one caramel brown. She couldn't stop laughing, even as Anna stared.

"He sent you earrings?"

Sarah nodded, putting the pieces of the puzzle together. He'd sent her iced tea and orange juice, paired in earring form. She didn't know what to say or what it meant aside from a gift to match the apology. He was nice, he was cute, but still. So many questions to answer, so many thoughts to sort out.

"Speechless over silly earrings?"

"They're not silly," she insisted before she realized what she was saying. "I mean…well…"

"So if they're not silly, what are they?!"

"A very adorable apology," she replied, even though she hadn't really decided what she thought beyond that.

Anna wasn't amused. "I don't believe that, but if you want to convince yourself that's all they are, I won't stop you."

"This was a nice gesture from a guy who knew he hurt me by banning me from the art exhibit. That's it."

"Like, nice what? Nice heart melt? Nice this guy is a cinnamon roll? What?"

Sarah blushed. "He's not a cinnamon roll. I'd call him…a rugelach, maybe? Like sculpted, hard-looking on the outside but sweet all over?"

"What is this hard-*looking* business?"

"When I spilled the tea on him, I spilled it on this white dress shirt he was wearing. Anyway, he ended up taking off the shirt and doing the show in the city in a white tank. And I actually liked *that* show better than the sculptures, to be honest."

Anna laughed. "Now this kind of content is what I come to Hollowville for," she said, settling into the chair in front of the desk.

"What time is Batya coming?"

Anna paused to look down at her phone. "She just texted me. She's on her way but she got caught up at her aunt's house. So you have time."

"Good. Because I need to send a thank you." And if there was anything else she wanted to say in the email, she'd figure it out when she was writing it.

September
Brooklyn

THE EMAIL FROM Sarah had come unexpectedly, thanking him for the earrings and accepting his apology. One email led to another and another and then a phone number, a text and an invitation to join him on a Saturday night for a trip to his favorite Brooklyn street food festival.

It had worked out perfectly; he usually went with a group of friends, but this year, none of them could find a date when they were all free. Which meant he'd been planning to go by himself, until he and Sarah had been talking on the phone, and he'd been inspired to ask. And that led to this moment. The one where she stood with him on a street corner not far from his studio. And whether it was Brooklyn or the way she looked standing in the middle of his neighborhood, he couldn't take his eyes off of her.

"Fried food in Brooklyn?"

He smiled. "Yep. Welcome to Streetfest." He gestured widely at the various vendors. "You should probably try everything."

And there was a lot of it to try. Quipes, empanadas, multiple varieties of fried chicken and French fries, mofongo, as well as plantains, gyoza, samosas, knishes and fried wontons. Food that smelled tantalizing, tasty, and so very, very appetizing.

"I do want to eat it all," she said.

She was dressed for early fall in sweater, a cute dress, and what looked like a more comfortable pair of shoes than she was wearing the last time he'd seen her in Hollowville.

"Let's do this," he said. His stomach also growled—his encouragement had been genuine.

And so they headed down the street, stopping at vendors, buying a few things from the booths, and finding a spot to eat it, before getting up and doing it again.

"I can't help myself," Sarah confessed, her eyes bright. "This is sooo good. I kinda don't want to stop."

"Who says you have to?"

"The clothing I brought with me," she said dryly. "I'd like to fit into it."

"Fair enough," he replied. "But I maybe should point out that we're walking and you have to head to the subway."

"I was going to take a cab to my friend Anna's place; it's not far from here."

"You have a friend who lives near here and you've never

been to a fair like this?"

Sarah laughed. "My sense of Brooklyn geography is non-existent," she admitted. "So by near here, I could mean a place that's clear on the other side of the borough."

He nodded, and he wanted to put his arm around her, kiss her, take her hand as they walked. Could he? Was this a date? A random outing he came up with as a tangible means of apologizing? A way for them to spend time together outside of the confines of Hollowville?

He didn't know at this point. But because he wasn't sure, he didn't want to push it. Dates came with strings attached; relationships would come with questions he wasn't ready to answer. And so he walked alongside her, not touching her. "I get it," he said.

He heard the sharp intake of her breath first, and as he turned slightly, he saw she'd tripped on a crack in the pavement. He moved and caught her, carefully.

He took a deep breath of relief of his own as he felt her arms come around him, circling his waist even after she'd regained her balance.

More importantly, he didn't want her to let go. This was a problem.

She bit her lip before carefully removing her arms from his body, leaving a chill where her hands had been.

"Thanks," she said. "I mean for catching me."

He nodded. "You're welcome. Glad I was able to." And being in a situation where holding her was possible wasn't so much of a problem after all.

"Maybe we should be careful?"

And there was the bombshell of reality again.

Careful. Entanglements. Heat. Kissing. Relationships. Gossip.

None of those went well together, especially when what had brought them together was so tightly entwined with the kind of expectations that would hurt more than just them if they failed.

So even though he'd gotten so used to telling Sarah no, the only word Isaac could say then and there, was a bitter-sweet, "Yes."

Chapter Twelve

Hollowville

THERE WERE MANY things Sarah could say about Isaac. He was cute, wonderful, and complicated in many ways, but the man knew his food. He knew who made it best, and why it was so important for people to share their favorites. Seeing his eyes light up as she tasted things she'd eaten before and things she was trying for the first time made her happy and melty inside.

"I don't get it," Anna said, a dubious expression on her face. She'd stayed over in Hollowville the night before, and now the two of them were lounging in Sarah's apartment, preparing to go out to brunch. "How did you go from writing a thank-you note to a quick trip to Brooklyn I didn't know about?"

She shrugged. "I don't know."

"Having a life."

"Harsh," she said, tempted to throw a pillow in her bestie's direction.

"Not so much," Anna returned, grinning back at her. "Besides. One of us needs one."

"You," she replied, "my dear judgmental bestie, should be focused on your upcoming conversation with your boss about the exhibit, as opposed to any other form of procrastination."

"Including helping you?"

Oh, Anna was insightful. She knew the lines, knew when not to cross them. "Oooh, that's harsh."

"It's true though. But I totally get it. You want my nose out of your slowly blossoming personal life. After I help you with this meeting."

Sarah shook her head. She didn't want to ignore or keep information from her best friend; there was a reason they were friends in the first place. "It's weird," she managed. "I mean, at this point, he's…nice. And there's no pressure."

"Stop examining it to death," Anna scolded. "You know, you might want to have a life that has nothing to do with this town and your responsibilities here. Not a secret, but something that's wholly yours."

Sarah sighed, stared out the living room window onto the sleepy Saturday morning streets of Hollowville. "You're right."

The nod her friend gave her was the encouragement she needed. "Maybe I just have to relax and enjoy myself." She pulled her cup of coffee toward her as she waited for her friend to look through papers she'd prepared. "So what do you think?"

Inspired by the Brooklyn street fair she'd seen the week

before, she'd made major changes to the food part of the festival. Mixing the latke vendors with the empanada, garlic knot, fried wonton, and quipes sellers; mixing the soofganiyot booths with the vendors who were going to sell churros and gulab jamun. And Anna was the first person to see the proposal before next Monday's meeting.

"I think," her friend finally said, "that this is a great idea. It's nicer than before. More open, more exciting."

Which was the reaction Sarah had only dreamed of. She felt as if the corners of her lips were curving up on their own, but they weren't, they couldn't.

"I'm not the one you need to convince."

"Well," Sarah said, sighing. "I guess I can hope that the rest of the committee is going to be as open-minded as you are."

"You can hope," Anna replied. "But I suspect convincing some of the people on the committee will be more difficult than others."

"True. I think Chana will like this. Hers is the most important mind that has to be convinced."

"Which means you have a few days to figure out how to convince the rest of the committee. But now? You need to feed me."

Brooklyn

IT WAS LUNCHTIME in Brooklyn, and Isaac was meeting his friend Oliver, a painter, at one of their favorite places.

"Did you make it to Streetfest last weekend?"

"Yeah," he said. "I did. Didn't want to miss it, you know."

"Don't remind me," Oliver quipped back, humor twinkling in his brown eyes, the sun through the window emphasizing the pink undertones in his skin. "I had a great time with Jamie, but I missed the food. Did you go by yourself?"

Oliver's inevitable question. "I…well."

"So," Oliver said, amusement clearly written on his face. "You didn't go by yourself."

And now he'd been backed into a corner by his own lack of desire to discuss anything. He had no choice but to admit the truth. "I didn't."

His friend snorted. "Feels like getting your answer is going to be like pulling teeth. Clearly, you were there with someone we haven't met yet."

There was some truth to that. He did want to keep his time with Sarah separate from his friends, mostly because he hadn't decided didn't know yet what he was doing with Sarah and how long it would last. "Not ready for you to meet," he clarified. "It's an important difference."

"It's a distinction without a difference." Oliver shook his head. "Especially considering how you asked Jamie to make her earrings."

Which was true. There would be no way of getting out of this lunch without telling Oliver the truth. Isaac sighed. "Yep. It was nice to hang with her at the street fair, kinda awesome to eat all the things with her, see her eyes brighten. It was cool to just...be with her, you know?"

"*Be*, as in spend time together, away from the town she lives in and all the people who place every social interaction under an electron microscope?"

Isaac laughed. "Yeah. Pretty much. But like...I don't know what I want this to be. I mean, yeah. She's cool. But...."

"I get it. You want to get to know this girl before we meet her and convince her you're awful."

"In some twisted way, and don't quote me on this it seems she belongs to everybody who lives in that town." Not to mention he was having difficulties understanding his own feelings, much less speaking about them. "And I guess I wanted her to have something of her on her own for five minutes, even after I banned her from the show."

"Wait, what? What were you thinking?!"

"Long story. Earrings were the apology, but they also ended up being the conversation starter, and we weren't going to go together to Streetfest this year, so I ended up inviting her, and it was amazing."

"Again, don't remind me. I think you may need to take me for Dominican food to make sure my stomach recovers from the fact I missed the quipes."

"Easily done."

"Good. Now the next question, and you can't dodge this. Are you seeing her again outside of Hollowville?"

Wasn't that a question he wanted an answer to? "I'd like to. It would be great. But I don't know."

Oliver nodded and took a long drink of his cold brew. "Got it. Leaving it up to her this time."

That was the theory at least. He was the one who initiated the first outing, so he'd leave it up to her to start the next. Unfortunately, he hadn't heard from her since she'd left Brooklyn and him behind. "If she wants to do this again," he told his friend, "that'll be for her to decide."

That was when his stomach decided to make its presence known. "Now I'd like to have lunch, okay?"

"Topic resoundingly dropped. Fine. Works for me."

Unfortunately, the fact that he hadn't heard from Sarah did not work for Isaac. And he didn't know what to do about it because waiting wasn't helping.

Hollowville

AS THE WEEK went on, Sarah hadn't been able to figure out how to handle convincing the rest of the committee of the merits of her proposal, nor did she manage to figure out what, if anything, she wanted to do about Isaac.

Finally, she found herself standing next to Chana, right outside the room where the committee would meet that night.

"You ready?" the older woman asked.

"No," she replied, knowing full well Chana would think it a joke. "But we don't have a choice, right?"

Chana clapped her on the shoulder. "We're as ready as we're going to be. And for what it's worth—which, let's face it, because I'm the chair of the committee, it should be worth a great deal—I like your proposal. I love the idea. And I love the kind of change you're bringing to the festival. If we want to bring more money and more tourists in, we have to make big changes, and I like this one."

Buoyed by Chana's encouragement, Sarah followed her into the room. Of course, she couldn't help but feel the jitters down to her bones. She could only hope that the committee felt as excited about her proposal as she did.

Unfortunately, the end of her presentation was met with silence.

Silence sometimes meant bad things. It also meant people were thinking.

Batya gave her a thumbs-up from her seat next to her aunt, who was making notes. Both good signs.

But those were some of the only good signs she saw.

The committee member who'd come back to fill Jack Lewis's seat, Mr. Bloom, had a stern look on his pale face. "I don't get it," he said. "We've run the festival food the same way for almost nine years. Easy to see what you want and get it quick. This just isn't right."

"If I may, this proposal allows for browsing, relaxing, and enjoying yourself as you do during every other part of the festival," Sarah answered.

"But," continued Mr. Bloom when nobody else on the committee seemed to support his query, "this isn't a street fair or an international food fair. Some of these items you're adding to the list of things on offer don't say Hanukkah to me. And having that kind of stuff, things nobody eats on Hanukkah at a Hanukkah festival, gives the wrong impression."

What Sarah wanted to do was yell. Instead, she pulled herself together, looked at Chana for approval, and then carefully took a breath. "The Hanukkah festival is about community," she said. "As we know, the only and most important requirement for a Hanukkah food is that it be fried. Jewish communities from all over the world eat different dishes on Hanukkah. Luckily, we live in an area where we can eat, enjoy, and learn about the wider Jewish community all at the same time."

Bloom still didn't seem satisfied, but thankfully Chana had also reached the end of her tether.

"As chair of the committee," she said while sending an icy stare to the rest of the committee, "I love the idea of having a bit of the world come to our festival. Who would we be as Jews if we didn't open the door, our hearts, and our stomachs to the strangers in our midst?"

There were a few more grumbles, but a glare at Bloom from Batya's aunt finally quieted him down long enough for a quick vote. The motion to permit Sarah's proposed changes to the food court area passed, in conjunction with a motion that would allow her to continue investigating food options under Chana's supervision. Much to everybody's relief.

Unfortunately, there was no relief for Sarah herself because the next item on the agenda was the sculpture. And she didn't know what to say or how to approach the subject in front of the committee.

"Any developments on the sculpture?" Chana asked.

"Well," she said, pulling herself together. "I've been trying to think of a way forward, and I haven't figured one out yet."

"I still don't see why we have to have a menorah anyway," Judith Goldberger said. She'd been so helpful on so many other issues, including spearheading the temple food drive, but her consistent lack of support for the idea of a menorah—and if Sarah thought about it, the festival itself—was upsetting. "I realize that this might be the last festival, but we've *somehow* managed to have a festival for nine years without a menorah at the core. Why is it so important to make sure we have one now?"

There were many different reasons why it was important to have a menorah. But any words she could think of to say were lost in the discussion that had bubbled up in the wake of Judith Goldberger's words. She couldn't hear the threads in the argument.

Chana put up her hand, the familiar exasperation clear in her eyes. As the committee came to silence, Sarah held her breath.

"We've had this conversation a few different times, and this time we have results."

There were gasps that made their way across the room, and Sarah knew at least one of them had been hers.

Chana shuffled a few papers before looking up at the committee "According to Shelly and Batya Averman's report, we're starting to get traffic from outside the community because we're one of the few specifically Hanukkah-focused festivals in this country."

"Yes," Batya said as she stood. "We're getting traffic from all over the country now. And by the way, Chana, you need to get answers to those questions I sent you so that I can send them back to the reporter from that airline magazine. There also have been questions about hotels." She paused and turned to Mr. Bloom. "A bunch of people have been directed toward the Hollowville Branch of Caliber Hotels."

Sarah couldn't help but notice that was a very nice touch, considering Bloom was one of the executives in charge of that hotel.

"I'll keep that in mind and make some Hanukkah packages available for guests if they wish. Maybe some things from some of the vendors."

Chana nodded, and Sarah couldn't keep the smile off her face. "Yes. That sounds great, Raphael, and thank you for reminding me about the questions, Batya. Anyway, as long as that kind of traffic and those requests continue, they should translate to the kind of dollars that the town and its businesses need, including the hotel. The money that *we* need. Do you understand?"

Judith didn't say anything, but Sarah took energy from the intense focus on Mr. Bloom's face as well as the smiles both Batya and her aunt were sporting.

"And yes," Chana continued, "I think we should still continue to search for a sculptor. But, as always, if anybody has ideas for a backup plan that still demonstrates the spirit of Hanukkah, I'm willing to listen."

Even though it hurt, Sarah knew Chana was right. The time for hoping or stalling had ended. As the festival was getting closer, she had to figure out something.

"The art department at Bruckner Community College might have a list of sculptors who could help," said Leah Hartog, a new member of the committee, excitement bringing out the pink undertones in her white skin. "Or possibly some of their art majors."

"Thank you," Sarah said. College students! Letting college students make their mark on the festival would be an amazing opportunity. "This sounds great."

She was excited to make the calls, but when the meeting

ended, Chana came up to her. "I didn't want to say this in front of the committee," she said. "But—"

"I understand," Sarah said. "We're coming down to the wire."

"Yes." Chana patted her on the shoulder. "You're doing an amazing job. The festival is coming together in a way that it hasn't before, which should bode well for us having a festival next year." She smiled. "And we'll do what we can to get a menorah. But in the end, if we don't have one, we don't have one."

"But I want there to be a symbol in the middle of this festival, and if nothing else it will be the festival's legacy. So that the town remembers we had a Hanukkah festival. Even if that menorah sits in a storage shed for years, when people see it they will remember. I just can't leave it empty."

"I know that you've been driving yourself hard recently. But you need to relax as much as you can. Life isn't a sprint, Sarah; it's a marathon. And you're just starting out." She paused and Sarah could see the concern in Chana's eyes. "Don't burn out. I'm looking forward to sharing the rest of the path with you."

Chapter Thirteen

October
Hollowville

SARAH SAT AT her desk, staring at the open email and the ten digits in the center she'd been trying to ignore for three days. But if she was going to make this awkward phone call, she had to do it soon. It was Thursday, the gallery show was on Saturday, the book signing was Sunday, and against her better judgment, as well as Carol's and at Anna's insistence, she was heading for the city on Friday.

The fact of the matter was, it was her turn to call him, had been her turn to initiate contact with him for weeks, if not more, and she'd been procrastinating. And still would have, except for the fact that the date had arrived where she had no choice.

"Did you call him already?"

Carol's voice rang through the halls, and she couldn't ignore her. "No."

The creaky hinges heralded the door opening, followed by the sound of boots on the carpet and a large sigh.

"Hi."

"Look," Carol said by way of greeting. "If you're going to call him, do it. Otherwise, stop staring at that email because you have others you need to handle."

There were benefits and drawbacks to having a boss who treated you like a granddaughter. "Okay. Fine."

Sarah swallowed, stared at the screen again, and picked up the phone. The numbers were easy enough to dial; she'd practically memorized them by this point. Now it was time for the wait. One ring. Two rings…

"Hello?"

He sounded uncertain, which of course was her fault for not keeping in touch. "Hi," she said, trying to insert joy into the situation. "It's Sarah."

"Yes. Hi, how are you?"

He was tentative, which was also her fault. And though the sound of his voice made her happy, his very obvious nerves didn't.

"I'm okay," she said. "I wanted to wish you good luck. I mean, break a leg or a hand or whatever for Saturday."

It took a long time for him to answer; she almost hung up the phone because she thought she'd lost him.

"Thank you. Really. I—"

"I get it," she interjected. "Absolutely. I know it's a weird situation." She paused for a second and decided to go for it, whatever it was. "So how about I take you to a meal or something as a token of how okay I am with this?"

"That would be great," he said. She eased her shoulders

down from her ears. "I'd like that."

"So when are you leaving for Hollowville?"

"Tomorrow," he said. "Tomorrow afternoon."

"I'm actually supposed to be getting into the city tomorrow afternoon. Is there a place we can meet near Grand Central?"

There was a pause, and she held her breath.

"Actually? There is."

The lightness in his voice was back. And as she jotted down the name of the place, she found herself looking forward to seeing him just that much more.

Manhattan

ISAAC STOOD BY the clock at the center of Grand Central terminal, his palms sweating. He couldn't believe Sarah had called him, but he was so glad she did.

He shifted his bag on his shoulder, checked his watch again. He was also thankful he was waiting alone, not with a group of his friends who'd be snickering and making him feel otherwise uncomfortable.

He didn't want anybody to see him like this.

Except her. As she walked toward him, his heart started to jump in his chest. She smiled, a tote bag on her jacket-clad shoulder, her boots pounding against the terminal's marble floor.

"Hey, sorry I'm late." She shook her head. "Trains are…trains."

The smile on her face almost knocked him to the ground. "I totally get it," he replied, shoving his words together. "The place isn't far from here."

She nodded. "Are we taking the subway?"

"Nope. It's walking distance, especially on a day like today."

As they headed through the terminal, they kept up a steady stream of conversation. He wanted to hear her voice, wanted to watch her eyes light up as they passed store windows filled with the oranges and black of early fall.

"I love this time of year," she said. "The pumpkins, the gold colors, the festivities, the shine of light that comes out of the darkness."

The bitter and the sweet. Which meant, "The candy. Sweet and sour."

"That too," she said her smile making him forget where he was. "I can't help myself when I'm giving out candy. I always tend to snatch a few. Okay, more than a few."

"It kinda helps, or possibly it doesn't," he confessed as they headed past a shop filled with a huge display of chocolate and icing, "that my favorite candies are the ones nobody likes. So the day after I can walk into any store and get them for half off. I have candy corn forever."

"A man after my own heart," she replied. It made him almost him trip over his shoes as they headed through the double doors onto the busy sidewalk. He hoped she didn't notice.

Of course, he wasn't sure what to say in response, except, "It's this way." He gestured toward the storefront he could see in the distance.

"I can't wait."

"I hope you like it," he said. "I actually came here for the first time with my *bubbe*." He paused, stopping at the door. "Here we are."

"This is adorable," she said, her face lighting up like a menorah on the final night of Hanukkah.

"Wait till you step inside," he continued, more confident in his words as he opened the door. This time, he knew to expect the powerful smell that reminded him of his *bubbe's* kitchen, the strong scent of tradition and of home.

"This is amazing."

"This is parve and meat," he said, beaming. "There are dairy-like dishes with all the milk substitutes, but it's mostly the meat side of comfort food."

"So no soofganiyot lattes?"

"I don't think he'd know what to do with—"

"Welcome, welcome," an older woman said. Her skin was wrinkled like his *bubbe's*. She gestured at the empty tables. "Come, sit."

He held his breath as he watched Sarah squeal over the menu and order a sandwich she hadn't seen in a long time.

"Oh wow," she said. "I could live here forever." Smile

wasn't the best word to describe the expression on her face. Smile was pedestrian. This? This was another level of happiness expressed through the sparkle in her eyes.

"Relax," he said because he couldn't think of anything else. "Relax, enjoy, and just be."

"But I'm supposed to be reassuring you. Not the other way around."

It was sweet but not necessary, and he tried to hold back the laughter that threatened to escape him. Yeah, he'd been nervous before, but that was because he wasn't sure she'd show up. "Reassuring me of what? I'm nervous about tonight, but I'm nervous before every show I do. Every time I put something I've done in front of people who are not me, I get nervous. It's life, you know."

She bit her lip. What was making her nervous? "So what calms you down, I mean aside from, you know, hanging out with people you want to spend time with?"

He felt the blush rising in his cheeks. "Well," he said, "aside from that, I think about things I like."

"What do you like?"

He thought for a second, then shrugged. "Crunchy latkes, sweet applesauce. Candles, the way they look against the snow."

"You think of Hanukkah?"

"Yeah. I know. It's weird, having Hanukkah as my favorite form of stress relief, but it is."

"You realize you're trying to justify this to someone

who's been given the nickname 'the Hanukkah fairy.'"

He grinned at the brightness in her eyes. "True."

"So call me curious, why is it such a stress relief for you?"

"It's when my family didn't travel, I think," he said. "We didn't go places for Hanukkah. Granted, my parents liked having parties with friends and a lot of people in the house, total chaos and high-stress wildness, but I loved the calm before the storm or after. The moments with my family or friends at a dreidel game. Someone always ate too many latkes, some wrong person always brought sour cream to the house. And we forgave them—sometimes. But the thought of a low-key Hanukkah has always been a fantasy of mine." He paused. "What about you? Why is Hanukkah your favorite thing?"

"It's joy we, as Jews, can share, whether it's family or friends or with the community," she said. "Light in the darkness. Fried, crunchy food. Fun whether with family or in a restaurant when you need a pick-me-up in July. All you do is order latkes and there you are."

"I can absolutely dig it." He grinned as their food arrived, his plate of latkes in early October and her indefinable sandwich. "So what are you doing tonight?"

"You mean tomorrow night."

"Yes," he said. He'd forgotten his show was tomorrow night. Tonight was just going to be a nice, slow Shabbat with his *bubbe*.

"Tonight I'm hanging out with my friend Anna. Tomorrow, we're going to this…thing. It's a craft fair with alcohol, I think."

"Oh!" Isaac sat back in his chair, feeling he'd heard about this fair from someone else. And then he remembered. "My friend Jamie—the one who designed the earrings?"

"I loved them, by the way."

The blush hit his toes. "I'm glad. Really glad. Anyway, she's going to be there, so you should say hello."

"I will."

And then Sarah looked down at her potato salad and the sandwich whose filling he didn't want to consider. Somewhere, anywhere but at him.

What was wrong? Something had to be.

"I tried to tell him not to, but my dad might be coming to the gallery tonight. Just ignore him, okay?" Sarah finally met his eyes.

Isaac nodded, knowing that was what he should do. And it made sense; her father was an important member of the community and was going to be at events to support the businesses in the town. "I understand."

"It's not going to be what you expect," she said, as if she suspected he was less fine than he said. "Otherwise, I will publicly disown him."

That was when he shook his head, smiled up at her. "You don't have to do that, seriously. I get it. He's protective. He's annoyed on your behalf."

"I guess I don't get it," she said. "I'm not mad. And if

I'm not mad, then—"

"Nah," Isaac said. "People get to have their own feelings. I understand that." He looked at her; he couldn't help it, even if his latkes were getting cold, even if her words made him nervous. Because her eyes twisted his insides in very happy ways. "Especially if I like the person."

"Like, huh?"

The glitter in her eyes made him want to say something he might regret. Except his stomach growled. "Umm, yeah. Anyway…"

"Yes." She nodded and slowly picked up her sandwich.

Had he seen regret in her eyes? Though that didn't seem possible when she was eating a sandwich she'd been craving. Strange that the latkes he'd wanted since he'd chosen this place for their lunch tasted like dust on his tongue. It made him hope that her regret and his lost appetite came from the missed opportunity for connection, though he doubted he was that lucky. Not even Hanukkah miracles were that convenient.

Chapter Fourteen

Manhattan

"YOU CAN'T AVOID the question forever about what's going on with Isaac," Anna scolded as they left the subway and headed toward the building that was being used for the craft festival they were going to. "At least not that one."

"I don't know," she finally said. "I honestly don't know what's happening. He's a nice guy."

"He's a *nice* guy. He sent you earrings and you went out of your way to see him yesterday before he had his show. Nice is probably not exactly what you're thinking about. But you're admitting feelings, so we're good."

We're good meant "for now," not a completely dropped subject, which was fine. They were heading into the building, and the noise of excited attendees burst through the front door.

"So what are we doing here exactly?"

"As it turns out," Anna said, grinning, "I have the night off. I've always wanted to go to this fair, but I've never had the chance till now. So you're here with me."

"Fair enough." She paused, decidedly not mentioning the fact that a friend of Isaac's was supposed to be here. "Any ulterior motives?"

"Motives? Me?" Anna smirked as they took the offered maps. A glance at the map showed the craft festival was spread out all over the warehouse floor; jewelry makers and artisans of all sorts stood behind long tables filled with their wares. A vendor was mixing alcoholic drinks filled with a new variation on a company's most famous liqueur, and others were selling cakes and sandwiches of all sorts. It was gorgeous.

Visions of future plans began to swim in her head; publicity she could give an author merged with ways the library might be able to fundraise, and programs the bookstore could use to reward loyal customers. "Oh my gosh."

"Isn't this great, though?"

"It is!" She beamed. "It would be great to reward regular bookstore customers with items associated with their favorite books, have a summer craft fair for the library and do so many things. I'm so inspired, Anna. Thank you for bringing me here."

"I adore all of those ideas," Anna interjected, "but you need to focus."

Sarah blinked. "What?"

"You're procrastinating by planning fifty million other projects."

Friends. Anna was the best one, the one who could read

her better than a book. Which was why Anna was able to see things Sarah did not want to admit aloud. Like the fact that she was allowing the inspiration for fifty million projects to keep her mind away from Isaac.

But maybe, if she allowed herself to think about it, maybe the problems she was having with the festival were also things she was avoiding. Maybe the idea of failing at the project she was worried most about inspired her to create new things—new things she couldn't fail at because they weren't yet started.

But instead of saying all that, she smiled at her friend. "That obvious, huh?"

"Yep. We've been friends since kindergarten. I know your techniques well."

She desperately wanted to keep it light. But she couldn't. The words wouldn't stop once Sarah looked into her best friend's eyes. "It's just been impossible. I've wanted to plan this festival forever, and I just—"

"You just." Anna smiled. "You always 'just.'"

She did. She'd move from one project to another, inspired, scared of failing, worried she'd hurt someone. "I do. I just wanted to make things better, to do better and maybe I got a bit…er."

"Yesss?"

"A bit…extravagant?"

"No. Not extravagant. Here's the thing." Anna put her hands on Sarah's shoulders. "You wanted to give the festival its best shot at succeeding. So you got Shelly Averman to drag her niece in to make a website, and Shelly herself to send out press releases, which looks like it's working. Next the food proposal was finally accepted and is going to be amazing."

"But?" Because there was always a *but.*

"You're running up against the wall and I think trying to convince a sculptor to make the menorah, at this late date, is going to be a hard sell if not impossible."

Sarah nodded. All of her queries came up with rejections, denials, 'we're sorry but...' Dead ends and closing festivals didn't match. And then she had to admit the truth. "Chana wants an alternate plan, and I have no idea what to do."

Because she'd failed. The Hanukkah festival would be over, and she'd failed.

And it would technically be Chana's legacy, but everybody in town knew it would be her fault. As the thought made its way into her brain, the crushing weight of failure stopped her breath and...

Anna threw her hands up as if she was directing traffic. "Stop. Seriously. Breathe a second and listen to me."

Sarah took a breath. She had the ideas; Anna was the planner. That was how it worked from the time they were little girls setting up a lemonade stand. And then a garage sale where Sarah made a ton of money off of perfume samples. Which was probably why she dragged Anna into unofficially-officially helping her with the festival in the first place.

"So here's my thought."

"Listening."

Anna turned a sculpted-glass earring a few different ways in her hand. "The festival has always sold items made by a small group of artisans. Not many, of course, but a few. But what if…?"

Sarah finished her trail of thought, their years of friendship making it easy. "What if we opened the craft part up a bit and commissioned a few tiny pieces instead, with the agreement that a small portion of those sales would go to the larger fund for the sculpture. I love it."

"Festival originals, though," Anna replied. "Has to be. You have to get value somewhere, right?"

"Jewelry, candle cases, specifically Hanukkah-related stuff though. With the festival logo."

"Does the festival even have a logo?"

"No," Sarah admitted. "I keep looking for artists who would take the commission but I can't find one."

"Considering we're in the middle of a craft festival that contains artists and illustrators," Anna said, "I suspect finding one will be a piece of cake."

"So very convenient." And the matching smile from her bestie was the best kind of gift.

"Perfect for your purposes."

"So logo, then shirts and other types of merchandise the local stores could sell to commemorate what was, long after the festival. And the money made after the festival is over, or if it ends up being canceled, would go to the community center or the library or something."

"I think," Anna said, though Sarah was somewhat bothered to hear a degree of smugness in her friend's tone, "that you found yourself a winner."

"Wait," said a young woman with hazel eyes, freckles and reddish blonde hair, who was suddenly standing behind the counter they'd been admiring. "Did you just say Hanukkah-related stuff with a festival logo for sale?"

"Yeah," Sarah said, smiling back at her. "I'm on the committee for Hollowville's Hanukkah festival this year, and we're looking to commission some things. Have you made Hanukkah-themed things before?"

"I'm still stuck on the phrase *Hanukkah festival.*" The young woman's eyes brightened more. "You really said a Hanukkah festival? Not a holiday festival?"

"That I did," Sarah said. "You can find holiday joy pretty much everywhere and Christmas joy even in more places. But Hollowville primarily focuses on Hanukkah this time of year."

"That sounds adorable!"

Anna grinned. "Tell her about the festival itself."

"Well," Sarah said, taking a breath, "Hanukkah has come to roost 24/7 in Hollowville for nine days for the past nine years, culminating in the final day of Hanukkah itself. Soofganiyot and latke-making contests, dreidel-spinning relays, ice skating on the river, hot chocolate, chestnuts. This year we're adding an international food fair, as well as hoping to add a bazaar featuring Hanukkah-themed jewelry and clothing. And a few commemorative items, so that no matter what happens next year, we'll have the memories."

"Oliver," the young woman said to the man next to her. "This sounds adorable."

"It does sound adorable." The man, Oliver, paused. "I'm still focused on the fact that you said you're from Hollowville." He leaned over the counter and stared.

What was he staring at? "Um…"

"Jamie," he said. "These are your design."

"So you're the one Isaac had me make the earrings for," Jamie, the young woman, said. "Oh my gosh."

"Yep." Sarah nodded, feeling the heat from the blush spread across her cheeks. "They're gorgeous," she said as she headed toward the front of the young woman's display. And found herself awestruck by the detailed work she'd done. "Isaac told me you were going to be here, so I was sorta looking out for you. I love your stuff, by the way."

"You didn't tell me that Isaac had friends exhibiting at the show," Anna pointed out, accusation in her tone.

"Don't feel too bad," the young woman said, grinning. "Isaac didn't tell us you were coming to the show either." She paused. "I'm Jamie Sawyer, by the way, and this is my boyfriend, Oliver Goldsmith."

"Nice to meet you both. I'm Anna Cohen. And this person who is horrible at giving information to others is Sarah Goldman."

Sarah managed a wave. "Hi. Did Isaac tell you anything?"

"He told me you existed," Oliver said, with a smile, "but only as a way of letting me know he'd made it to Streetfest this year. And to get me to ask you about the earrings."

"You're the one he took to Streetfest?"

Sarah could only nod at Jamie's direct question.

"Well, that makes sense." Jamie grinned. "I'm glad you like the earrings, and I'm glad you stopped by."

But Jamie's words flew over her head as she focused on a gorgeous glass star. "This is amazing," she said. "I absolutely adore it."

"Really?" She smiled. "It's one of my favorites. I saw variations of it as Christmas decorations and took a stab at a star. It's been a pretty good seller for the last few years."

Anna bit her lip. "Have you done a menorah before? And other Hanukkah things?"

"You can't have a jewelry business at the holiday season without including dreidels." Jamie reached into the case in front of her and took out a few items.

Sarah just couldn't believe what she was seeing. "Wow," she managed, unable to speak more than a random syllable that contained anything more than adoration. "I'm completely in awe."

"Well, thank you. And if the invitation's still open for

the bazaar, I'm so doing this." She turned to Oliver. "We're doing this no matter what Isaac does, 'kay?"

Oliver caught Jamie's eye and smiled. "Sure. Whatever makes you happy, love."

"Excellent. I have a booth boy." The look in Jamie's eyes was excitement personified. "Where do I sign up? And do you have the logo we're going to put on some of the new things? I realize it's already October, and yeah Hanukkah is in late December this year so we have some time—not much, but enough to get this done because it's important to me."

"We don't have a logo as of yet," Sarah began, thinking of the possibilities, "but if you know of someone who can make one, I'd very much appreciate the information."

"Actually," Oliver interjected, "I'm a painter, so I can make some kind of design if that works for you."

"Yes!" Sarah exclaimed, feeling the connections slam into place. She could hardly believe her luck, or the opportunity. Either way, both. Whatever. "I'd love that."

"And of course," Oliver continued, "the sooner the better, I'm guessing, so we can talk now and I'll work something up."

"Meanwhile," Jamie continued, "I'll give you a list of people who are here who'd be interested in participating in the bazaar and who'd have the kind of turnaround time as well as overstock to be able to do a good job."

"That would be wonderful!"

And as Sarah sat down with Oliver and Anna moved to take Jamie's list, she found herself wanting to tell Isaac what he'd put into motion—but she couldn't.

Instead, as she and Anna headed out into the rest of the fair, Jamie's list, and her instructions to head back to the booth once the fair was done in hand, she smiled. "This is fantastic, so much better than I'd dreamed tonight would be," she said. "You were right."

"I'm glad to hear that I was right in bringing you here, but if you think you're going to get away with not telling me about all the things, you are mistaken, *chaverah* mine.

"If," Sarah said, "there are any details to tell, I will give them to you."

"Good. Very glad to hear. Speaking of details, let's talk to the jewelers."

And full of purpose for the first time in a long time, Sarah followed her friend through the busy fair, searching for names on a list, and her future.

Hollowville

ISAAC MADE IT through Friday night and most of Saturday, catching up with his *bubbe* and finalizing details with Molly, the gallery owner. Together, they organized the pieces the way he wanted them displayed, and by the time his friends arrived, the display was ready to go.

"This town is adorable with a capital 'A,'" his visual artist friend Max Parker said. Isaac could see inspiration in his friend's blue eyes, excitement making his pale skin pink. "I want to catch the vibe of the gallery, but I think I might do something." Without another word, Max went off.

"Yep," said his friend Tom Walker, a photographer. "This is cool. I kinda dig the whole small town thing. Totally ripe for a show if the timing or mood is right." And again, before they could talk further, his dark-eyed, olive-skinned friend headed off into the crowd to do or see whatever he was looking for.

They were a mutual support society—he, Tom, Max, Oliver, and Liam, a comic illustrator who was working on the Shadow Squad Comics that were tied in with the blockbuster movies. And the only reason Oliver wasn't here was because he was supporting Jamie.

At the show Sarah was attending in Brooklyn.

Because he'd banned her from this one.

Isaac sighed, stared at the crowd. The gallery was *full.* People mingled and chatted over art, wine, cheese, and all sorts of desserts. His sculptures were well received, consistently and constantly at the center of attention.

"This is going swimmingly," Molly said, her green eyes sparkling with excitement, her pale skin rosy under the lights.

Isaac wished he could feel Molly's excitement. He wished despite everything that he could tell Sarah how excited he was at the energy that filled the air. She'd love it.

"I'm glad," he said, smiling despite his inability to enjoy himself. "Thank you for doing this."

"Me?" she said. "This is entirely my pleasure. And, if we're speaking truthfully, beyond my wildest dreams."

"What do you mean?"

Molly shrugged. "This sort of thing doesn't usually happen in a town like Hollowville. Musicians come to the theatre to warm up before they play concerts in larger venues, but artisans, artists? Not so much. We have moments of things, but rarely anything like this, where artists with an international name make original pieces to be shown in Hollowville. Not to mention..." Molly gestured toward the crowd.

"Yes?"

"People are excited to be here. The art is resonating with them. Which is usually a struggle. What you've done here is a wonderful mix of classic and contemporary styles." She looked around then back at him. "And then there's the other thing that happened tonight."

"What?" he asked, suddenly curious about what had put the sparkle in Molly's eyes. "Tell me, please. I would like to know."

"Your friends are lovely." Molly beamed. "In fact, I didn't realize who Mas was at first. But then he said he'd try to figure out how to do an installation here, and I got so excited I think your grandmother thought something had gone wrong."

"That's wonderful," Isaac said. "Not about my *bubbe*." He paused, searched the crowd for her, and was relieved to find her in a corner chatting with a few other people he didn't recognize. "But I'm so glad to hear that about Max."

"And your photographer friend?"

"Tom."

"Yes, Tom. He said he'd put together an exclusive exhibit of his photos here."

"That's also amazing." He had to thank his friends for being supportive of the gallery and what Molly was trying to do. "I'm so glad to hear that this place and your mission is resonating as well with them as it does with me."

Molly smiled and headed to mingle with the crowd. He followed suit in his own way, chatting with locals and people who came from the city to discover the art Molly had in her gallery.

"This is so wonderfully provincial," one woman said, her surprise on her face.

"Not provincial," he replied. "Art should be for everybody. And acting like it isn't makes you a snob, not a critic."

She blinked at him, as if his words didn't make sense to her in a fundamental way, before shaking her head and walking away.

"You did great, *tateleh*," *Bubbe* said as she came over to him. "I am so proud of you."

"What do you mean?"

"Those people believe Hollowville is at the back of beyond. I'd imagine they think anything north of Central Park is not worth attending."

Why would we go down there? That's...midtown where the tourists are. And why would we want to mix with them?

Statements like that, and others his mother made regularly when she didn't think he was paying attention, annoyed him. "I've never understood that attitude, nor have I understood the attitude that the city is the source of all evil in the world."

Bubbe snorted. "That too. Both sides of the same coin in the worst ways."

He nodded. "It's like...I can't stand the idea that people can be solely defined by one characteristic. No matter what it is. I'm a sculptor. An artist. It's fine when people don't like my stuff. Taste is taste, right? But there's a difference between not liking my stuff and not liking where they're seeing it and who they're seeing it with. The latter is where I draw the line."

"Ach," his *bubbe* said, putting an arm around him. "I look at them and I see the genius my grandson is."

"And that is why I love you." He let her lead him to the sculpture display. Not that he needed to see them, but he wanted to make a point. He wanted to show *her* off. Because if he'd do nothing else in his life, this moment, this perfect moment with his *bubbe*, was worth everything.

"So, genius," she said as they arrived in front of the

sculptures, "tell me about them. I want to know what you were thinking when you made them."

What was there to tell? He shrugged, but mostly because there was a crowd starting to form around them. Which meant his words wouldn't be just for her but for everybody. "Usually I'm a bit more experimental in my style. Partially because I love learning new techniques and seeing how they fit into the larger world. But every once in a while, I like to go back and do something more classic, but in a way that uses what I've learned through experimentation. These pieces are pretty much the result of that exploration."

She beamed at him. "Less intense for a small town crowd. You had the town in mind when you made these."

"I did," he replied. "But it makes sense to do that. Different shows, if I know the place where I'm showing, will have different sensibilities. I'll try different techniques for a Brooklyn show or a show at a gallery in Manhattan, for example, mostly because the people who are coming to see my work there are expecting that. But this? This felt like coming home."

"Fascinating."

He turned to meet a pair of inquisitive eyes. They looked almost familiar, as if he might have met this gentleman before. "Hello?"

The man smiled. "Robert Goldman. Big fan of yours."

Goldman. Sarah. The pang that had been hiding was now front and center despite his desire to focus on other things. "Sarah's father."

"Yes. Sarah, who's not here right now," he said pointedly.

"I know." Isaac's guilt mixed with the roiling mess in his stomach.

And maybe Sarah's father saw something in his eyes, because instead of keeping that tight, angry expression, Robert Goldman's shoulders softened along with his posture. Even his smile loosened. "It's hard in small towns," he said. "Everybody's close and tight."

Isaac turned at the random sound of someone, most likely *Bubbe*, clearing their throat.

"Yes," Mr. Goldman continued, a slight laugh in his voice, "I see you, Elsa. Anyway, everybody's in each other's business, and you never know who's connected to whom. So when something like this happens, it's hard for us."

"Yeah." He took his own deep breath. "It's difficult also because in the past, people have...well..." He paused, shook his head. "Let's just say people don't like it when I say no. So I've started to take precautions."

There was understanding in Robert Goldman's eyes as well as recognition. "I'm sorry," he said. "And I have to tell you I understand."

He felt stress and tension ooze out of his shoulders. "Thank you," he said. "I appreciate it."

"It's a difficult thing," Mr. Goldman continued. "I might be stepping on toes here, but I have to tell you. I worked, blood, sweat, and tears for nine years on this festival. But things change; people change. Times change. New boards of trustees that don't know town history arise, and sometimes you don't have the strength to fight. It's a wonder the committee, and my daughter, are still trying to find someone who can create a centerpiece, an original piece, for a festival that may not last beyond this year."

A gift. A gift of art to a town that usually found itself as a warm-up, a second choice, or even a runner-up. An original for a town that usually got hand-me-downs. He remembered the excitement in Molly Concannon's eyes when she'd told him about how his friends said they were going do original shows for her, to give her the first chance to see new art from them.

But the menorah was commercial; the festival was commercial, right? It wasn't just a gift but something designed to turn his favorite holiday into something that competed with the red and green, instead of being the kind of thing that was appreciated on its own.

Right?

Mr. Goldman shrugged, seemingly oblivious to the turmoil in Isaac's mind. "But it is what it is, right?"

"Right," he said. "Right."

As the night went on, Isaac started to wonder. What would it hurt for him to create a sculpture for *Bubbe* and the rest of the town she'd called home, for all these years and more?

Especially in these uncertain times when a community like hers needed something they could hold on to, and a part of their heritage they could share. Especially when trustees like Webster wanted to take it away.

What would it hurt?

But it was still a small step from a large menorah to a small one, then to special menorah collections in stores.

It didn't have to be.

Of course that was when he realized that the real reason he was even *thinking* of making this sculpture wasn't even at the show.

Chapter Fifteen

Hollowville

"WATCH YOURSELF."

Isaac's attention snapped back to the front of the coffee cart, to the older Israeli woman behind it. "Sorry," he said. "Daydreaming."

Which was part of the truth. He was still exhausted after breakfast at his *bubbe's* and last night's show. Now, he'd needed some air and space, so he'd volunteered to go and find the coffee cart and get some coffee for his friends and his *bubbe*, who were all waiting just outside the gallery.

"If you're not careful, you'll end up living here," the woman said. Wasn't her name Chana?

That was the last thing he'd expected her to say. He managed a laugh, which he hoped sounded plausible. "My *bubbe* does," he replied. "That's enough for me."

She raised an eyebrow. "But," she paused to look down at the list of coffee orders he'd written down for her, before putting the paper down and starting to pour. "You seem more interested in this town than you would if, say, you were *just* passing by to see your grandmother."

And that was the problem right there. More judgment instead of the less he'd expected.

Way too many people believed there had to be a firm dividing line between the city and the suburbs, where when you chose one of them, you ignored or even despised the other. And yes, some, like his parents, played along. But he didn't see geography as a zero-sum game. "I won't ever be *just passing by* as long as *Bubbe* lives here," he replied, maybe a bit too archly, maybe a bit too angrily.

"Just Elsa? And just as long as she lives here? Because I think there are questions there."

Of course there were. Yes. He liked Hollowville because his *bubbe* lived here and it served as a beautiful visual contrast to his Brooklyn neighborhood. But it also retained some of his favorite things about his corner of Brooklyn; everybody knew each other, people watched out for each other. People helped one another. The regular street fairs and block parties were the neighborhood's equivalent of a festival to share traditions and foods and culture.

And that brought him to Sarah. What drew him to her, the way he desperately wanted to be the kind of person who'd make space for *her*. And, of course, how he hated the fact she couldn't be at the show last night.

But instead of saying all of that and opening the door to further questions he wasn't comfortable answering, especially while in the middle of a line in front of a coffee cart, he shrugged.

"So is that a shrug of dismissal or a shrug of something else?"

"Definitely not dismissal," he said. "You do a great deal for the town, so the last thing I want to do is offend you."

She smiled at him. "Ach," she said. "Which is a lovely way of saying mind your business."

He laughed. This time it was easier.

"But this is a small town, and me, if I can't meddle, I can't breathe." She sprinkled some chocolate over what had to be a mocha, then sprayed some whipped cream on the top of one of the other drinks before adding some raspberry syrup. "I pay attention," she continued, opening a container of almond milk and pouring some into a large paper cup. "So. I'll just say I see how much she smiles around you and how much you change with her, hmm?"

Meddling. His parents didn't even meddle, mostly. *Bubbe* smiled and nodded at necessary moments, expressing her disapproval in others. But communities, like his friends and the members of the *minyan* he went to once in a while? They cared about their own. And Sarah? There was a space for her in the Hollowville community, where people cared about her. Or at least paid attention to her. Sometimes a bit too much, but that was life in a small town as part of an even smaller community.

He didn't say that to Chana, because any and all of those words would have unleashed an extended discussion he didn't have time for; heck, nobody had time for that kind of talk on a chilly Sunday morning. Especially when he was getting a whole bunch of coffees for friends who'd made the drive up to see him. So Isaac defaulted to a very polite smile and a nod; Chana, thankfully, got his meaning, because she smiled at him as she gave him the tray with the drinks, as if to say she understood.

"Here are two black coffees, one with almond milk, two soofi lattes, a soofi latte with an extra espresso shot and a gelt mocha, with extra whipped cream for Elsa."

"Thank you," he said. "I very much appreciate it." As his payment went through, he made sure he gave extra for a tip.

"You," she said again, "are a *mensch* when you want to be."

"Thank you."

"You should be one for Sarah," she said.

He blinked. "What?"

And then another woman came over to join her. "Chana. It's nine a.m. and the setup..."

The words flew out of Chana's mouth, fast and furious. He might have recognized one of the Hebrew words he wasn't supposed to have learned when he was studying for his bar mitzvah.

"I can't believe they didn't!"

"What's going on?" he couldn't help but ask.

"Move off the line," Chana barked. "Talk to Carol and help fix the problem. I can't right now because half of Hollowville is waiting for coffee."

He nodded, and followed the instructions and…Carol?

"Carol Thomas, proprietress of *Tales from Hollowville*," the woman said. "We met a while ago. But forget all of that. We have an emergency. You have how many people with you?"

His brain froze for a few seconds as he tried to count. "Five, I think? And my *bubbe*."

"That should work," Carol continued, nodding her head as if she was making some kind of tally. "Six people and your grandmother to supervise." And then she paused, cocking her head. "Have any of your friends supervised an event setup before?"

"One of them is a visual artist, so he's definitely organized things, and one of them is a photographer if you need photos?"

"Good enough." Carol paused. "It'll have to be."

"For?"

"Go get your friends and meet me back here," was all Carol said, leaving him even more confused than he'd been before he'd started.

What did she mean?

He let his thoughts carry him as he walked down the street toward the place his friends and *Bubbe* were supposed to be waiting. Of course, he could hear them from a mile away, their voices and laughter intermingling in the fall air.

Finally, he saw them, sitting on the bench in front of the gallery, enjoying the morning and each other's company.

They weren't bothered at all at the fact that he'd been at the coffee cart for as long as he was.

"So, was it the line at the coffee cart or someone you saw there that took you so long?"

"Doesn't matter," he said as he passed out the coffee. "Long line, small town, and caffeine. But more importantly, we've been recruited."

"Recruited for what?" His *bubbe* took her latte from the container. "Who recruited you?"

"Carol," he replied. "Some kind of emergency involving setup?"

"We're here for you," Tom said, grabbing his coffee. "Whatever you need."

"You might need to take photos," Isaac said, before turning toward Max. "You've organized event spaces before?"

Max shrugged. "Probably don't have to work with much, just need to know the flow of the space that they want. But I'm guessing we're talking bare bones because no time?"

"We schlepped all the way from my parents' house this morning after driving there from Manhattan last night." Jamie said. "We felt guilty about missing the show. Now we're here and you're giving us coffee, which is amazing. So we're here to do whatever."

"Do they need signs?" Liam asked, his brown eyes focusing, the sun highlighting the golden undertones of his brown skin. "Ol, you can give color to an illustration, right?"

"Haven't done it in years, but I can put my inking fingers to good use," Oliver said, nodding. "We can also lift if needed."

Soon after, he, his friends and his *bubbe* made their way back to the spot where Carol was waiting.

"We were supposed to get the signing set up but the people who were meant to do it fell through," Carol said. "Can you people organize a signing?"

"Do you have an idea of how many people are coming?"

Isaac sat back and watched Max ask Carol a litany of questions.

"I never knew," his *bubbe* said, "how intricate a balance that was. I always thought it was easy."

Max shook his head. "Event setup sounds like it's easy but it never is. Flow, number of people, and all of these other intangibles have to be included in the prep."

"Exactly," Carol replied. "If you're setting up a huge signing, you have to think about a bunch of different things. Is the author speaking? Is the author expecting to sell a lot of books or a few? Will there be snacks?" And as she turned back to Max, she smiled. "Good."

"Most important question is how much time we have."

"It's now nine a.m., so we have about two hours."

Isaac saw the flash of…something pass across Max's face.

"Two hours," he said, nodding. "It's going to be tight but we can do this."

And that was when the group headed up the walk, into the library, on a mission.

SARAH WAS EXHAUSTED. But there she was, heading to the library to see what needed to be done before the signing.

Carol and Chana had reassured her that things were on track to be settled by the time the event was supposed to begin, but she still wasn't convinced. And that made her nervous.

Breathe.

She forced in a breath, then another one. And once she'd gotten to the point where she didn't have to force it, she took a long swallow of her precious soofi latte. The drink was sweet and dark all at once—the taste of the coffee and the sweetness of the cream and the raspberries balanced each other perfectly. Which was the push she needed to get to the library, only a few long steps away.

She hoped for excited noise in the library to drown out her nerves, or at least a curious librarian to redirect her attention. Yes, libraries were supposed to be quiet places, but small town libraries, like Hollowville's, were community centers and as vibrant as the communities they served.

Unfortunately, as she opened the big wooden and sculpted metal doors, Sarah was met with silence. It was semi early on a Sunday, and yes, there were patrons shuffling in with books, DVDs, and other bits of media to return. But nobody behind the desk or otherwise stopped her, for any questions or for bringing in her latte.

Who knew what was going on?

Either way, latte in hand, she headed upstairs to the set of meeting rooms where the signing was supposed to take place.

That's when she noticed the carpet.

And the crowd.

The library staff were staring at the group of people in the middle of what was the most intricate setup she'd ever seen at the library.

The chairs were organized just so, drawing people's attention to the display of photographs on the wall, just behind where the registers were set up.

Just over the boundary line into the next room was the lectern. The separation between the two areas gave people space to look and purchase books before walking into the space where the lecture would actually happen. Each inch was used to its best advantage.

And beautiful signs were everywhere, illustrated and colorful, directing patrons and other attendees around and inside the space.

Oh wow.

Looking closer, she could see Elsa Lieberman. And Dr. Marylise Rodriguez, the library director, of course. And in the middle of all of that was a tall guy with hair that curled just a little bit. Isaac.

She didn't want to disturb them, except she had to say something.

"Sarah?"

A single voice echoed through the space.

"Hi," she said as a dude taller than she was but yet not as tall as Isaac approached her. "Yes?"

"Max Parker." He paused. "I...organized the space and I wanted to make sure it was okay with you."

"It's wonderful," she said. "It's gorgeous. I love the way it directs people through the space."

"You do this all by yourself?" Another voice. Isaac of course.

"Usually?" Sarah said, smiling, trying to make sure it wasn't that big a deal. "Mostly. I don't do it this intricately; I don't have the capacity for that, but usually."

"Still," Isaac said, as he moved closer to her. She was so glad he was here. "It's a lot of work."

She didn't want to think about how long it usually took, nor did she want to think about how easily she fit under Isaac's arm, and how easy it was to lean in. Before she pulled back.

"But you guys did a great job," she said as she reminded herself she was there to work.

"And you shouldn't have to do this all by yourself," Elsa interjected. "You should make a committee. This is Hollowville. We help each other, or we're supposed to anyway. What time does the event start?"

"At twelve-thirty, I think. So there's a bit more time." She took her tablet out of her purse and moved to check her spreadsheet. "Dr. Abraham is supposed to be here at around twelve-fifteen. The books are..."

She paused when she heard the rumbling of the elevator, then the slow creak of the doors as they opened to reveal...Oliver, from last night, with Carol and another guy. The guys were pushing carts full of boxes tethered to the bottom, and Carol was holding a sheet of paper.

"There's been a change," Carol said, getting everybody's attention. "The publisher sent the wrong book, so I've been on the phone for an hour trying to figure out what was going on."

She had to breathe. She tried to breathe.

There was suddenly a weight on her shoulder; she turned slightly to see Isaac's arm around her, and the simple fuzziness of his flannel shirt against her cheek as he pulled her close. "It's going to be okay," he said.

She went still at first, utterly still, and he dropped his arm completely, as if he thought he'd crossed some invisible boundary.

But she didn't move. She needed the reassurance and if he was the one who was going to give it to her, she didn't have a problem with it. "Thank you," she said to him before she turned to Carol. "So what's the problem?"

"You're not going to believe this." Carol paused. "Dr. Abraham isn't talking about local myths."

"So...what is he going to talk about?" Sarah held her breath, as she suspected did the rest of the room.

"Hollowville is going to be the first stop on Dr. Abraham's 'The Story of Hanukkah' tour."

"What?"

That was all she could manage. A simple question word wrapped up in way too much emotion. A lot of it. Like a waterfall of confusion and excitement that hit her all at once. What was going on?

"Yep." Another woman entered the room, boots clicking on the tile floor. Pencil skirt, brown eyes, close-cut brown hair and brown skin with cool undertones. "Dr. Abraham's a few minutes away, so I figured I'd brief everybody on what's happening and why." She turned to Carol. "Jesse Watkins here, and I work for Dr. Abraham's publisher. What happened is that someone named Shelly...Aber..."

"Averman," Sarah interjected.

"Yes. Shelly Averman sent a press release to the publicity department and we approached Dr. Abraham, who jumped at the chance to release his new book here. For whatever reason."

Sarah's hand flew to her mouth. "What?"

Jesse, meanwhile, nodded. "Yep. Book's not officially releasing until before Hanukkah. Press release went out today, and this is the first event he's having for it."

"So how do we explain to everybody what's happening?" Dr. Rodriguez said, shaking her head, questions in her brown eyes. "I mean everybody came here to hear local history, not about Hanukkah. Not that they won't mind, necessarily."

"Except for that *fakakta*, Webster," Mrs. Lieberman pointed out.

She was not wrong, of course. Sarah laughed.

"We like Hanukkah in Hollowville, no matter what that hipster Webster says," Carol added. "But we do need some kind of explanation. So what do we do?"

Then Carol, Dr. Rodriguez, and Mrs. Lieberman were all focusing on Sarah in a way she wasn't comfortable with.

"We have the 'Hanukkah fairy' here," Mrs. Lieberman interjected.

They were going to ask her to introduce him. She knew it, The thought of it made her palms sweat.

"You can introduce him," Carol continued. "You're the link between this event and the committee and the festival. It'll make more sense that way."

She was not prepared, and the sudden pressure from being the first stop on a famous non-fiction author's new book tour was making it worse.

"It has to be you," Dr. Rodriguez said. "You're the only one who can get them to understand."

"You can do this," Isaac said. "You can really do this. I have faith in you."

She met his eyes and nodded, took a deep breath. Show had to go on, and it was up to her to take care of it. "Fake it till you make it, hmm?"

Carol nodded. "Yep. That's it."

And in the minutes that followed, Sarah desperately hoped for a miracle. Hanukkah was a holiday filled with them, of course, and hopefully a last-minute Hanukkah book substitution would give her a miracle of her own.

SARAH WAS RESPLENDENT, her dark curls hanging just below her shoulders, a blazer with a cute menorah on it, a light skirt, and dark tights with the Hebrew word for love written in various ways. She glowed.

But she wasn't smiling; she wasn't even looking at him. Her knuckles were white as snow; her focus was on her tablet. She was writing a speech, and he was useless with words.

"Isaac, *tateleh*." *Bubbe*, of course. "We should go and sit down, yes?"

He nodded, even though what he'd really wanted was to wait with Sarah, reassure her that was capable of saying the perfect words to introduce the author.

But she was working, needed to compose the speech and he didn't want to bother her.

"Isaac?" Sarah's voice.

He looked up to meet her eyes.

"Thank you. Thank you for everything."

"You're welcome," he said. "I'm glad we were able to help. I mean it wasn't just me."

"But you had a lot to do with it," she replied. "And I thank you."

He wanted to touch her, hug her, somehow physically transfer some degree of his faith in her so that she'd realize how he was beginning to see her, how so many saw her.

And then as if someone was reading his mind, she stepped forward and put her arms around him. "Thank you," she said, squeezing him briefly before letting him go and then stepping back. "We'll talk later?"

He nodded. "Yes. Absolutely." Then he took a chance. "I'll save you a seat?"

There was a pause that stretched longer than it should have, went awkward from settled and then, when he'd started to turn away, out of the corner of his eye, he saw her nod.

"Thank you," she said.

Then he waved and walked away, heading toward his friends and his *bubbe*, who clearly would have questions. And for the first time in a while, he didn't care.

SARAH FORCED HERSELF not to watch as Isaac walked away; instead she went into the corner, hoping to find some inspiration and privacy to pull together her speech.

What could she say? How could she explain the complete topic change and how inapplicable the advertising and the décor and everything else they'd organized now was?

"Excuse me."

She looked up and saw an older man smiling up at her. "Hello?"

"I'm Leonard Abraham," the gentleman said, holding out his hand. "I'm so happy to be here, and I'm so glad you're having me speak. Letting me speak."

His smile was infectious, his brown eyes bright. He wore a bright blue bowtie covered with menorahs and dreidels, a blue suit and a yellow shirt. His eyebrows were bushy, and his bald head gleamed, the olive undertones clear under the fluorescent bulbs. "I'm so sorry," he said, "but I've been following the Hanukkah festival—"

"Wait. You've been following our festival?"

He nodded. "I absolutely have. I love how it's become a way of pulling your town together, and serving as a beacon. There are times we feel so alone, but a festival like this? It make us feel…no, reminds us that we have a community. That we're part of something bigger than ourselves."

And somehow, the author had managed to articulate what she loved most about the festival. That amid the hustle and the bustle the end of the year brought, it was a way of reminding their community that they weren't alone. "Thank you," she managed. "That's wonderful to hear."

His smile brightened his wrinkled face. "And when Shelly Averman's press release was brought to my attention, I couldn't help myself. I had to reveal this book here. I also would love to do a reading or two at this year's festival, sign some books maybe. Of course this is subject to what the festival chair would say, of course."

"Well," she said, hope blossoming inside her chest, "I'm actually the vice chair of this year's festival. So I think you might have a bit of an in."

"Oh, that's lovely. I'm feeling such…nachas, right now. Anyway…" He smiled a bit more. "Whenever you want to get started."

"Well," she said, the excitement inside her giving her wings, "how about I introduce you?"

"That would be lovely."

And then, heart in her throat, she headed up the aisle, past the rows of perfectly aligned chairs, past the signing station at the front, and stood behind the behind the lectern. She held on to the sides of the lectern, opened her notebook, closed her eyes, and took a breath.

"I want to welcome all of you to the Hollowville library," she said. She opened her eyes. She was surrounded by people who knew her, loved her. Chana was there, at the back, staring at the refreshments table; her parents had arrived, sitting together, her mother trying to keep her father from falling asleep. The mayor had staked out a spot in the front row, his wife's hand on his lap.

Out of the corner of her eye, she saw another group together at the back of the room. Elsa Lieberman was surrounded by Max, Jamie, Oliver, Isaac, and a few other people. They were grinning up at her, their thumbs raised in the air in the unified sign for good luck.

And then there was Isaac himself. His focus was intense, but his eyes were like beacons of light in the darkness. His steady smile gave her confidence, his presence made her beating heart slow just a little. And when she caught his eye, he gestured toward the empty seat next to him on the aisle.

"As you know," she began, "Dr. Leonard Abraham is here. He's an accomplished historian, and his books have received wide acclaim from both fellow historians and the non-academically inclined. He was originally supposed to talk about local history, but I'm proud to tell you that we've had a change in subject matter."

She held her breath as the audience chattered among themselves, before she pressed forward.

"Even though we haven't yet finished putting away our fall decorations in Hollowville, Hanukkah itself has become an integral part of life here. We're known as the little village that teaches the larger world about the beauty of candles gleaming in the snow, of fried food, and of the miracle of togetherness."

Nods and sighs filled the audience.

Yes.

They got what she was saying. And that understanding gave her the energy she needed.

"So," she continued, "it's fitting that award-winning, bestselling author Dr. Abraham has chosen our village as the very first stop, a pre-publication stop, for his brand-new book, *The Story of Hanukkah*. It tells the detailed story of how, and why, Hanukkah is celebrated in this country. But not the story we know. The book is about the stories we don't hear, things like the origins of instant latke mix and why soofganiyot haven't made their way here yet and who's trying to change that. He also delves into the most persistent Hanukkah battle ever: the question of applesauce versus sour cream and which dipping sauce is best for latkes. The book also covers the group responsible for the first public menorah lighting, and so many other stories."

Now she could see the audience sit a bit straighter, their eyes wider, their hands ready to clap. "Which means that right now, I have the honor, the privilege, of introducing to you: Dr. Leonard Abraham."

And as Dr. Abraham came into the room, the assembled crowd was almost as excited as she was.

What she was expected to do was go and sit next to her parents. Instead, she took the aisle seat next to Isaac, where she could see everybody and enjoy the lecture with all of them.

And she could steal some time of her own for a while.

Chapter Sixteen

THE LINE TO get into the Caf and Nosh went out the door, winding through the sidewalks of Hollowville.

"So what's this thing?" Isaac asked. He, Oliver, Jamie, Max, Tom, and Liam had joined Sarah and her best friend for some kind of dinner.

"It's kinda a town thing."

"A town thing?"

She nodded. "The Caf and Nosh does a preview of its Hanukkah menu as a way to raise money for charity. It's called the Cavalcade of Latkes, and this year it's tonight."

He blinked. It was the most amazing thing he'd ever heard. "Cavalcade?"

She laughed. "Yeah. The Caf and Nosh Hanukkah Cavalcade of Latkes. Latkes made from a ton of different vegetables and in a ton of different ways. Applesauce, of course, and that other stuff."

"Glad to know you're an applesauce lover."

"Of course I am. Because it's the best."

He nodded. "Absolutely." Usually being around long lines bothered him; on them was even worse. But here, and right now, he was filled with anticipation. "How long has this been going on?" he asked.

"A few years. Three maybe?" She paused. "I kinda see this as the real beginning of the holiday season, you know? Some people think of a parade and a red suit; I think of sizzling latkes and an entire town ready to eat them."

"I love that image," he said. "I can see it, and it's so great."

"What's great, Mr. Lieberman?"

He turned to see Chana standing in front of them. "That the entire town seems to be here tonight," he said. "That my friends and I are going to get the chance to have a wonderful dinner."

"That's all well and good." The older woman turned to Sarah. "I understand the whole *be a good citizen* thing, but, Sarah Goldman, you're vice chair of the festival! What are you doing in this line?"

Sarah bit her lip, and he wanted to shield her under his coat, protecting her from what she wanted to hide from. "Waiting? Like everybody else?"

Chana shook her head. "*Fakakta*," she said. "Absolute stupidity. Thankfully, I came out here looking for a big table and our Hanukkah fairy should *not* have to wait on this line. Especially when your parents, Sarah, and Anna's, wherever she is, and Elsa are already inside."

He turned around, to his friends and Anna, all of whom were attempting to put their hands in their pockets, trying to cover up whatever shenanigans they were involving themselves in.

"It's cold out here!" Tom said, laughing. "Come on. Bring us to food!"

"Also," added Anna, "you can't forget the most important rule."

"Which is?" he asked.

"Never naysay a restaurant owner when she wants to make her own rules."

They both laughed, before Sarah gave an imperceptible nod, which was Chana's cue to lead them all up the hill to the restaurant. And dinner. And whatever else was going to happen in the Caf and Nosh, that night.

AND BECAUSE SHE was smart, Sarah leaned into Isaac as Chana led the group up the hill to the restaurant. It was decorated with blue lights, some patterned to look like stars of David, some dreidels and gelt. Menorahs lined the countertops that led the way into the restaurant, and the smell of frying oil made her remember latkes her own mother made.

"Now, here's your official welcome to the cavalcade," Chana said, full of pride. "For those who don't know."

Sarah heard a few of Isaac's friends snort as well as Anna's distinctive laugh.

"We have multiple variations this year: three different potato as well as a bunch of variations that don't have any potato at all—Brussels sprout, leek, turnip, two different squashes and a few others."

"You have outdone yourself," Sarah said, beaming. "I am so excited."

"It's a nice thing we do." Deflecting praise as usual. But that was Chana, and as she did the same, Sarah didn't blame her. "And part of this year's proceeds go to the local food pantry as part of their fund drive."

"How many of these are going on the official menu?" Anna wondered.

"There's an official menu?" Surely one of Isaac's friends, of course, asked the question. But that was the fun part of introducing people to your customs. Seeing their reactions.

"The day after Thanksgiving," Chana replied, as if the question didn't matter. "That's when it shows up. That menu will pretty much contain all of the variations we have here tonight, with a few surprises rotated in until the end of the year."

"A few surprises?" Anna asked, even though Sarah recognized the conspiratorial look in Chana's eyes.

"I have to have a few tricks up my sleeve." Chana beamed before turning to the entire group. "So. Do you want chai – one pass at all of them, with a select bunch of soofganiyot for $18, or do you want the all-you-can-eat double chai for $36?"

"Double chai for Jamie and I. Tom?"

As Isaac's friends excitedly went down the menus, choosing what they wanted, most of them settling for the double, Sarah debated which would be better for her mood and her waistline.

"Double chai," Anna said. "I want all the things."

That was when Isaac looked at her, and the sight of his smile was a *shamash* candle. "Double chai for me too," he said.

And whether it was the excitement of sharing this perfect tradition with Isaac, whether it was the understanding that the money would go to charity or even the taste of the food, Sarah matched his smile with as much of her own. "Double for me too."

"Excellent choice all around. Seven double chais. Let me get all of you to a table."

As they stepped into the recently expanded central dining room, there was laughter and the sound of clinking silverware, of families and friends together sharing moments of the holiday season.

Which stopped, almost suddenly as the large group made their way through the tables.

"What?" Chana interjected, shaking her head. "Have you people never seen a festival vice chair eat before? Keep eating or I'll think you don't like the food."

And as if she'd waved a magic wand, the conversation started again.

"Anyway," Chana continued as she ushered them to the long, extended table in the back of the restaurant, "ignore the *Chelmites* who clearly haven't seen a large group of people eat latkes. Enjoy your dinner and *chag sameach.*"

And as Sarah sat down, she looked across the table, filled with the joy of old friends and new. And Isaac. This would be fun, even if it meant she'd be the topic of conversation in Hollowville for the next year.

ISAAC COULD BARELY stand. He'd eaten more than his fill of latkes and soofganiyot and managed to drink his gelt mocha without losing his marbles. Barely. But sitting with Sarah and his friends, and her best friend, had been such a perfect end to a wonderful weekend. "Wow," he said. "This was…"

"Perfect," she said. "Absolutely one hundred percent perfect." She'd shared recommendations, and he'd even really liked the strawberry despite his desire to eat only raspberry. But the dazzle in her eyes when she ate the lemon and the custard swayed him to try something new.

"So where are you guys parked?"

"Over by the library," Jamie said, grinning. "So good to walk off this excess."

"I'm carrying a ton of bricks," Max pointed out, "all of which are sitting at the bottom of my stomach."

"I need some kind of mobility vehicle because I sure as

heck am not walking, or I at least need to wait before I do," Oliver added.

"You're driving back to the city?" Anna interjected.

Jamie nodded. "Yeah. You want a lift?" And then she paused before meeting his eyes. "You going back to the city tonight, Isaac?"

The question, innocent as it was, hung in the air like a bee: small and potentially dangerous. He smiled, trying to find a better answer than the one he had. "I'm not sure," he said as honestly as he could.

"Well," Jamie said, "Tom, Max, Liam? You guys have a car?"

"Yeah," Tom answered. "We're driving back, too. So we have space in the car if you don't."

"Are you guys leaving now?"

"I still have to get my car. Tom?"

Tom nodded. "I'll go with you. I moved to park near the library, too."

"So you guys wait out front. We'll come back with the cars, 'kay?"

"That," Oliver said, giving his girlfriend a kiss on the cheek, "is the most amazing thing I have ever heard."

But as time continued, and bills were squared, Isaac realized that he hadn't heard what Sarah thought. And he wondered why.

THE HOLIDAY LIGHTS and the streetlights seemed to be fighting a losing battle against the dark of the night sky. It was the beginning of the season of light and miracles after all, the elements that combined in each of the holidays celebrated around this time of year.

Usually dark came with quiet outside the city, but here in Hollowville it didn't. The door of the café opened and closed as people came up the stairs to eat or left the restaurant with their families and friends. Happiness, joy, and footsteps broke through the winter silence.

Oliver, Liam, and Max dragged Anna off through the town, and so he and Sarah found a bench to sit on. The cold had brightened her cheeks, drawing his gaze toward the bright smile on her face. He had to smile back.

"Heading back to the city then?"

"A bit later," he said, then paused when her expression didn't soften. "I want to spend some time with *Bubbe* before I head out."

She nodded. "Makes sense." She paused; he wondered what she was going to say, what words were so difficult for her to form that she took his hand. "I'm sorry," she said. "I mean about the shenanigans when we first walked in."

He shrugged. "You're a local celebrity, you're organizing the festival."

"Don't want to talk about the festival tonight," she said. "But yes. I'm part of this town, and in a lot of ways you are too. I guess we need to figure out what that means, you know?"

Which was true, but when he went to answer her, he noticed that he and Sarah were no longer alone. In fact, they were surrounded; he could see Jamie and Oliver, as well as Max, Anna, Liam, and Tom, Sarah's father and a woman who had to be her mother, and another older couple that must have been Anna's parents.

"Hi, guys," he said, grinning in an attempt to break up the sudden silence. "Guess we're all heading out, hmm?"

"Mmmm."

Sarah's non-committal noise was clear in his head. But she showed no signs of moving away from him, despite the expressions on everybody's faces. He took that as a win.

"Were you guys up to anything interesting?" her father asked, pointedly staring at the space between them.

"Well," she managed.

"Digesting," Isaac said, smiling. He brushed a hand toward the part of his stomach where it felt like the latkes, the lattes, and the soofganiyot were sitting. "I'm so stuffed."

"We do latkes quite well in Hollowville," her father said.

"You do Hanukkah quite well," Max replied, smiling. "It's really a lovely town."

"Why, thank you," her father said. "We try to keep up the spirit, you know, community and rededication and all."

"And we're welcoming to those who need a place at the table," Sarah said, grinning, brushing her hand against his yet again, as if she was trying to tell him something.

"Yes," said a woman whose smile reminded him enough of Sarah's that she had to be her mother. "We are. We embrace everybody who lives here, and," she paused. "So many people who don't."

"It's what we like to hear," Tom added.

"What is this *freyliche* gathering?" his *bubbe* asked as she joined the group, a huge smile on her face. "My *tateleh* and so many wonderful people around, just outside the café."

"It's Hollowville," Sarah's father said. "It's what we do. And we're celebrating togetherness."

"*Nachas*," his *bubbe* said, beaming. "Yes. All the best sort of *nachas*."

Jamie interjected. "I don't mean to be a bummer, but this beautiful scene needs to end shortly if some of us are going to make the train. That, or whoever's coming in the car and wants to get back to Brooklyn before traffic erupts."

"Am I going to be able to get a ride?" Anna asked.

Jamie paused, looking at him, as if she was budging him toward an answer before turning away and back to Anna. "I mean if you're going to stay a bit longer, Isaac, I've got space in the car for one more."

And with everybody staring at him, he smiled. "Yeah. I'm going to stay a bit longer."

And he wasn't dreaming when he realized that Sarah had squeezed his hand.

"*Tateleh*," his *bubbe* said, "I'll take you to the train a bit later, okay?"

"Thanks, *Bubbe*," he said. "I appreciate it," even though it was the last thing he wanted.

And as people started to say goodbye, he stood and lingered with Sarah. "I'll call you?" he said.

She nodded, her eyes bright. "Looking forward to it."

He wanted to kiss her, desperately so. For so many reasons, this wasn't the right time, not yet. But for the first time, he wondered what the right time would feel like.

SARAH WASN'T SURE how the scene had ended; Jamie made her announcement, and then people scattered like they'd been on a timer. There were hasty goodbyes from her parents, who she'd talk to tomorrow, and a lingering goodbye with Isaac before he and his *bubbe* headed home. Now she and Anna stood with Jamie, Oliver, and the rest of Isaac's group of friends, not exactly sure what to do next.

All she could think of was the lingering moment with Isaac, both too short and too long at the same time. Sitting with him, chatting with him, had been the most comfortable thing in the world, and they'd sat together in the library, in the Caf and Nosh and even on the bench afterwards.

She wanted more of it.

What did she want from him? How did she see him?

"This is going to be interesting," Anna said, breaking the silence and busting into her thoughts, "because you're not really here."

"Can I be blunt?"

Sarah looked away toward the sound of the voice, only to meet Max's eyes. Max, the visual artist, the one who'd organized the signing. "Sure?"

"Don't worry about Max," Jamie said. "He's harmless, even though I'm not sure he's capable of being anything other than blunt."

The group laughed, even as they all turned toward Max. "So," Oliver said. "What's this minute's pronouncement?"

Max smiled in a way that reminded Sarah of how close to this group he was, this group of Isaac's friends. "I'm not sure what your intentions are toward Isaac, but my suggestion is that you figure it out before someone decides for you."

"Gotta say," Anna added, "he's right."

Sarah nodded. He was right.

"The town's already pushing you two together, or at least thinking about it," her friend continued. "No matter what happens, no matter what decisions you two make, you need to make them before the runaway train takes you both on an express to disaster."

"Yeah," added Liam, the illustrator; the one who'd made comments about being part of the version of the *Shadow Squad* comic that was made to tie in to the recent movies. "You're not the only one who's gonna pay the price if they're pushing you places you don't want to go."

She nodded, because that was all she could do. There

were so many questions she needed to answer, not only for herself, but for him. Isaac was becoming…something. Whatever it was, she needed to figure out how she felt about it. And him.

"SO WHY DID you leave so abruptly?" The question fell out of Isaac's mouth as he and *Bubbe* drove up the hill to her house. He didn't mean to ask it, but he'd been wrestling with it for a while.

There was silence, of course. He was probably as prepared to ask as his *bubbe* was prepared to answer.

"I have a question for you, *tateleh*."

Of course his *bubbe* answered his question with one of hers. And of course he was going to answer it, no matter what it was.

"What are your feelings toward Sarah?"

That was a question he'd anticipated at some point, but not now. "She's nice," he said, knowing his words didn't encompass the depth of his slowly blossoming feelings. "I like her," he finished.

His *bubbe* nodded as they pulled into her driveway. She didn't say anything as they got out of the car and walked up the steps to the front door. The silence lengthened and made him nervous, made his heart beat against his chest.

Finally, as they were sitting down with a cup of tea, she

smiled at him. "Hollowville is a small town," she said, her eyes sad. "The Jewish community here, the people who are in my circle, the people Sarah works with at the library, the people at the bookstore, the people who see her every day—they know. They pay attention to what people are doing. They pay attention to what she does, who she does it with."

Images of the sudden hush that came over the Caf and Nosh like a wave greeted his memory.

I'm part of this town. You are too. I guess we have to figure out what that means.

"I had a great time with her when we hung out in Brooklyn. She was different, more relaxed."

His *bubbe* nodded. "Now," she took a deep breath. "One of the things that's been happening in town is the festival. It's important to all of us; it's important to me, *tateleh*."

"I know."

"You say you know, but today? Well, you saw how everybody came out for the book signing and the cavalcade. That's just a small percentage of the people who are going to take part in this year's festival."

"But what does that have to do with Sarah?"

"Chana is technically the chair, but Sarah is the heart of the festival. She clearly isn't bothered by the fact you're not doing the menorah, but you can help her, you can take some of that stress off of her shoulders."

He sighed, drank some of his tea. "But, what good would this menorah do, *Bubbe*? What exactly? The town comes to celebrate together, not—"

"That's the thing, *tateleh*. The village doesn't have to let us have this festival. The village can hide behind people like Webster who turn good ideas into a sharp sword."

The festival tree dude. The one who wanted to prematurely end the festival before this group had a chance. Right.

But *Bubbe* wasn't done.

"*Tateleh*, you saw how close these events bring people, and you, well, you can bring your heart to a menorah. Because whatever you make will be from the heart. Your heart. With you making that menorah, it could be more. It doesn't have to be commercial in the way you don't like. It could help people *remember*."

Help people remember.

Remember what?

The holiday? The festival didn't need him to help remember; if the festival had forgotten the holiday, nothing he could do would help.

Family? No matter how you celebrated it, Hanukkah was really about rededicating yourself to your life, to your family. To your faith and everything you'd lost along the way. But Hollowville seemed to be a family. Filled with people who had strong ties, who knew each other by face if not by name. Who shared in each other's cultural heritage, even if it wasn't their own.

But what kind of menorah could he make to help people remember what was important about the holiday? What kind of thing would do the town, their festival, and Sarah justice?

And would he be able to make it in time?

And did he want to?

"I'm not sure," he said. "I have to think about it."

"You don't have to tell me now, *tateleh*," she said, still urgent. You can tell me soon."

"As soon as I know, you'll be the first to know," he said. "I promise."

She grasped his cheeks with warm hands and kissed his forehead. "Good."

And he thought about it on the train to Brooklyn, on the subway back to his apartment and all through the night. He thought of his *bubbe*, standing outside, the snow in her hair as the brightness of a menorah he'd built lit up her face as brightly as her smile.

And maybe Sarah's bright smile alongside hers.

Maybe.

Chapter Seventeen

Brooklyn

MONDAY NIGHT WAS game night. Oliver, Jamie, Max, Tom, and Liam arrived at Isaac's apartment, bearing food, drink, and art supplies. There were rules, of course, including drawing with their non-dominant hands, instituted to keep things somewhat on the level. It was fun.

"Well," Liam said, reaching into his messenger bag and pulling out a thin magazine, branded with the name of an airline. "That festival's publicity committee is doing its thing."

"What?"

To be fair, Isaac had been thinking a lot about the festival and about what he'd seen over the weekend. But he didn't expect this, on game night. He'd gotten the impression that the festival was having trouble getting publicity, which was why they needed him.

"I was flipping through this," he continued, putting his bag down on the sofa, "and I saw an article about holiday festivals. You know those lists, the ones with biggest tree, and the one with the best cookies..."

"Yeah?"

"Anyway..." Liam flipped through the pages and looked up at the group before passing the magazine around. "They went into explicit detail about how homey Hollowville's Hanukkah festival is."

"Were there photos?" Tom wondered. "Because someone named Batya made a comment about how few photos there were. I said I'd take a few, send them to the web designer..."

"Yeah, but there was an article." Liam paused. "Reads to me like they got a press release, which is what Anna had said this weekend."

Press release. Photos. Articles. Major publicity. And more publicity associated with Dr. Abraham's latest title.

A festival in the spotlight, no menorah, and a trustee bent on filling the empty space with a tree.

Did they need him?

"Wait." Oliver pointed to the bag and the foil that stuck out of the opening in the top. "Why are you not touching the *banh mi* I went all the way to Manhattan for? What's wrong?"

How could he answer that question? "I..."

"Oh come on," Tom said, grinning. "Admit your conflict, dude."

"Why is he conflicted?" Liam wondered.

"Yeah, Isaac," said Max. "Why are you conflicted? And if you're not touching the *banh mi*, I'm taking it."

Isaac shook his head and swiped the sandwich from the

plate in front of him. "So I've been asked to do a sculpture, but I'm not sure. Still. Like I thought I was vehemently against it, but I...well...I don't know."

"What sculpture?" Liam asked. "Is it some random animal for a fast food company or for Wall Street?"

"No animals, no randomness." He stood up, started to pace, sandwich firmly in hand. He took a bite, let the spicy goodness enter his mouth, forcing his thoughts to calm down and focus a little bit. "Have you guys ever done anything out of the ordinary? Hmm..."

"I mean," said Oliver, stealing one of the large sushi rolls and dipping it into his soy sauce. "I've done a sketch for some strange parties friends of mine threw. But nothing that gives me that much pause. What's the story?"

"So," Isaac said, as he continued to pace around the room. "There's this thing, and I was asked to do something. For humanity? For charity? And I'd have to get a large-scale sculpture done in about a month."

"Last time I did a project on a whim like that," Liam said, "I was in my early twenties."

Jamie snorted. "That was four years ago; you make it sound like you're an old man. Dude."

"Fine." Liam laughed. "Fine. Anyway, it was a special charity project, raising funds for disaster relief. It sold huge and the proceeds funded a lot of little things that helped people's lives. We did another edition a few months ago, the proceeds of which went to Puerto Rico."

"Oh that's awesome," Isaac said. "But, this isn't on that kind of scale."

"It's what?" Max wondered. "Like that huge Christmas tree someone made?"

"Wait," Oliver interjected, incredulous. "Someone asked you to make a Christmas tree? No wonder why you're balking."

Isaac shook his head. "No. Not exactly like that." He sighed. "Sarah…the Hollowville committee asked me to make a menorah for the festival."

"So *that's* why her father was all like 'We do Hanukkah well,' hint, hint." Oliver shook his head.

"And," added Max as he looked over his glasses, "why the dude made a big deal about the girl not being at the show and how it wasn't good or whatever."

"Wait, wait." Jamie threw up her hands as if she was directing traffic. Which, Isaac reflected, with this group she usually actually was. "So I made earrings because you screwed up and said no?"

He shook his head. "No, the earrings were because I…banned her from the show."

"Which is how I ended up meeting her and her friend, who recruited me to the festival." Jamie shook her head. "You need to *talk* to people, Isaac. You really do." She sighed.

"So what's really the problem?" Max interjected. "You like her, you love your grandmother."

What wasn't the problem? Where did he start?

"It's not that simple," Isaac managed, trying to pull his thoughts together. "Yeah. Sarah's great and I love my grandmother. And I don't want them to cancel the festival. I just...I don't want to participate in the commercialization of the holiday."

Oliver raised an eyebrow.

Jamie cleared her throat, before folding her arms. The room went silent, and his heart pounded against his chest. "Are you judging me for exhibiting?"

He shook his head. "No, no, not at all. I'm glad. It's just a different conversation."

Jamie sighed. "See, Isaac, this is the thing. I don't always have a chance to celebrate my heritage. Yes, I make *Judaica*, but they're vanity pieces. For me. Not for a dedicated audience of people who would want them. So that they can be reminded of where they came from, of who they are, and celebrate it proudly. As if they're taking proactive steps to identify themselves as part of a community. So it's not just a small town bazaar where people sell things. This is a physical representation of Hanukkah and of people celebrating it. That's why I'm doing it, not to make a few dollars and spend the day with my boyfriend in a small town."

"Yeah," said Liam. "Gotta tell you, doing that second edition for Puerto Rico? Easiest decision I ever made. Not because it was a good thing or because it was the right thing to do or even because it was an easy way for me to help a good cause. No. It was also for the community, for my family, you know?"

He did understand both of their points. Community, family, and tangible, visible representation of the community.

Not just money.

"I guess," he said, "I could take a look at the background, maybe, really learn about the festival and its history before making a decision?"

Liam nodded. "With my charity project, I had the advantage of knowing what it was for in the beginning. This, you only have your view of it, not the history. Is there someone you can ask for more insight?"

"And," Oliver added, "not just your *bubbe*?"

Liam grinned. "Not to mention, there's a special occasion coming up very soon where you can invite a few people to your apartment in Brooklyn who you can ask to come and enjoy life for a little while, before you ask them about history?"

Isaac laughed. He'd been volunteered to host Liam's birthday party a while ago, and so he'd slowly been planning. It was going to be on Friday night. "Too late to invite them?"

Liam shook his head. "Never. Blame me for insisting whoever they are come."

And as the rest of the night continued, thoughts of parties, invitations, and nerves danced in his head. He couldn't wait to send the invitations to the three extra guests. Especially Sarah.

He hoped she'd make it.

Hollowville

AFTER A LONG, wild day at work, Sarah finally left to grab a quick dinner before heading to the committee meeting. Her papers were organized, put far away in a folder deep inside her tote bag.

As she stood in line at the Caf and Nosh's takeout counter, she heard a familiar voice.

"Well, hello, stranger."

She turned around with a smile. "Hi, Daddy," she said, accepting an embrace. "How are you?"

"Good," he said. "Enjoying the freedom of not being in charge of the festival this year," he confessed. "Though I don't like how it's been worrying you so much. I don't like what Webster and his ilk are trying to do and I hate the fact that I'm not involved with you to make it easier. Take more of the heat."

She shrugged, stepping out of the embrace. "It was time," she said. "Not to mention I'm working with a great group, and Chana is such a perfect chair to deal with Webster, though I promise that if things come up where we need you, I'll let you know."

"You're right," he said. "And I thank you for that."

She nodded, and in the space between phrases, she pulled together what she'd wanted to say to him since she'd seen him try to guilt Isaac about the sculpture. "You know, speaking of festivals and difficult things…"

Her father nodded, bit his lip. "Town gossip network is working overtime, hmm?"

She laughed. "Not overtime. Overtime would have been a late-night text from some random person telling me my father was breaking the rules at the gallery."

Her father folded his arms, suddenly defensive. "Any rules that keep my daughter from the best art exhibit Hollowville has ever had deserve to be broken."

"Dad," she said, rolling her eyes. "If I'm not offended, you shouldn't have been."

"I'm not offended," he replied.

She reached out to rub his fuzzy-sweater-covered shoulder. "You were being my loyal, brilliant, bright light of a father."

It was his turn to laugh. "If I'm going to be called out for something, let it be defending my daughter. That I'll always admit to. And you know what?"

She couldn't help but smile. "What?"

"I won't stop defending you. You deserve it."

"I love you and appreciate you, but you know it's not always necessary to step in. Besides, that one show brought a whole bunch of artists to the gallery and Hollowville in general. Which is amazing."

Her father raised an eyebrow. "Why is it so amazing?"

"Apparently the artists who came to the show are going to do a bunch of things all over town. There's going to be," she paused, and tried to remember each of the things she'd heard. "A photography show at the library as well as at the gallery. There's going to be a visual art installation at the gallery and a few mixed media painting and drawing shows. And before I left for the night, Carol got an email from one of the most talented comic artists as of late, who wants to do a signing at the store and maybe teach a class or two at the library."

"That is wonderful," her father said, pausing as the information she was giving him sank in.

"Yes." She smiled. "And I'm so excited for Molly and the gallery."

"But still no menorah, huh?"

She laughed. "No menorah, and I think we're getting to the point where we should probably stop looking."

"Why?"

She shrugged. "I mean...I want to be hopeful but I don't know what's happening for the future and the festival is a bit less than two months away, so I've got an idea that can be flexible. Which I'm going to bring in front of the committee tonight."

"And you've been spending some time with that sculptor. What's his deal?"

She shrugged. "I honestly don't know. I mean it's fun, and wonderful and he's a nice guy, and I like spending time with him both here and in the city."

"But you're not talking to him about the festival?"

"I should, shouldn't I?" She sighed. "I mean I feel like I don't want to push the issue. He said no, and I like him, and I like how I feel when I spend time with him."

"You like him, huh?" He laughed. "Probably not the kind of thing you should be saying to your father, but as I am your father I'll tell you something."

This probably wasn't the conversation most fathers and daughters had, she knew. Especially after her father had made comments about always defending her. But her relationship with her father was special, and uniquely theirs. "What, Dad?"

"You need to be happy, Sar," he said, reaching out to rub her shoulder with one hand. You deserve it. Every second of joy, no matter what else happens. If this sculptor makes you happy, that's good. Really good."

Which, she decided, it was. It wasn't going to make the meeting any easier, but it was nice. "Thanks, Dad."

She hugged him.

"Are you two going to order?" Chana interjected, a smile on her face. "You need to do so quickly if you're going to make it to the meeting on time."

"Well, Madam Chair," her father said, smiling. "Give us two specials to go." He turned to Sarah. "Coffee?"

"Large soofi latte with an extra shot of espresso, thank you."

"And I'll have the sugar-free version." He grinned. "Good for my diet."

Chana rolled her eyes. "Yes. Yes. Of course. Extra espresso on one and sugar-free on the other. Got it. Let me make your coffees, and I'll see you at the meeting."

Of course, the prospect of presenting at the meeting wasn't exactly exciting, considering the kind of doomsday bombshell sort of news intrinsic in the proposal. It was realistic, not giving up. Right?

Right.

"It's going to be fine," her father told her as he took his bagged dinner to the back of the room.

"You're going to do great!" Elsa Lieberman said, smiling at her.

She smiled back. "Thank you," she said. "I don't know what I've done to deserve your faith in me, considering you haven't even heard my proposal, but I appreciate it."

"The Hanukkah Fairy," Elsa replied, "has as much heart as she does spirit. Considering I've known you since you were a little girl."

"Oh, Mrs. Lieberman," she managed. "I—"

"Oh hush, *mamaleh.*" The older woman beamed. "If anybody deserves my faith on an unseen proposal, it's you."

"Thank you." She gave Elsa an embrace before heading over to her seat. "I appreciate it. Even though I don't feel I deserve it."

Elsa's warm smile didn't ease the increasingly explosive bits inside her stomach.

Because Sarah couldn't quite shake the feeling that she was letting the entire festival committee down, and not even her even her egg salad sandwich was making her feel better.

She sat down in her usual seat around the central table, reaching for her soofi latte as if it was a caffeinated, sugary lifeline. The sweetness and the caffeine followed each other down her throat, wrapping her in a blanket full of the kind of energy she'd need to get through this meeting.

Sufficiently caffeinated, she put the cup down, moved the agenda in front of her and grabbed a pen. As the meeting went on, she made notes in her notebook in a desperate attempt to keep her mind on the meeting instead of the horrible news she was about to deliver.

"Finally," said Chana, her distinctive voice breaking through the silence, "we've reached the agenda item that concerns me the most. I have to tell you, Sarah, that you've been amazing as our on-the-ground person this year. A lot of the committee members, the vendors, and others we've spoken to have said great things about your abilities."

She took a deep breath as the pressure rose up again. "Thank you, Madam Chair," she said, trying to find the right words that didn't show how unworthy she felt of that kind of praise. "I appreciate your confidence in me."

"As your chair, I could not have had a better vice chair.

This year has been difficult, possibly more difficult than we expected. Whether dealing with trouble from outside or inside the committee, Sarah has been steadfast. And whatever she's got, I'm looking forward to hearing."

"Thank you," she said once again, glad for the mood change in Chana's words. If the chair had continued to make her feel like she was capable of the impossible, nothing she'd say would be acceptable. But listening to Chana being realistic about things made her feel a little better. And so she passed her papers out to the committee.

Chana took her folder and smiled. "I like this already."

She bit her lip. "Thank you, Madam Chair."

"Now you can proceed."

Sarah swallowed.

All you have to do is leap, she reminded herself. *Leap, close your eyes, and hope you land.*

And if you don't? That's what your friends and family are there for.

"So yes," she began, taking a quick drink of her latte to soothe her throat and maybe show her heart down a little bit.

Maybe.

"We are in a very particular spot. We are less than two months away from what could be the very last Hanukkah festival in Hollowville history. But according to Shelly Averman's email, the efforts of the publicity committee have been fruitful. Ad buys are up, the traffic on the website is up too. There have already been a few high-profile pieces written about the festival, so those are now up on the website, and our new contact at *Empire Daily* informs me that there's coverage coming from there as well. We also have contacts at a few of the other papers now, and some of them have committed to providing coverage, some of the others have committed to put us in their 'what's going on' sections."

There were bits of conversation as the committee reacted to the information. But there was more to say. "The vendor test nights are settled, and the vendors have responded, so final invites are going out to the congregation. We're expecting a high turnout there.

"We also have a wonderful logo, done by Oliver Goldsmith. It's now on our website, and has been added to all of the email we send out."

There were excited noises, a few claps. And she paused to let herself soak in the good reactions. She was going to need to fill herself up with them in order to deal with the meat of what she had to say. "Which is all amazing news, and these are all great things. But there's one obvious thing missing. A menorah. We all know that. And as much as I wished any of my queries would have come back positively, none of them did. For whatever reasons, be it financial or philosophical or any other reason you can think of, we don't have one."

There was a flurry of silence, small bits of quiet that slowly built into a raging storm of nothing.

It hurt.

It was misery.

She had to continue, and walk straight into the blizzard, hoping she'd find shelter. Hope. "But we need *something*. Whether that something turns into a thing by which we remember the Hanukkah festival as it was, or whether it turns into a fund for a sculpture next year. So here is my idea. Commemorative items."

As she explained, some of the committee members brightened, their eyes wide with the excitement at the possibilities. Some of their eyes narrowed, confusion and questions deep beneath their surface.

"We're a not-for-profit organization," one of the skeptical members said. "How can we engage in this kind of commerce?"

Sarah shook her head. "This isn't for profit."

"So what else do you call selling things specifically under the festival label?"

"A percentage of the sales will go to either a future sculpture or a cause we'd vote on to be named later. Maybe the library."

"Or," said one of the other board members, "it could just be a temporary fund for a sculpture, and then we decide what to do with it once that is completed."

"This is a great idea," Chana said, looking smug. "Do you have any interest in this? Have you polled any of the vendors?"

Visions of Jamie's bright smile and the smiles of the other crafters she'd met at the craft fair in the city went through her head. "I actually have, because you can't do something like this without vendors who don't have a sufficient quantity of items and time to add the logo. One of the vendors, Jamie Sawyer, is knowledgeable and was able to guide me toward vendors who not only were interested in participating, but also had the inventory to do it. As part of the package of papers I passed out, I have two different lists of vendors. One list gave me commitments, pending the committee approval. The other is comprised of vendors who are capable of following through, but who want details I can't give then until after this vote."

This time, the room was full of hopeful sounds, of papers rustling and whispering committee members. "Most of the vendors on both lists are already signed up to be part of the festival, and will be showing their wares at the jewelry and accessories test night."

"What about the businesses who want to get involved but don't create things?"

"Well." Thank goodness she'd thought of this angle. "You can turn to page three of the proposal where I talk about this, but basically, the businesses who are exhibiting at the fair can either sell the items someone else creates at their stores or create a special something on their service menu that could contribute."

The owner of the copy shop, Mr. Mendelowitz, tapped his fingers on the table. "For every 613 copies made, Hollowville QuickCopy will donate a percentage to the Hollowville Hanukkah sculpture fund?"

"Yes. Exactly," Sarah replied, relieved that she didn't have to explain the proposal in further detail.

"Ten percent of each 'soofi shake' will be donated to the sculpture fund," Chana said, slamming her hand on the table, punctuating her commitment. "I love this. This is perfect. And yes, we'll figure out the shake recipe and introduce it shortly—as long as that's acceptable to everybody here?" She paused, and Sarah held her breath. "Vote. Hands. In the affirmative?" All hands were raised. "Okay then. The motion passes."

Pure sweet relief filled Sarah's veins. All she had to do was make it through the next month and a half without someone putting a tree in the empty space where the menorah wasn't going to be.

Chapter Eighteen

THE TUESDAY AFTER the meeting was hard. Sarah brought a gelt latte back to work as an incentive to prepare for the next few events.

"What do you have on the docket?" Carol asked.

Sarah sat down at her desk before answering. "Well, organizing signings for the days around the festival. And..." She trailed off, the sound of an incoming email breaking through her concentration.

"And what?" Carol wondered. "What's going on?"

"I don't know," she admitted. As she clicked into the other email account, she realized the email was not only from Isaac, but also sent from one of the many different websites that provided event invitations. "I've been invited to something."

"Invited?" Carol asked as she stood from her chair, walking around the corner of the desk. "To what?"

She shrugged, then turned back to the screen, clicking on the invitation.

I know it's short notice, but I'd love to see you. You don't have to bring a present for my friend, but he also wants to see you. And just so you know, your friends Anna and Batya are also invited.

"Apparently I'm being invited to a birthday party for someone by the guy who's hosting it?"

"Isaac is hosting a birthday party?"

"Yes," she said. "But I don't know if I want to go.

"When is it?"

"Friday night?"

"You should go," Carol said. "Give yourself time to breathe. You don't work on Saturdays anyway, so you don't have that conflict."

"And let me guess. You'd make sure, as my boss and owner of the store, that even if I did have a conflict, it would be nonexistent."

"What kind of a gossip would I be if I didn't make things easier for you after that committee meeting last night. Must have been rough."

"It was necessary," she said, grabbing her gelt latte and taking a long drink of the chocolaty beverage. "I didn't expect the reaction, but it's done now. And I'm so tired. And so scared, but I've done all I can. I think."

"Now, go to that birthday party, have fun in Brooklyn and then come back for work and the first of the vendor test nights energized and filled with vitamin L."

She tapped her fingers at the corner of the desk. "Maybe I'll run over to Rosen's Art supply during lunch, or after work to get a gift."

"That's the spirit. And make sure you remind Mr. Hernandez that he should bring me a signed copy of his first second-generation *Shadow Squad* book when he comes here in July. Want to see his signature near the thing kids these days are calling 'the treasured tuchus.'"

"I will remember," she said, knowing if she didn't, there would be trouble. She adored her boss, and wondered if she could get Carol an early signed copy for a birthday present, even if Liam's signature was the only one near the cartoon version of Mr. Shadow, and of course, actor Sam Moskowitz's, aka Mr. Shadow himself, prized butt.

Wheels racing in her mind as the idea got clear and stronger. Now, she had yet another reason to go to this party.

Along with, of course, the most important reason. Seeing Isaac.

Brooklyn

FOOD, CARDS, FRIENDS, music, warmth. Isaac's apartment was full, on a Thursday night, and he was happy.

Or he would be, once everybody was there. Sarah was supposed to come, and she hadn't yet. And with every passing moment, he was more worried she wasn't going to.

"She'll be here," Jamie said, as she organized a few napkins. "She said she'd be here when I saw her this week. Did you talk to her after you sent the invitation, or did you just send it and hope she'd reply?"

He bit his lip. "I didn't. I didn't want to push her or anything. Or pressure her."

She shook her head. "You need to use words, dude." She smiled. "You realize why Oliver and I made you host this party, right?"

"Because Liam needed a bigger party than pizza and sugar-fueled karaoke?"

Jamie laughed but Isaac knew he wasn't even close to the truth.

"Try another one. Like how you hibernate while working, and when we planned this party you weren't working. Maybe it's a good thing," she said, smiling as she grabbed a bottle of water.

"What?"

"You had something to invite Sarah to."

He laughed. "Yeah." He ran a hand through his hair and stared at the wall, willing the speaker to announce someone was downstairs, or his doorbell to ring with the announcement of a new arrival.

Finally, the deep rumbling of the bell heralded someone, and he'd never moved so fast to answer, whether he was excited to see who it was, or whether he was blocking someone else from leaving the chaos of his living room. He didn't know.

His friends were quiet, thankfully; they knew what was at

stake here. His heart probably…no. His mind definitely knew how important this was. Sarah was coming to see him in his space, with his friends. That was the most exciting and dangerous thing he could think of. A miracle of its own.

And as he opened the door, he lost his mind. Plain and simple. Shut down.

Sarah stood there, a large winter coat, hair mussed from a hat she must have taken off, cheeks pink from the cold and bright lipstick. Her eyes were alight with excitement.

"Hi," she said, reminding him he was on earth, in need of words to say. "I…"

"Come in," he said. "Let me hang up your coat. Do you want tea? Can I get you something else?"

She smiled. "Some room?"

He laughed. Lord did he laugh. "Yes. Right." He stepped back, remembering he was a gentleman, not an unsociable idiot. "Sorry," he said. "I meant to…"

"It's fine. I'm here."

She was, and it was, thankfully. Now he was able to really enjoy the party, knowing she'd come down on a Thursday. Yes, to celebrate Liam's birthday, but to celebrate with *him*.

SARAH EXPECTED THE situation was going to be horribly awkward. Yes, she knew his friends. Not well, but well enough to recognize them and chat with them like she had last weekend. But this was a strangely private party; friends, tea, silly stories she hadn't heard about Liam, the guest of honor, or even Isaac.

Isaac, who watched over her to make sure she was okay—was she warm? Was she enjoying herself? Did she want a drink? Did she want something to eat? Sweet, hovering, nervous Isaac. So completely different from the guy she'd spent time with in Brooklyn and in Hollowville.

"I still can't believe you got this notebook," the birthday boy interjected. "I mean, seriously."

"The guy at the art supply shop talked about how great these were," she said. "I like certain notebooks for writing, but he was saying he drew. So, I asked. He told me he liked the paper in this, how it didn't let the ink bleed through, so I figured you could use one."

"Totally impressed," said Liam. "In fact, I'm so impressed that I want everybody to lift a glass to Sarah."

And everybody lifted teacups, water glasses, the occasional wineglass or beer bottle. "To Sarah," he repeated. "Who is smart, a great event planner, and who is wonderful enough to wake the hermit from his fiery solitude."

Her cheeks burned, and as she looked just to her right, she watched Isaac swipe a hand across his brow. Embarrassment? Nerves? Worry? Either way, she smiled at him.

"May I make a toast?" she asked.

There was discussion and conversation, which came to a

halt. "Of course you can," Liam said, his voice bright. "You absolutely can."

"Okay then." Everybody raised their glasses and she grinned. "To friends, old and new; to birthdays, and to our host, for being a beacon of warmth in the November cold."

"Cheers!"

Glasses clinked, voices rose, and all of the noise made her feel at home. And she found herself enjoying the party, falling into rhythm with his friends and him, and most importantly, realizing what about this group made him smile.

And as they all headed out much later, they made sure she knew where she was going.

Including Isaac. "You. You're going to be okay?"

She nodded. "I will be. Thank you," she said, smiling. "But will I see you soon?"

"I actually have a question for you."

He was hesitant, and she wondered what he could ask her that made him that nervous. "What?"

He bit his lip. "I want to know more about the festival. Like the history. Because I don't know anything about it, but I know it's important to you and my *bubbe*."

Her breath stopped.

History. Festival history.

They hadn't talked at all about the festival since he told her he wasn't going to make the menorah. And now he wanted to know about festival history.

"Are you okay?"

No.

His voice wrapped around her, pulling her back to reality, or at least the version she was standing on.

She forced herself back in vice chair mode. "There's something happening, if you can come up to Hollowville on Saturday night."

There was a long pause, which was weird considering the fact he'd asked the question out of nowhere. Did she come on too strong?

Did she give him enough time? Too short notice? "Maybe another time."

"No, no," he said, as if to jump in and reassure her. "Saturday is fine. I'll come up tomorrow night, have dinner, or...no. I'll come up Saturday morning, spend the day with my *bubbe*, and meet you..."

"At the HHC," she said, smiling. "Meet me at the HHC at seven. Don't eat...I mean, don't have dinner, okay?"

"That sounds great," he said. "It really does. See you Saturday."

"We're *leaving*," a voice shouted. Oliver probably—the voice was male and seemed loud enough for the purpose.

"Which means I should too, then, right?"

She should. She *definitely* should.

"Yes," he said. "You should."

The disappointment in his voice hit something inside of her. Not regret, but a wish that this could be longer. More.

But it couldn't.

He put his arms out and she stepped into the space between them. Being in that embrace made her feel like she was part of something bigger than herself, part of a pair. Like being home.

And when he broke the embrace, she felt almost lost.

But when she lifted her head, the look in his eyes grounded her. They were bright, once again reminding her of a *shamash* candle. And his smile…his smile was sweeter than any soofganiyot she'd ever tasted.

"See you soon?"

"Soon. Hear from me sooner."

And as she walked out the door, she couldn't help but wave and watch him as he closed the door behind her. She followed his friends to the subway, only to feel a buzz from her phone. She pulled it out and rolled her eyes because it was from Isaac. Of course it was.

Seeing the text unleashed a flood of warmth inside her on this cold, early November night. She didn't know what was happening, but what she did know was that she didn't want it to end.

Chapter Nineteen

ISAAC MEANT TO get to Hollowville on Saturday morning, but a call from his agent, the realization he needed to do laundry, and the stink in his fridge kept him from leaving until the afternoon. He reached Hollowville with enough time to drop his stuff at *Bubbe's* house and chat for a little while before heading down to the temple.

They'd been chatting about a whole bunch of things, his parents and their preparation for the cruise, as well as one of the new tapestries his friend Cecile was making. But as they reached a stoplight near the temple, she turned to him. "Where are you supposed to meet her?"

"At the temple," he said, sheepish about the fact he didn't email to clarify between Thursday night's conversation and now.

His *bubbe* rolled her eyes as they pulled into the HHC parking lot. "Well," she said. "I suspect it will be easy to find her, considering she's running this."

He raised an eyebrow. "What?"

Bubbe turned off the car and pulled the key from it, her grin as bright as Sabbath candles. "You'll see. You'll also understand why she didn't want you to eat, and why I didn't even suggest dinner."

He nodded, zipped up his coat, and smiled. "Well then. Let's see what she's got planned."

The grin turned from the two candles to the final day of Hanukkah. "Oh, I've been looking forward to this," *Bubbe* said as she got out of the car.

Interesting.

This was a pre-festival tradition. It had to be. Why else would Sarah suggest he meet her here if it wasn't? But what was it?

Bubbe was also was wearing her "comfy dress pants." The very same pants she brought out when they were going to a restaurant that had an all-you-can-eat buffet of her favorite foods, not something she'd wear anywhere near the temple.

So this was a special occasion involving lots and lots of food.

Things just got more interesting.

"Isaac," *Bubbe* said as he felt the jab of her elbow in his side. "*Tateleh.*" He stopped, and met the stony expression on her face.

"What?"

"*Tateleh,*" she said, sighing as if he was a little boy who'd run afoul of the rules. "You are not paying attention and you need to. There will be questions and you need to focus in order to answer them."

He raised an eyebrow. "What kind of questions?"

"You've been spending time with Sarah. She means something to this community, to the Jewish community here, to the readers in town. Heck, to anybody who knows who she is, she makes a difference."

Ahhh. More gossip, more judgment. But this time by the people who actually had known her since she was little.

"But more importantly, you're making her smile."

He was. He loved putting that smile on her face. The one that made him think she wanted to spend more time with him.

"And they notice when she smiles. Because these people, they notice she spends way too much time making everybody *else* smile."

He knew that about her, too, knew that about the town, and about life. People kept telling him that, and their inability to realize he understood was starting to bother him. But this was his *bubbe*. So he nodded.

"That's why they'll notice you, *tateleh*. The more time you spend with her, the more they notice she wants to be around you. So they'll be around you, too, making sure you keep making her smile."

So these people, the ones who really knew her and understood her, were in favor of his…whatever was developing between them. "Okay," he said. "I don't have a problem with that."

"Most people would, but then again, I need to remember that you, *tati*, are not most people."

He shook his head. "Nope. Not most people. I'm your grandson. Made of sterner and more determined stuff."

She laughed and put her arm around him. "Just remember," she said, "the most important thing is to talk to *her* first. Let Sarah be the first to know what you want to say, whatever it is."

He nodded, following her up the stairs and into the building. Excited noise and beautiful smells emanated from deep inside.

"What?"

Bubbe beamed. "You'll see."

He hung his coat and headed into the entranceway. But he turned around and *Bubbe* was gone, leaving him alone.

"You're here!"

He came alive at the sound of her voice; Sarah simply glowed. Her eyes were brighter than a sky full of stars. "Hi," he managed. "I…"

"I'm glad you were able to make it," she said. "This going to be fun. I think."

"Fun, huh?"

"Actually, it might even look somewhat familiar."

He raised an eyebrow. "Really?"

Her earrings, a familiar mix of orange on one ear and brown on the other, dangled as she moved. "Yeah. This has been a thing for a long time," she said as she took his hand, leading him toward the entranceway into a large room. "Was actually where the festival started, you know."

And that's why she wanted them to start there. "Tell me the story."

"Many years ago, the temple used to have a night, just like this. A little bazaar. Some jewelry, some food, some other things. Local merchants. Tiny. Just the temple community."

"It was here?"

She nodded. "The bazaar itself was right here." She pointed in the social hall. "The food in here." She pointed at the cocktail area. "And when they added the games, they were just outside in the yard."

"That's amazing," he said. And he could feel her excitement in every word, her breath on his face.

She squeezed his hand, bringing him back to reality, back to the temple. Back to the questions he knew he'd be getting.

"This was so small when it started. And people—the temple congregation, the committee—didn't expect anybody to come, not when it was a separate holiday, not when it wasn't commemorating the end of the hurricane, 10 years ago. I'm…"

"What?"

"I mean that's how the festival started. A hurricane knocked out power in the Hollows, both Hollowville and in North Hollows. twelve years ago."

He nodded. "I remember that."

"Anyway, the temple and the library both sheltered people, and when it was all over, people gathered on the temple lawn to thank the Temple for their hospitality. And then a few months later, they came back, because of the community the temple had fostered, to join the congregation in celebrating Hanukkah. They came *back* together because of the community."

But she'd started to lead him further into the room, deeper into the mouthwatering smells. "What's going on?"

He lifted his head, looked around, and realized she'd led him into the temple's social hall. And in front of him, there were long tables, filled with all sorts of food. "Take a whiff," she said, gesturing widely. "Smell all of this amazing food."

"I do," he replied, as did his stomach. "Yeah. I definitely do."

"Wonderful, huh?"

"The smells are, yes. The food looks amazing, but what is this?"

"Well," she said, swallowing in a way that told him she was about to tell him a story, "the festival has changed so much in the ten years since it started, but the viewpoint has always been that if a festival forgets where it came from, it won't do very well in the future."

He nodded, taking in the scenery. "Right. And tradition is what you guys are really celebrating, right?"

"Right. Anyway," she continued as they stopped off to get plates and napkins, "the festival is huge. Tons of vendors sign up to get involved. Food vendors, non-food vendors."

He knew that; he'd seen that as he'd spent time with her,

and the one vendor he knew personally—his friend Jamie. "How do you even decide who gets in?"

"Well, the committee gets an idea from the list—people who've participated in previous years, and other sorts of recommendations, but we need to make sure we've chosen the right people, and with enough time that if someone doesn't work, we can replace them." She paused, and then beamed. "Which means we have to try all of our vendors out in some fashion, so we do preview nights for the temple congregants: one for the food, one for the non-food. This is the first of the two—the taste testing."

It had been hard not to look, but once he did, he couldn't look away. Tons of different food vendors, each of which had a line in front of them, people milling around the hall, smells intermingling with smiles and laughs.

The best part of it was her smile, and the way she lit up as she took him around the social hall, along the maze of the tables and flavors. His eyes brightened at seeing the quipes alongside the latkes, and spaces where soofganiyot and *gulab jamun* sat next to each other. Empanadas sat next to Chinese soup dumplings, and bowls of hot chicken soup with matzah balls.

"This reminds me of the day I took you to Streetfest," he said, smiling. "Like the way everything is mixed. And is that kosher kielbasa over there?!"

She nodded, a slight blush riding up her cheeks. "Yeah. You can say I was inspired in a lot of ways, you know."

"Really?"

She met his eyes with hers, sparkling green, focused and bright all at the same time. "You're inspiring."

"Well," he said, "maybe we…"

"Sarah, hello."

The moment suddenly stopped as she dropped his hand, and stiffened next to him. "Mom?"

He'd seen Sarah's mother before, from far away. But up close the resemblance was unmistakable. But this time the older woman wasn't smiling. In fact, she was staring at him as if he was the worst person on the face of the planet. What had changed since the last time he saw her?

Had he done anything since then? Or was this just an example of the dynamics his *bubbe* had warned him about in the car?

"Very nice to meet you," he said. He held out his hand.

"Is it now?"

"Mom, this is Isaac Lieberman."

There was a nod, and a bit of a softening as the older woman took his hand. It was clear she was annoyed, but there was something that altered her reaction to him. He didn't attribute it to his own personality, but to the way Sarah had touched his shoulder, almost like she was making an endorsement.

"Well," Mrs. Goldman said as she shook his hand. "It is nice to meet someone who makes my daughter smile."

Just like Bubbe said.

There was tension in the air, just for a moment, before it dissipated. He figured he'd hear why later. "Just as long as you keep doing so."

And once again, she'd made a comment he was ready for. Like his *bubbe* had warned him before he had even arrived in the temple building. "I will," he said. "To the best of my ability."

Mrs. Goldman nodded, though there was that suspicious look again. He knew he'd be watched; heck he'd always been watched. But he wasn't that worried. And even though there was relief when her mother walked away, Sarah's hand still rested on his shoulder.

"I'm sorry," she said. "I don't know what to say"

But he cut her off with a smile. "It's fine. I understand. She's your mother; she's protective. This whole town is, which makes me happy." And then he took her hand when she offered it. "There's so much more you need to show me, after all."

And as they walked through the rest of the social hall, trying different things as they went, he saw her start to relax. He hoped she'd stay that way.

SARAH HAD BEEN having a great time with Isaac, leading him through the tasting, watching his reaction as he tried the different savory dishes, and watching the sparkle in his eyes as he surfed the wave of flavor.

Of course, her mother had to come and ruin it all. She'd been tame, but she'd done enough, weaving a web of nerves in a public setting. A cherry on top of a whole bunch of anxiety-producing things. She'd been able to deal with it for a while, as she focused on Isaac and the smells.

Unfortunately, the wave of anxiety hit her again once she realized exactly where she was: with Isaac at a small table, plates of samples in front of them, surrounded by people who had known her since she was a girl, each of whom had seen and heard her mother's comments. And in that moment, the food she'd been eating, a great example of kosher kielbasa, suddenly turned to dust on her tongue, and she couldn't breathe.

"That kosher kielbasa would definitely warm my stomach on a cold day."

She looked up to see concern in his eyes, a smile on his face. The fact that he'd noticed the change in her mood made her feel slightly guilty even as it reassured her.

His eyes were brown with a hint of green, his smile comforting and soft. As he breathed, somehow she found a reason to breathe with him. And finally, she could speak. "It's good. Layers of flavor."

"There's been a lot of that," he said, looking at her plate, acting as if nothing had happened, as if they were just hanging out in one of the best buffet restaurants. "Are those the remnants of the hot dish?"

"Yeah." She nodded, picking up her fork and stabbing a bit of the tater tot. "I'm savoring it, honestly. What did you think about it?"

He was amazing, letting her slide into the kind of conversation that wasn't going to stress her out. Talking about food was so much easier than talking about how awkward her mother, and, honestly, most of Hollowville had made her feel.

"I liked it, actually."

"What was it?"

Not to mention the way his enthusiasm about food made him glow, and not just food, but innovations and different foods he hadn't seen before. "Tater tots at the top, matzah farfel at the base, chicken in the middle, with an applesauce dip on the side..."

She watched him as he thought through it, as if she was watching the wheels turn. "It's like a layered latke or something."

"It's not what we usually see here, but that's the point."

She watched him as he took a long drink of his water and smiled back at her. "You ready for dessert?"

"Oh my gosh yes."

The two of them headed away from the group of people and the tables, back to the area full of smells and people who were paying more attention to the food than to her.

"The smells," he exclaimed as they walked, his excitement making her gleeful again. "Although," he turned back toward her, his expression somber. "If you want to go somewhere else to eat or something, I'd be up for that."

"The fact that you even asked is sweet, but I can't." She sighed, wishing for a second she could take him somewhere else. "There are moments where I want to, but at the same time, this is part of my responsibility for the festival. But I'm sorry for dragging you into my emotional miasma."

He laughed. "First of all," he said as he took her hand back in his, "my *bubbe* lives in this community, so trust me: I'm very well aware of the dynamics. And right now, I wouldn't have it any other way. You, dessert, and a cool moment in the middle of the wildness."

And as they stood just in front of the dessert area, the happy sounds of vendors mixed with sweet smells: the rugelach cookie salad next to the soofganiyot, some Sephardic-style cookies, and at least one version of flan, she smiled back at him. "This is a cool moment in the midst of it all."

"And honestly?"

She held her breath as he started to speak; she wasn't sure what to expect or to plan for.

"There's nowhere else I'd rather be."

She bit her lip and squeezed his hand. That was certainly not what she was expecting in any way, shape or form. "I'm glad to hear that," she managed. "I..."

"Yes?"

"Nothing. So what do you think of this part of history?"

"I'm enjoying it," he said as they stopped to grab dessert

plates. "It's bright and beautiful and sweet."

She smiled back at him, suddenly relieved their conversation had returned to festival stuff. Considering she had a great deal of it to share. "You know that the only Hanukkah food requirement is that it be fried, right?"

He nodded as she grabbed some flan from two of the different vendors. "Yeah. I was wondering about that."

"I was thinking about the festival this year, changing it up a bit. And my mind immediately went to who's going to be here, who lives in Hollowville, you know? So what we decided is that the food we're going to sell at this year's festival is representative of who Hollowville is. And what we eat. And yes, all of this is fried in some way."

"This is wonderful," he said. "It's so not what I expected when I first heard about the festival."

"What did you expect?"

He laughed. "I mean, don't get me wrong. I love latkes and gelt, and macaroons but like...we know there's more than that in terms of Hanukkah food. Tradition is great, but it's better to learn and understand more than what's at the tip of your fingers." He paused. "It's why I like this interpretation of it so much."

She could only follow as he reached around her to take her full plate, and led her to the back of the room. They stopped just before the door, right in front of a small couch. She hadn't been involved in the religious school for a long time, but she'd wager large amounts of money it was where parents waited to watch their kids as they played on the playground just outside at the end of the day. But it was far away from the gathering, so it was empty.

She sat down next to him on that couch, his jean-clad leg rubbing up against her leg through her tights. Making her breathe hard, her dessert plate on her lap.

"Not that I'm complaining, but what is this?"

He smiled. "Aside from the promise of more rugelach with vanilla pudding and soofganiyot and churros and…"

She grinned back at him. "Yes. Aside from that."

"You keep talking about community," he answered once he'd stopped laughing, "and it's clear to me that it means a great deal to you. Except when it's…"

"Yes, I know. Except when it's ignoring my personal space."

"Well, that's the other side of community. It matters to you, and you matter to the people who are in the community, right? Like you do things for everybody and they see you. They watch you and they take care of you in their own way."

She nodded. That was true. "And you?"

"Me?" He laughed. "I'm a Brooklyn boy who wants to make sure you know you matter. And who wants to make sure you have enough iced tea."

She laughed. Of course, he'd mention iced tea.

"So let's have our dessert, have our moment away from everybody, be just us. For as long as we can."

She couldn't help but smile. She had to. Even with the absolute certainty they could be interrupted, she didn't want to trade the minutes she'd be spending with him for anything.

Even when Elsa found them an hour later, their dessert plates long emptied as they just enjoyed the silence, she was smiling too.

"Sorry to break up this party," Elsa said. "But I feel like I have to go."

He squeezed her hand as he got up, half helping her up as he stood. She smiled back at him. And then she got an idea.

"What are you up to tomorrow?"

"Nothing really." And then he met her eyes, and what she saw in his was magic. "Want to tell me more history?"

"Yes. Meet me tomorrow morning at the Caf and Nosh, and I'll tell you the rest of the story."

"It's a date," he said, as a smile completely transformed his face from interested to excited. And warm.

"Looking forward to it," she said, trying to speak and process what happened as Elsa...Mrs. Lieberman came over to give her a hug. "Night, *mamaleh.*"

"Night, Mrs. Lieberman," she said, as she embraced the older woman.

And as Elsa led Isaac away and outside, memories of the gift he'd given her swirled around her mind. He'd given her solitude, time to breathe, which was more precious than anything he could ever have spent money on.

She couldn't wait until what Sunday morning would bring.

Chapter Twenty

IT WAS STILL dark when Sarah woke up. Or rather, when she gave up the battle she was waging with sleep. Excitement and anxiety warred in her veins; visions of what the day could mean ran through her stomach.

The aftermath shoved her into a beauty routine, complete with a sheet mask before going into the shower. But it wasn't enough to deal with all of it, so she dragged out her armor, the Hanukkah-themed jewelry and clothing she'd accumulated over the years. There was a lot of it, but she'd probably wear just enough to make her smile. She hoped.

A few hours later, she was as ready as she was going to be; warm sweater, comfy boots, jeans, and earrings in the shape of dreidels that could be seen beneath her curls. She'd gone for subtle, but she suspected someone else might not agree.

Better not subtle than pale-knuckle nervous.

Her phone vibrated against the kitchen counter. The nerves in her stomach jumped. Grabbing it, she saw a text from Isaac.

"Couldn't sleep. Early. Can't wait to see you."

He wasn't going to bail on her, wasn't going to leave her

behind like she'd feared, which was good. Instead he was apparently so excited to see her that he'd gotten up as early as she did.

But he'd been a good guy about it, not insisting or assuming she'd be early, just told her that he was.

She looked at herself in the mirror again. Yes, the Hanukkah hat one of the clerks at the bookstore had bought her would serve her purposes. This was going to be a great day, if she didn't fall asleep halfway through.

A SIMPLE TEXT completely upended Isaac's plans and his thoughts.

"Also up early. On my way. See you soon."

Nine words. He could barely breathe. He was excited, tired, couldn't wait to see her and spend this day with her, learning about the vision she had for the festival. What made her so excited about it and...

Whew.

He had to keep cool. Had to not completely play to the stereotype of the artist who could barely see the forest through the trees. Nope. He had to be the open, relaxed someone she may have thought him to be at one point in time.

He failed miserably at the sight of her.

There were no words he could think of to describe the

laughter that came up from the depths of his toes at the sight of her hat. That was what he saw first, after all, the fluffy cotton blue menorah, sitting tall at the top of her head, highlighting the curls that fell to her shoulders. She was a sight to behold against the bright lights of the early morning, her green eyes inviting him closer, the cotton flames making him smile.

"That is…" he managed.

"Both warm and the most perfect icebreaker ever created for two people who were too nervous to sleep."

Laughter and appreciation for a good quip mushed together on top of his tongue. "I was going to say magical," he said, "but that works too."

Her smile lit up her face in a way he really wasn't prepared for, not yet, not this early. "I'm glad. You ready?"

Was. He. Ever.

Instead of saying that, he nodded. Vehemently. "Tired, but definitely ready." He started to take her hand; instead, she took his fingers in hers.

"So you don't get lost," she said by means of explanation he didn't really need.

But he appreciated it anyway, the explanation, the excuse, whatever it was. "I love this."

And, of course, having been deprived of food for way too long, his stomach voiced its disapproval. "I guess it's time for breakfast?"

She nodded, not bothered by the noise, which made him

feel better about himself. Instead, she just led him to the Caf and Nosh, her hand letting his go for a single moment as she pulled open the door. Like the gentleman he tried to be, he reached out to hold the door, letting her enter first before following her into the cozy restaurant. He let the smell of the place overwhelm him.

"To stay?"

Even though she'd asked him, he had a strong suspicion she'd already decided. But that was more than okay with him. "That sounds good to me."

She smiled back at him, taking his hand once again as she made a beeline to an open table. "We have to plan," she said. "And we need fortification to do it."

His vision of the day made him smile in a way so very few things had recently. "What kind of fortification are you looking for?"

She shrugged. "Basic stuff. A large soofi latte, with egg and avocado on a bagel."

"Perfect," he said. Especially considering he'd wanted most of the same things, if not all of them. "Sugar and caffeine on the one hand, balance for it on the other, and still mouthwatering. Breakfast of champions."

She raised an eyebrow and he got nervous.

Did she think he was judging her and her choices?

Because if she did, he had to make it very clear that he wasn't.

"Does that mean you're going to have one too?"

Immediately, and without pause, he nodded. "But I'm going to add orange juice and some hash browns. Breakfast is not breakfast, in my particular view, without those two things."

She laughed, and he liked the fact they might possibly be starting a joke they'd be repeating for the rest of their lives. "My shirt might feel jealous."

"No tea to keep it company, but that's okay. I'll have more orange juice for lunch."

"And I'll have some iced tea," she replied, smiling up at him. "Glad that's settled."

"What's settled?" Chana asked as she joined them. "Your breakfast order?"

"Yes, actually," Sarah said. "Two soofi lattes, one large with an extra shot of espresso, two bagels with egg and avocado, one with home fries, and a glass of orange juice for my breakfast companion."

The older woman turned, grinned at him. "Nice to see you this morning, Mr. Lieberman. Keeping our Hanukkah Fairy company on an early Sunday morning?"

"Yeah." He smiled, nodded. "She's got a whole bunch of things she wants to show me this morning. I'm looking forward to seeing them all."

The older woman looked between the two of them as if searching for some invisible subtext. Which, he realized, she probably already had from listening to their conversation.

"I'm showing him the festival history, for his purposes,"

Sarah said quickly.

But he recognized the look on Chana's face. Sarah may have deterred one set of purposes, but he clearly didn't see them dispelling any other anytime soon.

"Oh really?" the older woman said, crossing her arms. He was right. "And what would those purposes be, hmm?"

He smiled. "Nothing that would worry my *bubbe*," he replied. "And nothing that would alter anybody's plans. Just spending time with someone, seeing things through their eyes."

Chana raised an eyebrow. "Searching for artistic inspiration."

He laughed. "Always. Absolutely always."

WHEN TALKING TO Isaac about the festival and trying to harness her excitement about the holiday, Sarah was well aware that the line between interested and obsessed was thin. After all, Hanukkah was her favorite holiday, taking the vaulted place of honor only a few years before. It was a holiday she could wear, and celebrate, with pride. She just hoped Isaac wasn't overwhelmed by it. The fact he'd taken her hat in good humor was a good sign.

And so was the toe-curling smile on his face. "I have to say, I'm looking forward to seeing what's inspired you so much."

She felt the heat rise in her cheeks.

No. She had to fight past the nerves and focus, not just on Isaac's expression, but on what he wanted to know. He'd asked for the story she had. He wanted the information. And only she could give it to him.

"Well," she said, putting down her latte, "I think the biggest change between the beginning and now is space. We've had the festival for nine years now, and this is our tenth. I showed you where the first festival was. But they outgrew that space within two years."

"So what kind of space are we looking at now?"

"Well," she said, "we've got a lot of it. That's the short version. The longer version is that the festival takes up most of the town's business district and has expanded down to the marina and lake area this year."

"Do you have a map or something? I'd love to see how it looks and maybe see the way it expanded?" He paused. "I mean, I love listening to you talk, but I think it'd be easier for me to visualize if you have something tangible."

She nodded before carefully reaching down to grab the notebook she'd shoved into her purse. "The map isn't to scale, but you can get an idea, and it'll be easier for me to show you the way the festival has expanded."

She carefully avoided the obstacle course of their breakfast dishes to put the notebook down.

"May I?"

She wasn't sure what he was asking at first, but then she

realized he wanted to actually hold the notebook. She passed it over to him, her fingers brushing his, callused fingers touching her smooth skin. His eyes met hers, and he swallowed, held his breath in time with hers.

His smile brightened as he took the notebook, letting his fingers linger on her palm. But then he was all business as he focused on the pages in a way that made her nervous.

Of course, he was a sculptor, not a painter or anything like that. But he had enough of an eye to potentially poke holes in her horrible drawings.

"Not judging," he said, as if he could read her thoughts. "You have this great vision and I cannot wait to see it as we walk through town. But this way I can understand it better."

"So you're not going to be annoyed if it's not to scale?"

"I'll be annoyed if I don't get lunch or dinner," he said, laughing in a way that made her lips curve involuntarily. "Don't care too much about the scale of maps."

A weight left her shoulders and she nodded back. "There's a cute place we'll go for dinner down by the river."

"Looking forward to it already," he said. "Now you said you expanded to the marina and the lake?"

"Yeah. The high school hockey team wanted to do something, so they're supervising the ice skating, the boosters are helping a few extra food vendors to sell hot chocolate and pastries down there. They also are talking about some kind of surprise, but the word on the street is that someone has some kind of connection with the Empires or the Legends women's team so there's going to be something..." She paused, trailing off, suddenly convinced that she'd bored him. "Sorry," she said.

"No, no, no," Isaac interjected, his hand covering hers like a warm glove. "I'm excited. This sounds wonderful. And that's going to be where the dreidel races are?"

She shook her head. "No, they stay back on the lake, on the other side of town. I'm just excited to see what people are going to think about the new layout."

"Are some of the changes because you're expecting more people than in years past?"

"Yeah. To a degree." She paused, drumming her fingers on the table as she tried to find a good way to answer his question that didn't sound weird or strange. "Part of it is that it's always better to not let a festival get stagnant as it grows. Tradition is great and important, but it's also important to give a gift of newness to people who come every year, you know?"

"I guess."

"Also," she continued, ignoring the skepticism clear on his face, "yes this might be our last festival, but we're also getting more attention than we have in years past. For whatever reason, the fact that Hollowville throws a festival dedicated to and solely about the holiday of Hanukkah is fascinating to people. So, if fascination turns to attendance, we'll need more space and more things to do, not just to diffuse the crowd but make sure that no one area gets over capacity in a way that keeps people from enjoying themselves." She paused. "At least that's the hope."

He shook his head. "That's both amazing and weird at the same time. I wonder what's so special about this year?"

She shrugged. "Aside from threats by the board of trustees and the fact that we actually have a functioning website and publicity committee?"

He laughed. "Right. Aside from that."

"My best guess," she said after thinking for a second, "is that people are grabbing on to Hanukkah, the light in the darkness that it is, as something reassuring. These days, people are in desperate need of something that celebrates the triumph of good over evil. And the fact that miracles can happen for everybody, even them."

He nodded. "People are searching for things that make them smile, because on so many days they can't do it on their own."

He got it. He truly got it. The light in his eyes, the smile; they both shone with an excitement that matched her own.

She had no choice but to smile back and hope she didn't explode in joy all over him. All she could manage was a single syllable. "Yeah."

ISAAC HAD LEARNED so much during the day, not just about the festival but about the town and Sarah and the way she saw the world. It was magical just spending time with her.

And now they were having dinner, alone, at a small place by the river. He couldn't believe his luck.

"This is where the ice skating is going to be," she said absently, pointing out the window.

He followed her finger and closed his eyes. He could see it: a slight step beyond the pictures he'd been shown, the natural forward-moving development of the festival from where it had begun. And when he opened his eyes again, he shook his head in amazement. "I can't believe how far the festival has come," he said. "It's…"

She smiled, her eyes bright. "I know, right? Like from a small bazaar to…this. I guess we started at a time when people were looking for something to grab on to, you know? To help them smile."

He nodded, took a drink of his water, and felt the warmth of the holiday inside of him. Even though the story of the festival was making him smile, it was the company that made it perfect. "Yeah," he said. "There are times where it's so dark outside that you can't remember when it's ever been bright. But each night of Hanukkah brings one more candle into the window, or into public display wherever that is, and it's just a little bit brighter, until the entire menorah is full of light."

She smiled back at him, but it was shy. She was half focused on cutting into the marinara sauce that sat on top of her eggplant parmigiana. "I'd like to think that the festival committee sees the festival as a beacon, you know? Like if you need light, come find us. We're here. We're community, and if you have it, or even if you don't, you can find it in Hollowville."

He smiled, took a bite of his lasagna and nodded. He'd definitely found a great deal in Hollowville. Community, warmth, light, and maybe love. More than maybe. And he didn't want it to end. And maybe he wanted to make some light of his own for Hollowville.

Chapter Twenty-One

SOMEHOW, SARAH MANAGED to convince Anna to come to Hollowville for a girls' night out at the jewelry preview.

"Of course your GNOs involve the festival," Anna said, rolling her eyes as they headed up the stairs to the HHC. "Though at least there is wine and crafty things."

"Yes," Sarah said as they headed into the coatroom. "That there is, but you're helping me do an important job."

"Which is?"

"Making sure everything looks as good now as it did on websites or at random crafts fairs and things."

The sound of Anna's laugh made Sarah smile. "Making sure someone doesn't do something weird?"

"Pretty much."

"Speaking of weird," Anna interjected as they headed into the social hall, having hung up their coats, "what's been up with you?"

What a loaded question. But a fair one. "Well," Sarah began, "I'm not sure. But we're going to have to walk the preview as we talk about this."

Anna nodded. "Sounds good. But start from the beginning, please."

She sighed as she took the conversational volley back from her friend, proceeding to tell her the story of the last weekend.

"He came to the tasting and you didn't tell me?"

Sarah shook her head. "I don't know why, I just got caught up in stuff. Besides. You've been a bit busy, otherwise occupied."

Anna took a pair of candlesticks from one of the tables, inspected them before putting them back down. "Yeah. Not gonna lie. Things have been busy recently, and won't go back to normal until at least March after this exhibit opens."

"Is there anything I can do?"

Her friend shook her head as she grabbed a glass of diet soda from one of the trays. "Nope. Just listen and help provide distractions to make me not think about what's going on. So okay. He was at the tasting. Anything happen?"

She thought for a second. "He made my mother smile."

"Your mother *smiled*."

Sarah laughed. "She liked how was able to keep me from the gossip."

"Ahh, yes. The traditional gossip chain that passes along random things like the fact that you were banned from his art show at Molly's gallery."

"Yes. That gossip chain." She rolled her eyes and grabbed a glass of iced tea from one of the trays. "He was able to buffer me from it for some reason during the tasting and I really liked it, so he…well, he spent the day in town on Sunday."

"Okay, spending the day is good. You may have told me this, but forgive me because my brain is Swiss cheese with work and nonsense. Anyway, he spent the day. How did that go again?"

"It was great, fun, wonderful."

"Did you wear the hat?"

She eyeballed a challah cover.

"Wait. He took you around town wearing that hat? That menorah hat?! Are you serious?"

"Not kidding. Not at all."

"Whoa. Well, then we'll discuss the implications of that later. Right now…"

"Sarah!"

Sarah looked up into a familiar pair of eyes. It was the jewelry designer who was also Isaac's friend. "Jamie! Hi," she said. "I'm so glad you're here."

"Wouldn't have missed this for anything," the designer replied, sweeping a hand across her booth. "Don't have my booth boy tonight, because I figured I would only bring a small selection, but by the looks of everything, I'm going to be completely cleared out by the end of the night. Which is great."

"Of everything?"

Jamie shook her head. "Nah. Of everything I brought.

Which, I gotta say, makes me happy I only brought a small sample and catalogs for the store." She gestured, her short nails pointing at the brightly colored booklet. "Tom came over, took some pictures, and then he, Liam, and I designed the book. Speaking of Liam…"

Sarah raised an eyebrow, watching Anna stare at the earrings Jamie had in the case. "These dreidels are beautiful," she managed, staring at the beautiful blue pieces in front of her.

"They're glass," Jamie replied. "I've seen other holiday symbols made in this method, so I decided I'd make a symbol of Hanukkah that way."

"Oh my God," Anna squealed, "this is just amazing."

"Thank you," Jamie said, her eyes bright and joyful.

"So, what else do you have?"

"Well," Jamie said tentatively as Sarah stared at the counter. "I've got stars done in this way too. I thought of doing a menorah, but I settled for an actual menorah."

"They're gorgeous," Anna replied, staring at the hand-lettered earrings. "Really."

Sarah nodded, glad Anna had fallen in love with the set. Truth to tell, she wasn't surprised Jamie had brought her A game to Judaica. "They are."

"Well, thank you." She smiled at both Sarah and her bestie. "I have something for you, for your boss?"

"Oh. For Carol. Thank you."

She took the paper-wrapped package from the other

woman's hand. "This is going to be fantastic."

"Liam also made me promise that I'd tell you Carol got a treasure in that comic, whatever that means."

She didn't even want to think about the fact that Liam had gotten Sam Moskowitz, *the* Mr. Shadow of the Shadow Squad movies based on the comics, to put his signature on a cartoon depiction of his *tuchus* for Carol. "Tell him I said thank you."

"I will. Also…" Jamie bit her lip. "Did you tell Isaac about the commemorative stuff?"

She shook her head. "I didn't."

Jamie nodded as she reached into her case, and pulled out two different pieces. A keychain with candles, a dreidel and a menorah that looked just like the festival logo, and a small mirror with the logo etched in the metal.

"Those are perfect," Sarah said. "Thank you, Jamie. Really."

"I've seen a few of the others, and they're gorgeous too. But do me a favor," Jamie continued, as if Sarah hadn't said anything. "Tell Isaac about this as soon as you can, okay? Like next time you see him."

She nodded. "I will."

And as she and Anna left Jamie's booth to explore the rest of the preview night, she wondered why telling Isaac about the commemorative merchandise was so important when he wasn't interested in participating in the festival.

Brooklyn

WORDS HAD BEEN running through Isaac's mind since he got back from Hollowville, Words like community and light. So he woke up early Tuesday morning to sketch out an idea for a sculpture. But nothing seemed right. Not at all.

Which meant after catching up on emails and a whole bunch of other things, he invited Oliver over for dinner and told him to bring his drawing pencils.

Oliver arrived around five p.m. with drinks and Indian food.

"Hey," Isaac said. "How are you?"

"Starved. Glad to see you. Life is good."

Isaac put the takeout bag down on the table along with the drinks container, and the two of them sat down. He opened the bag, and the fragrant smells of the food permeated the apartment.

"Good to see you, too, and especially your good choice of dinner. Jamie's working late?"

Oliver nodded. "She's so excited about this festival, you know, that she's working overtime to get pieces made. Putting stuff on her online shop, then sending things to people she'd had agreements with, and then working afterward to try to pull enough stuff together for this festival."

"That's—"

"Dedication? Who knows? Either way, when I leave, I'm

taking home a carton of ice cream and some hand cream to soothe her hands."

Isaac nodded, removing his bright, sweet *mango lassi* out from the cardboard drink container. "Good man."

"Yeah." He grinned. "I'm a very lucky man." There was a pause as Oliver rummaged around the bags and took out a few things. "So, you and the gal who's running the festival?"

Thankfully, Isaac hadn't yet sampled his *lassi*. "What?"

"Yep. You and the gal who's running the festival. The one Jamie made those earrings for and, you know." He paused to take the top of the container off of his curry chicken and took a strong whiff. "Yeeeep. Best ever. Anyway, that."

Isaac raised an eyebrow. "What?"

"Come on, dude. I'm the only one of the group in a long-term relationship, and you asked me over for dinner on a Tuesday night."

"What?" He laughed. "You think I'm asking for relationship advice?"

Oliver took a drink of his own. "Dunno. But the last time I saw you, which was a few days ago, you were making last-minute plans to spend two days in Hollowville, and now you're here, and here I am. So what gives?"

He blew out a breath, taking out the saag paneer and the naan from the bag closest to him. "I'm thinking about doing a sculpture."

"Good on you. What made you change your mind? Is it

the girl?"

Was it Sarah? Not totally.

"Partially. Partially it's my grandmother, partially it's...I don't know."

"You got feelings, huh?"

"Artistic feelings, romantic feelings for Sarah, yes, and love and family feelings for my *bubbe*. I also learned so much over the weekend, it was kinda amazing."

"So this is why you were in Hollowville? This is what you were talking about with Sarah at Liam's party, when we were trying to get her to the train?"

He nodded. "Spent Saturday night and Sunday in Hollowville. Spent Sunday with Sarah." He paused a second. "It's as if my view of everything changed. The festival turned from something that seemed like it was trying to turn Hanukkah into something it isn't at all to a symbol and a beacon."

Oliver crossed his arms and took a long drink of his soda. "A symbol? Of what?"

Isaac counted out the reasons on his fingers. "Community. That became a way to start a conversation, you know?" He paused for a second as Oliver nodded. "To build bridges and share traditions and spend time together. Once the festival got too big to hold in the temple, people started adding space and offering to help and stepping in, and it was apparently kinda mind-blowing, you know?"

"Yep."

He swiped another samosa and bit into it, the crunch making him smile.

"Not to mention I have a feeling it's a way of showing the town what Hanukkah was instead of making everybody explain it all the time."

Oliver laughed. "Best example of show not tell ever invented, apparently."

"Yep."

"What about the beacon?"

"According to Sarah and my *bubbe*, because they're like the only festival in the area that focuses solely on Hanukkah, people are searching them out. Jews from all over the state and the country are starting to come."

"Like the article Liam brought up during game night?"

"Exactly like that. Which means this year is going to be a kind a watershed moment. Like what they do, how they handle it. And whether or not it ends up being their last."

"And this is a wonderful story, dude. Really. But. Most important question. Why me?"

"Samosa?"

"Yes, of course." Oliver shook his head. "I mean, I'm hungry and won't turn down a samosa, but you're stalling, dude. If I wanted something that stalls this bad, I'd grab my car from the garage."

Isaac snickered then calmed himself. "I think I may need help."

His friend rolled his eyes. "Why do you need my help for

a sculpture?"

How could he explain it? "Well," he began. "I've got this...vision, this idea. And I can't manage to get it right on the page. Maybe you can draw it for me?"

"Dammit, Ike." His friend took some a bite of his samosa before diving into his curry. "I'm a painter, not a cartoonist!"

Isaac snickered and drank some of his *lassi*.

"But seriously. You know someone who draws regularly. Liam would be a better choice than me. Which again, leaves the unanswered question of why me."

As the sweet drink went down his throat Isaac tried to organize his thoughts.

"Liam brings his own perspective to the art, which is great, but not what I'm looking for right now. Besides, a great deal of what I'm leaning toward in this sculpture are some of the concepts you've explored in your painting."

Apparently, judging by the way Oliver practically snapped to attention, his friend was in. "Which ones?"

He grinned. "Flame and hearth and home and beacons."

Oliver nodded slowly. "That's awesome. Like that idea." He paused and dipped his fork in the biryani sitting in front of him. "Wait. This is going to be a menorah?"

"Yep," he said, grinning back at his friend, "I'm definitely going to do it."

Oliver nodded. "Good to hear. Absolutely."

"So." Isaac smiled. "I'm also going to need your help onsite, I think."

"You mean when I'm not being Jamie's booth boy?"

He laughed. A full-blown one that made him remember why he was so lucky to have friends like his. "Yes. Exactly. I kinda want this easy to work with, but that might mean assembly onsite and adding a few things when we get there."

"Sounds good to me," Oliver replied. "You got my hands onsite when I'm not helping Jamie."

"Thank you," he said, as he ripped off a piece of naan.

There was a short pause and Isaac wondered what was going on.

"You know," Oliver finally said, "I also drew the logo, right? For the festival?"

"I didn't," he said. "But now it makes more sense. Maybe I can work your logo design into the sculpture a bit."

"That's what I was thinking." And then Oliver paused. "When are you going to tell her?"

Sarah.

Of course. "I'm not sure if it's actually going to be possible to get this thing together on time, but I'm going to try. So I guess what I'm saying is that I don't want to tell her until I know for sure. I'll tell *bubbe* and you and Jamie but I don't want to give Sarah yet another thing to worry about."

The strange noise Oliver made almost defied description. It sounded awful, like a hiss got stuck in a vacuum cleaner.

"What?"

"Just don't. Be smart about this, please, 'kay?"

"But?"

Oliver shook his head then reached to pull out his drawing pencils. "I know how this works. Process and life and all of that. But at the same time, you don't want to keep her out of this when it's important she knows. This isn't just a commission, dude. This is your life, and you can't screw it up. Not twice."

"But now," he said, "we turn a logo into a sculpture.

And as Oliver took out some paper, he nodded. He *would* tell Sarah. Eventually.

Chapter Twenty-Two

Hollowville

ELSA LIEBERMAN'S HOUSE wasn't far from the house Sarah grew up in, but she felt every inch of the drive deep in her stomach.

Of course this visit wasn't the only source of stress she'd been dealing with. There was regular work stress, as well as best friend stress. Anna was nervous about going to Rockliffe Manor, the town where her grandparents lived, for thanksgiving with her family and was convinced it was going to be a disaster.

If that wasn't enough, Sarah was avoiding questions from Chana about Isaac. It had gotten so bad that she'd even offered to host a romance book club at the bookstore and library to keep Carol and Dr. Rodriguez from delving deeper in her love life. Though she strongly suspected the latter had been a setup, not to mention Carol and the library director probably had their own thoughts about what had been going on between them since that special Sunday.

"You okay, Sarah?"

And there she was, back to her childhood, sitting in the

back of the car as her father drove, her mother navigating. Both concerned. "Yes," she said. "Fine. Thank you."

Which was when she realized they'd arrived at their destination.

Elsa Lieberman had always been lovely, friendly, sharing moments with her parents and other friends over the years, but never this. Never opening her house for a small dessert party the night before a holiday during which she was known to spend hours over the stove.

The pumpkin pie her mother had been conscripted to bake sat on Sarah's lap; she could focus on it as a distraction, and the smell grounded her.

"You ready?"

Grounded but not calmed. Of course. But as ready as she'd ever be. "Yes," she offered.

But the smile and the worried eyes she saw on her mother's face weren't wholly unexpected. "Are you sure?"

She nodded as her mother opened the car door, holding the pie as Sarah undid the seat belt and got out of the car before retrieving the pie again. "Fine," she said. "It'll be fun. And if it isn't, we have pie."

Her father laughed, a twinkle in his eyes. "You should be so optimistic about the rest of your life."

"Soofganiyot cures everything," she said with a laugh she didn't feel. "Right?"

"Right," her father said as he put his arm around her. "And if not, we fake it until we make it."

And as she walked up the steps to the house, she held her breath, rang the bell and hoped for the best.

ISAAC HAD TRIED to hold his breath, to act like everything was normal, but it wasn't. Sarah was there, in his grandmother's house. And she was perfect. Smiling, eyes bright, looking like she'd stepped off the cover of a fashion magazine. Comfortable, gorgeous and just…

"You're staring," his father said, the smile on his face drawing attention to the olive undertones in his skin. "You need to look a little less focused on her and more focused on the rest of the world, otherwise your mom might notice."

Too late. She'd noticed. "Who might notice the fact that my son is taking way too much interest in a girl from here?"

He smiled, caught off guard but sure of the world, sure of the sun, sure of Sarah. "Yeah. She's great. I like her."

Then his mother made a noise that was too dignified to be a snort as she raised a sculpted eyebrow. "What does she do?"

"She works with the library and the bookstore, coordinating events. She's also vice chair of the local Hanukkah festival."

"She works with books, which is good. But she's…embedded here, established, hmm?"

His mother looked unbearably uncomfortable amid the

soft cushions, the warm paint, and the familiar smells of his grandmother's house. Isaac knew she preferred her own modern, clean lines, open and artful. Not this. Not homey. "She likes the train," is what he said instead of going into the details of how deep Sarah's connection went to this town, and how open she was to having adventures in the city.

"Mmm." His mother's extremely well-manicured alabaster hands went across her pants, wiping any trace of imaginary dust or crumbs off them. "The train won't last forever. And this town will pull you in, change you, and make you different. It will take everything from you and treat you differently because you aren't like *them*."

Before he was able to reply, explaining his life was not his mother's, his fears and approaches were not hers, and that Brooklyn and Hollowville were not as far apart as she thought, she left.

And as he turned toward his father, he realized he'd been left alone. That meant he had to find the one person he'd not had a chance to talk to yet. The one person he wanted to talk to the most.

SARAH WOULD ADMIT the food and the company were wonderful. Mrs. Lieberman had outdone herself.

But there was one problem. Isaac.

His family had kept him close, a woman who she could

only guess to be his mother intercepting him as he moved anywhere near Sarah. She wasn't unaware of social cues; she could see what the woman was doing. It was starting to bother her, but at the same time she didn't want to spend the entire evening mooning over the fact she couldn't talk to him.

But as she headed into the kitchen to get herself a glass of water, his mother blocked her path.

"Hi," she said, offering a hand to shake, deliberately ignoring the way the older woman's arms were crossed in front of her elegant sweater, her eyes storming beneath her perfect makeup and coiffed hair. "I'm Sarah Goldman. I know we haven't had a chance to chat—"

"No," she said. "We have not."

She kept the hand out, kept the smile as a shield. "Well, it's nice to finally meet you," she said.

Isaac's mother made the barest motion, shaking her head like the interaction was beneath her. "I can't say the same, and I suspect you understand that."

For a second, Sarah wondered whether she'd stepped into a historical romance, where the hero's mother was about to warn the potential heroine away from the hero because she wasn't *enough* for her son.

Instead of saying anything, Sarah dropped the level of her smile from genuine but nervous to the professional mask she used when she was dealing with recalcitrant publicists and literary snobs. And braced herself.

"You know," Isaac's mother continued, clearly focused on her goal and ignoring the fact the game had changed. "He's never going to stay here, never going to be fully invested in this place. He's much better than what it is. And I've been watching. I know my son."

Instead of letting her emotions loose, Sarah nodded. "That's all well and good, ma'am, but I suspect your notions about Hollowville, and your son, are as out of date as a set of encyclopedias."

"What?" And instead of reacting the way most snobs did, the woman snorted, sounding more like a pig than anybody with pretensions of elegance.

"Of course you know my son better than anybody, right? You *know* he'll come home to you at the end of the day, like a good small town wife, and he'll leave the city and be okay with the limitations of small town culture? Of people and of their opinions?" The woman snorted again, as if the writer telling this story had fallen in love with the term. "Please. Next you'll be asking him to work a *conventional* job."

"I wouldn't ask him to do anything he doesn't want to do," she replied, sighing, shaking her head. "Only people who don't know the kind of person he is would even try. But honestly, the one I see attempting to keep him from something or someone he wants, is you."

"Keeping him from doing things that would irreparably harm him is my job, and it doesn't end."

She shook her head. Smiled, even when she didn't want

to. But she wasn't sad. She was exhausted. "I'm sorry," she finally managed. "All I can say is that feel sorry for you." And then without another word, she headed into the kitchen, got her water glass, and sat down at the kitchen table, watching as the snow fell outside.

ISAAC HAD ENJOYED himself at the party—tons of dessert, tons of great people. Except he hadn't been able to have a conversation with Sarah like he'd wanted. Which made him feel like there was a gaping hole somewhere inside of him. His mother was, of course, trying to manipulate everything, but at the same time, the fact she'd even come had been a small victory.

Okay. Not small. Large. Big. Huge. Humongous. Momentous. Except for what she was doing, but he shrugged as he made his way through the crowd. Trying to follow his father's advice and not focus too much on Sarah. But he was failing. Miserably.

Especially when Sarah had disappeared for what felt like an hour but was probably actually only a few minutes. He was nervous, down to his bones. Worried about what she might say. Worried about what might have happened.

And when he found her in the kitchen, she was staring outside into the slowly falling snow.

"It's snowing," he said, unnecessarily.

She turned toward him, and the look in her eyes froze him. She was tired. Exhausted. Not afraid.

"I was looking for you." The words came out of his mouth even though he hadn't meant to say them.

"You were?"

He wanted to pull her into his arms, wash the hurt out of her face. "I was. I'm glad you're here."

She bit her lip. "You are?"

Was she still nervous around him?

If looks could kill, his mother wouldn't survive the next time she saw him.

At least, he thought it was his mother. If he was wrong, he'd own that. But right now, there was only one person he could blame for putting that kind of fear into Sarah's face. "Yeah. Always."

He reached out his hand, and she took it, squeezing his fingers with her own.

"I don't know," she said. "I don't know what I'm doing here, with you."

"Hanukkah miracle?"

She laughed, and the sound made his heart spin like a dreidel. "I don't know. It's not even Hanukkah yet."

"Not even the real start of Hanukkah season. Isn't that tomorrow?"

Sarah nodded. "Yeah. The Hanukkah menu at the Caf and Nosh starts tomorrow in earnest."

"I wonder what it'll taste like," he said.

She stood, looking up at him. "Some of what you had at

the cavalcade and any other ideas Chana has up her sleeve."

He put his arms around her and took a deep breath as she leaned in.

"Can we not think about Hanukkah for a second?"

He was surprised she'd said it, but he'd take it. "Okay."

She smiled. "It's weird that my favorite holiday has been causing so much stress, but as long as I'm here, with you, it's okay."

"More than okay."

He wondered what she was looking for; she was inspecting his face as if she was searching for treasure or a flaw. "I…"

"You're too far up," she said. "It's bothering me."

Far be it from him to deny her anything at this point. And so he leaned down just a little bit, so that his eyes met hers directly. Their lips were so close they could touch.

Lips. Touch.

He had to be sure. He had to be sure they were ready. "Yes?"

She nodded slightly and he leaned in, touching his lips to hers.

Magic, the sweet taste of his *bubbe's* soofganiyot and her mother's pumpkin pie mingled in his mouth, the soft sensation of her fingers on his cheek.

It was a moment, and he didn't want it to end.

But it did. And as she pulled back, breaking the kiss, he was glad he'd had this moment even if he had to steal it. And if he was lucky, he'd have more of them.

Chapter Twenty-Three

Brooklyn

BETWEEN HOURS AT the forge, he'd turned on some Hanukkah music, songs about lights and miracles and blessings, made latkes, and dove into the soofganiyot he'd found at a local bakery. He drank soofi lattes each morning on the way to the forge and in the afternoon on the way back home, purchased from a local coffee shop that equalized the seasonal drinks.

Finally, he was ready to tell his *bubbe* what he was up to. She answered the phone on the first ring.

"*Tateleh*," she said. "You haven't called me since Thanksgiving. I was starting to worry."

He wasn't going to argue with her; he'd run out of the house that night like a man on a mission. Which he was. He barely spoke to his parents on the ride back, jumping on the subway to his apartment in Brooklyn, headphones on.

He'd started working on the menorah the next day and the deadline, which was the day before the festival—as well as the festival itself—was racing toward him. So he'd been spending way too much time working and not talking to anybody.

He knew that was a bad thing, but that single-minded focus had gotten him here. "I'm sorry, *Bubbe*," he said.

"You should be sorry." His *bubbe* paused as if there was something else. "There's a trustee meeting tonight. The regular meeting of the board of trustees, open to the public. The final one before the festival, where the standing committee makes its final report."

He swallowed. Right.

"So," he said, pushing himself to get to the point. "I wanted to tell you that I'm at a point where I can confidently tell you..."

"Yes?"

"I'm making a menorah."

"Oh that's wonderful, *tateleh*." His *bubbe's* excitement came through clear on the phone. "That's absolutely wonderful. What did Sarah say? She must be overjoyed!"

"Well..."

"You should probably tell her soon."

"But she's busy," he said lamely. "I don't want to add another thing to her plate."

His *bubbe* groaned. If he were a betting man, he'd say that she slapped the center of her forehead based on the noise he heard. "Oy, *tateleh*. You cannot do that." She paused, and he wondered what she was thinking. "I think something might happen tonight, and so do I have your permission to mention that you're doing this if need be?"

He nodded then remembered she couldn't see him. "Yes. You can."

"You should do it first, though," she said. "Because you don't want her to hear it first from someone other than you."

And so after saying goodbye to his *bubbe*, he rushed off a quick email before heading back to the forge. He had work to do.

Hollowville

SARAH WAS TRYING to access her email and failing. Apparently she had a new email but she couldn't read it. She hoped that it wasn't that urgent, knowing she'd have to deal with it later. Business? From Isaac, wishing her luck?

It could be anything. She tapped her foot against the floor in Town Hall where they had the evening meetings and tried to access her email again. No luck. She sighed.

"We'll be fine," Chana said. "We'll present to the trustees, and they'll vote in favor and we'll be ready to continue."

Sarah sat in her seat next to the committee chair and bit her lip, trying to think about good things. But all she could think of was the clock ticking down toward the end of the festival despite everything she did and could have done.

The room and the folding chairs soon filled up with people, people she'd known for years and people who'd been part of the festival since it's inception. And as the mayor gaveled the session into order, the room came to a sudden silence.

"All right, everybody," began Mayor Erlichman. "What do we have on the agenda?"

As the meeting progressed, Sarah looked at the agenda, checking off items and wondering what Isaac was up to.

"We'll be fine," Chana whispered as Sarah tried to get into her email again.

Sarah nodded absently, trying to figure out the best way to approach the trustees. She reached into the bag at her feet and pulled out the papers she'd copied and stapled in preparation for this night.

"Finally," boomed the mayor. "It's time to hear from the Hanukkah festival standing committee. Is there someone here from the committee who can speak to us?"

"Hello, everybody," said Chana, clear as a bell from her seat. "My name is Chana Levitan. Some of you may know me as the owner of the Caf and Nosh, but I'm also a proud member of the Hollowville Hebrew Center, and chair of the festival committee. From everybody at the Hollowville Hebrew Center, I want to wish you all a happy holiday and to pass the proverbial podium over to Sarah Goldman, my vice chair, who will tell us more about the festival."

Sarah nodded and stood, heading toward the podium, placing the papers she'd brought on the place designated for plans and handouts. "Thank you, everybody. I have some prepared handouts that detail what this year's festival will look like."

"Mayor Erlichman?"

Sarah looked up from her notes and followed the voice to the table where the trustees sat. Webster was waving his hand as if it were a baton, trying to get the mayor's attention.

Mayor Erlichman rolled his eyes, adjusted his glasses. He looked annoyed, and Sarah was trying to figure out what was going on. "What is it, Trustee Webster? You're not letting the vice chair speak. What's so important about what you have to say that warrants an interruption of a speaker?"

"Well," Webster continued, shuffling papers and making Sarah's stomach twitch nervously. "It's a pretty important question, because it concerns a particular lack of space. And if we need to fill that space, it behooves the council to fill it. Wouldn't want a festival to have a central space that's...empty, now would we?"

He met her eyes with those last words, the deceptive openness that made her cringe. "I..."

"That's fine," Webster continued. "You don't have to answer the question, but we know it's true. So, Madam Vice Chair, do you or do you not have a sculpture to occupy the central spot in the town square?"

"We don't," she said, looking down at the paper in front of her. "I'm afraid we don't have a menorah to fill the space."

"Can I be recognized?"

Mayor Erlichman adjusted his glasses and rolled his eyes, turning to the older man who stood a few rows away from

Chana, his large graying beard and flannel shirt familiar to her as her own face. "What, Mr. Fitzgerald? What would you like to say?"

"Name's Pete Fitzgerald, resident of North Hollowville, owner of Fitzgerald Tree Farm. Got a call from Trustee Webster, and I wanted to tell him that I want no part of puttin' a tree in the town festival. We got trees everywhere; this is a place is where a tree don't belong."

Sarah could barely hear herself think as the claps resounded. But order was called quickly.

"Never mind this year then," Webster said. "We'll put a tree in the yard next year."

She didn't look toward Fitzgerald or the mayor or Chana or anybody else. She held her breath.

But suddenly the doors burst open, and the steady footsteps she'd heard most of her life rushed in. "Can I be recognized, Mayor Erlichman?"

"Welcome to the floor, Elsa. You should go ahead and speak because"—he laughed—"apparently the entire town is speaking, so why shouldn't you?"

"Thank you, Mayor Erlichman," she said smiling in a way that Sarah didn't know how to react to. "For those of you who don't know me, I'm Elsa Lieberman, Hollowville resident, member of the Hollowville Hebrew Center. I'm also a proud grandmother, and it is under that title that I am here, to correct the record."

Webster raised an eyebrow. What could be confusing

him?

"What part of the record would you like to correct," the mayor asked, "and why would you be able to correct it because you're a grandmother?"

"At this point in the evening, I'm guessing the record states that there will be no menorah in the central town square. Am I correct?"

Mrs. Ledesma, the secretary, nodded. "Yes, Mrs. Lieberman. The record says that in response to Trustee Webster's question, the vice chair, Sarah Goldman, stated that the committee doesn't have the means to fill the space."

Elsa nodded. "Well tonight, I've received news that says the information you have is wrong. And that yes, the Hollowville festival committee will have a sculpture to display in the center of town."

The rest of the meeting was a blur, and Sarah didn't know what to think. Of herself, of Isaac, or anything.

Was the festival saved? Why did he decide to do this?

Was it because he kissed her?

Why didn't he tell her?

And why did the victory she'd wanted feel so oddly bittersweet?

Chapter Twenty-Four

THE FESTIVAL WAS starting to come together. Days after the meeting, merchants started arriving in town, and the traffic snarling the village streets and parking lots was much easier to deal with once you saw the new faces in the restaurants and other stores.

"I'm proud of you," Chana said as she stared out the window at the trailer delivering the series of tables that would serve as latke central. "You did good."

"Only because I was working with you," she replied. "It's your committee, after all."

But as Sarah watched everything fall into place, she tried to organize her feelings.

She'd sent basic texts to Isaac to try to get to the bottom of things, but he hadn't responded. All she'd heard was that he was working on the menorah and it would arrive.

But what if it didn't?

What if he never spoke to her again?

What if he was telling everybody things but not her…as if he'd banned her from his creative process?

And that was when her phone buzzed.

Isaac: Can't talk. Taking break. Making menorah. See you when I'm done. Sleep soon.

"Any news about the sculpture?"

Sarah bit her tongue, then her lip, trying to ignore the look on Chana's face. "Well," she said finally. "He says he's making it, but we've still got the commemorative stuff and we'll go ahead with the plan regardless."

"And what makes you doubt him?"

"This festival," she said after thinking a bit. "The whole thing with this festival is that everything has been falling apart the entire time, and I don't want to believe for one second it could be better."

"Sounds to me like someone is afraid of optimism. And believing in people."

"I'm more afraid of," she paused. "Making my happiness the responsibility of one person or thing, you know? Because the festival and then oh, Mr. Webster, of course you want to turn it into a Christmas festival. And oh… *Oh.* I kissed someone and then he…"

Chana cocked her head, put her hand on her hip, and raised an eyebrow. "Kissed?"

Sarah nodded. "I did. I kissed him. And it was beautiful and then he made a decision I needed to know about and he didn't tell me."

"Did you talk to him?"

She shrugged. "I mean I tried. I didn't manage to. He texted."

And to head off any attempts at having this conversation for any longer, she led Chana away from the center of town, toward the lake where they were setting up the ice rink.

Brooklyn

HE'D FINISHED. ISAAC had finished. The menorah was done.

He sat against the wall in his area of the forge, looking critically at it. It was different than anything he'd ever done before, but the pieces were finally cool enough to touch and test. He'd hopefully managed to create something larger out of the smaller pieces and make a memory Hollowville could use forever.

And maybe at least one person could smile at.

He wiped his brow and grabbed a bottle of water from the counter, studying every weld, every curve and every cut he'd made. Twisting off the cap, he put the bottle to his lips and drank heavily. He finished the drink in barely one breath.

One more look at the final product of all of his hard work. And, yep, he'd done a good job, making what he'd set out to.

He was proud of himself.

He left the pieces together in his room, locked up behind himself and headed to his apartment for the first time in weeks. It was snowing in Brooklyn, white over the torn-up streets, kids running up and down on the sidewalks, grinning excitedly.

There were strings of lights on some of the brownstones and apartment buildings, menorahs and bright blue Jewish stars mingled with the red and green of Christmas. Winter in Brooklyn was beautiful and celebratory.

And as he headed into his building, he waved to everybody he met, passing the large Christmas tree and the beautiful menorah that stood side by side in the lobby, the dreidel and the stockings dancing together on the walls. He smiled as he sorted through the overflowing bits of his mailbox, a large pile full of gorgeous cards on expensive stock and flimsy notes and bright photograph paper. Then he headed upstairs and into his apartment, dropping the mail on his dining table.

The closest chair was comfortable and once he was seated, he pulled out his phone. It was yelling at him, of course; there were messages and emails galore. His voicemail was probably full, but he wasn't going to take care of those messages until later. Out of the corner of his eye, he saw the date. Only a few days till the festival and he was ready. He had leeway, not much, but enough to get the Menorah to the festival on time.

All he had to do was call someone.

Hmm.

Who was going to be able to help him get the menorah to Hollowville without incident? *That* was going to be key.

That and letting people know he hadn't fallen into the forge this time.

He wondered what Sarah would think of the finished menorah…Sarah and his *bubbe*. He wanted to call both of them. He knew Sarah was probably sleeping at this point, so he sent her a text.

Isaac: Done. Done. Done. It and I will see you soon. Miss you.

Instead of taking a risk and possibly waking up his grandmother with a too-late text, he decided to call her the next day, and instead order his dinner from the Thai place that was always open. After his food arrived, he'd eat then he'd sleep, but he'd set all the alarms in the world because he needed to get up on time. Hopefully he'd manage it.

Otherwise, he wouldn't be able to get the menorah to Hollowville the next morning. And if that couldn't happen, he'd be in serious trouble, the work he'd done completely worthless. As would his word, and his *bubbe's*. And the very last thing he wanted to do was to make his word worth nothing.

THERE WERE NOISES at the door. Loud ones.

Isaac blinked, ran a hand across his face, grabbed a sweat-shirt, and headed out of his bedroom to his dining table. It was early. He hadn't slept through an alarm, but the noises wouldn't stop.

"Coming," he said, hoping they were knocks.

He headed toward his door, opening the chain and then the lock before realizing all his friends stood on his doorstep. "Good morning?"

"We bring coffee and bagels," Liam said, poking Oliver in the ribs. "Jamie's leaving tomorrow for the fest, but she sent us to see where you were on the sculpture since you didn't talk to anybody."

Max smiled and put a large bag of bagels on the table. "Here you are. We need to eat and go to the forge."

"I finished yesterday. Home last night, couldn't tell you when though." The taste of the Pad Thai he'd eaten had been dust, but it was enough to satisfy his stomach. Now, looking at the bagels, he was ready to eat. "Juice anybody?"

Each of his friends shook their heads. "Nope. You can have your juice, thanks."

A little over an hour, and a shower later, the guys had made it to the forge, with Oliver going back to his apartment to tell Jamie the good news. Or, it would be good if his friends liked what Isaac had done.

The menorah was huge, perfect and gorgeous, as far as he was concerned. It could be easily disassembled so the town could annually store it, reassemble it and display it without worrying much about space. It was also easy to transport in a disassembled state. Which meant he'd need time and help onsite to put it together. All the same, he held his breath and waited.

"Wow, dude," Liam said. "I like it."

"The balance is fantastic," Max added. "Perfect."

Tom nodded. "Now all we have to do is figure out how to get it to Hollowville."

Which was the least of his problems. Sarah hadn't responded to his texts, and he had no idea what kind of welcome he'd get when he got to Hollowville. He hoped the menorah would be enough to sway the town in his direction.

And if it was, all he had to do was convince Sarah that he was serious about exploring what that kiss had started.

Chapter Twenty-Five

Hollowville

THERE WAS COFFEE to be drunk, conversations to be had, and Sarah was ready.

Of course, she wasn't ready for the three different groups from the temple choir who'd decided to sing Hanukkah songs on the streets of Hollowville a week before the festival or the lights and the "Happy Hanukkahs" that filled everybody's ears two days before the festival.

"Sarah." Jamie ran over to her, her eyes darting everywhere but at her.

"What's going on? Is everything okay?"

"Look. I really have to tell you something."

Sarah nodded, looking at the jewelry designer. "Okay?"

"Did you have a chance to talk to Isaac, tell him about the commemorative stuff?"

"I didn't," she said. "It's been so crazy here and I was worried the sculpture was going to fall through, and the festival itself still could and...it just wasn't something I thought of to say to him at any time."

Jamie nodded, bit her lip. "Well I didn't get a chance to

either, but it's probably something you should tell him at some point before he sees it. He knows Oliver did the logo, but we really haven't had a chance to talk since Thanksgiving. I've been working so hard to try and get things organized."

She tried not to allow her thoughts to travel down a road where everything was going to fall apart. "Do you know where he is?"

"Oliver and the guys have a separate car, they needed space for the menorah. One of them is driving and…" A pause as Jamie's phone buzzed and she looked down to check it. "They're parking somewhere. Oliver is sending me a pin of their location if you want to come with me."

"Okay," she said. "That's probably the best thing at this point." And all she could do was hope she'd catch him in time.

OLIVER PULLED INTO one of the spaces in the village parking lot, one that had a blue bag with gold writing over the meter.

"Sweeeet," Max said as he unbuckled his seat belt.

Isaac nodded. It was a Hanukkah parking miracle, something he hoped boded well for the rest of the day.

Except as he opened the door to get out, Trustee Webster was right there. The man wore flannel, weird circular glasses, a huge red hat with a pom-pom on it, and his beard looked like he'd spent hours on it.

"Hello, Trustee Webster," he said, despite his wish to ignore the man, or even worse, punch him into the middle of the nearby Hudson River. "What can I do you for?"

"It's not what you can do for me, Mr. Lieberm...Isaac, if you don't mind?"

He shrugged. Being petty with someone who could have an effect on the lives of those he cared about, even remotely, wasn't his idea of fun. "Sure," he said.

"More importantly, Isaac, it's what I can do for you."

He shoved a hand into the pocket of his coat. "Not sure I follow."

Webster nodded, folded his arms. "So there's a very interesting story going around town, and it says that you're making one of those candle things for the festival, right?"

Isaac nodded. "I made a menorah, yeah. It's ready to go. Just waiting for instructions on where to put it."

"That's so disorganized of the committee. Those people should know better about how to treat the person who's giving them a centerpiece they didn't have the means for."

"Not a question of means," he said. "Question of doing the right thing. People need to see symbols like a menorah, centered in a way that says they and the holidays they celebrate mean something."

"Holiday exclusivity, but let's not have this sort of same-word, different-thing conversation, shall we? I wanted to let you know that it's probably a bad idea to have worked so hard on the sculpture, only to find out that it's not needed."

The phrase 'holiday exclusivity' sounded wrong, but what really hit him in the gut was the back end. "What do you mean? Not needed?"

"Well," Webster said. "There's an interesting conversation to be had about this. Because of course, next year's festival isn't going to be a Hanukkah festival. Nope. It's going to focus on trees, and Santa and all the things that make other small town festivals special. So…" He smiled. "We won't need a candle thing. Which is why the committee—and this is the important part—has been using the logo on merchandise. Things you sell, things that you, and I may have heard wrong, but you don't like commercialization of the holiday. You don't like it when spirit gets exchanged for filthy *luchre*?"

The walls were closing in, the air leeching out of the atmosphere.

The logo Oliver made.

The logo he turned into a sculpture.

They were doing *what* with it?

But he had to be clearer. So he forced air into his lungs and asked the question. "Using the logo on what?"

"Selling things. Things that are…what's that word the advertising people make such a fuss about? Right. They're *branded* with the festival logo. So that the festival committee makes money for…profit for themselves once they no longer exist. Which means," Webster beamed, "you don't need to take that there candle thing out of that van. Because I figure they don't need it, and you don't want to associate with that kind of commerce anyway, right?"

"I..." He paused. Tried to make the whole thing make sense. Tried desperately to figure out what was happening and what he should do.

Disappointment and indecision warred in his head.

If that information had come from anybody else, his decision would have been clear. He would have gotten back in the car and brought the menorah back to Brooklyn.

But this was Webster, someone who'd been actively trying to destroy the Hanukkah festival and the spirit of those who cared about it. He had to be wrong. Had to be.

Had to be.

"Well," Webster continued, a look on his face that made Isaac want to punch him, no matter what the consequences would be. "If you won't take my word for it, there are people you can speak to, you know, to confirm what I'm telling you. They may not like to, but they will."

With that, the trustee turned on his heel and walked away, seemingly uncaring about the trouble and pain he left in his wake. And leaving Isaac well aware he had to ask some questions he didn't want answers to.

SARAH WAS STARTING to panic. She and Jamie were heading

toward the pin, and the parked car. She desperately hoped she had enough time to find Isaac before someone else did.

"Now where are you going so quickly, Miss Vice Chair? I mean if I were you I wouldn't be in such a rush. Especially on a day like this one."

Webster. Standing in front of her, forcing her to act as if she'd put on a mask. She couldn't show him panic. "Sorry, Trustee Webster," she said. "So much to do and so little time."

"Especially when you might not have that candle menorah whatever in the end."

She swallowed. "I… What did you say?"

Webster shrugged. "I couldn't help but look through the papers you gave me…rather the board of trustees at the last meeting; very educational actually. And I remember the conversation at that ridiculous restaurant that has way too little eggnog. Anyway."

"I'm not sure I follow, but continue."

"Well, the most important thing is that your sculptor needed to know that you were using the logo to sell commemorative items. Basically, that you were operating on a plan that didn't take a sculpture into account, so you didn't need him or his work."

She bit her tongue, trying to compose herself somehow.

"Speechless, I take it? Yes. I know. You gave me good information, and I am so very glad you do your due diligence and ensure that your committee has an interest in keeping the board of trustees informed of all these very smart details." He paused and smiled in a way that felt like he was stabbing her. "And by the way, you should probably follow your friend because the sculptor is standing in the parking lot, not very far from here."

And instead of saying anything further, he left, whistling a Christmas tune she'd heard just that morning. And this time, parody lyrics about menorahs and applesauce didn't make her feel better. They made her feel worse.

ISAAC'S HEART POUNDED as he saw Sarah walk up the stairs toward the parking lot. Jamie and Oliver were having a conversation, and it wasn't going well. Max and Tom were standing back, not sure what to do.

"Sarah," he said as she approached. "I am so glad to see you. Just tell me that what Webster told me was a mistake, that you're not selling merchandise."

"Isaac," she said, pain flying across her face. "I can explain..."

His heart stopped. "You didn't tell me."

"When?" she asked. What was that in her voice? Was she confused? Apologetic? Angry? "When was I supposed to tell you? In response to the random texts you sent me at like two a.m.? In a letter I gave to your *bubbe*? Where you told everybody but me—"

"I told two people. I told Oliver, and I told my grandmother. I told my grandmother so she could walk into the council meeting. I also sent you an email. Or did you not check that?"

"You had my phone number. You could *call* or text me if I'm not responding."

"I didn't want to disturb you. I *never* want to bother you."

"That's lovely, but when you wanted to do something before you had no trouble calling or texting."

"But you knew. You knew how I felt about commercializing the holiday, and as soon as you thought I was going to make this menorah—"

"You told me nothing. How could I even pull out of thin air that you were going to make this menorah? I asked. You said no."

"I asked you tell me the *history* of a festival I'd wanted to nothing to do with. It should have occurred to you that something was going on."

"I thought you were interested in my perspective, not doing something you'd been vehemently against." She threw her hands up in the air and he tried not to notice the tears at the corners of her eyes. "Someone confronted you at the train station. The very last thing I wanted to do was come within twenty feet of asking you about the festival."

"But you were always different," he said. "You were always special. I asked you about the festival. You showed me a map and we walked the festival setup. You should have asked me about the sculpture."

"We were having fun; you kissed me. And all I thought was that we were getting to know each other, learning about each other."

Isaac shook his head. "Most important thing about that statement is the tense. Whatever was happening between us? It's over. Past."

He tried not to see the way she shook herself as if trying to pull herself together. "I guess my first impression of you was right. You're a Hanukkah snob. Just like your mother."

And then for the second time that day, someone turned and walked away from him.

Chapter Twenty-Six

SARAH CLOSED THE door of her apartment behind her and reached for the first blanket she could find, then put it down when she realized it was covered with menorahs. Then she got up and went into the kitchen, turning on the burner and making herself a cup of tea.

Halfway through her third cup, the sound of the buzzer went off, and she got up to tell whoever it was that she wasn't fit for company. "Go away," she said into the speaker.

"I've come with Chinese, and you're turning me away?"

The sound of her best friend's voice made her burst into tears. She pressed the button, letting her friend up, and then headed to unlock the door.

"I came as soon as I could," Anna confessed as she put her arms around Sarah. "Chana couldn't find you, and Elsa told her what happened, and so here I am."

As angry as she was with so many in the town, she couldn't be angry to see her friend. "Thank you," she said. "I—"

"You're a mess. I see. Something happened?"

The simple kindness of her friend's words triggered another round of tears. When she'd gotten halfway through telling the story of what had happened, the shock on her friend's face surprised even her. "What, Anna?" she asked. "What's got you so surprised that made you ignore your soup?"

Her best friend shook her head. "You didn't think he was debating for a second when he told you he wanted to see the festival grounds?"

"*I'm on* the festival committee; I'm supposed to talk about the festival. I thought he was indulging me. You know, reputation as the Hanukkah fairy and all of that?"

"He'd been so against it, Sarah." Anna sighed and swiped a bite of her egg roll. "And I adore you, but also think he fell in love with other things, so he decided to listen to you about the festival."

"We were…deliberately not talking about the festival."

"What, when he said *can you tell me the festival history and show me how it began*?"

"I honestly just thought he was indulging me," Sarah said, taking a long drink of her tea. "I mean especially after what happened at the train station and what people had done to him in the past."

"He did a great deal of festival history research for someone who wasn't going to involve themselves in the festival, hmm?"

That was interpretation, wasn't it? She'd wrapped herself in the feeling of him so much that she didn't second-guess anything, or leave it up to analysis, she admitted. "I was enjoying spending so much time with him that I didn't want to make him feel uncomfortable because I misinterpreted what he was interested in." And then it was time for her to drop the bombshell. "Especially after he kissed me."

Anna closed her eyes and covered them with her palms before blowing out a breath and shaking her head in what looked like exasperation. "Oh my God. You two are going to be the couple that ends up fighting because neither of you knows how to communicate. Like seriously. Neither of you seems to know how to use words."

Sarah paused, looked at her friend, confused. "I have to admit that this seems an interesting turn of events. You're usually upset that I hide behind the festival to ignore and avoid romantic relationships."

"Whatever it is," Anna said, "all of it ties into the problem where you need to stop being afraid and talk about what you want. If you don't talk about it with people, it's never going to happen."

Something in Anna's eyes stood out and made Sarah nervous. "You okay?"

Anna sighed then nodded. "Just being back in Rockliffe with my family for Thanksgiving has given me a bunch of feelings I'm not sure how to deal with."

Sarah raised an eyebrow. "Like what kind of feelings?"

"First loves, missed opportunities and things I thought I'd buried in the past. But I spend way too much time dealing with history to not brace myself for anything."

"I'm sorry," she said. But hey, food was their love language, and Anna was obsessed with wontons. "Here. Have another wonton."

"I will, actually." The smile that had appeared on her friend's face dissipated for a moment as she took the wonton from the container. "But I have to tell you how important it is to talk about what you want instead of assuming it's there."

"I promise," she said. That was the best she could say.

Long after Anna left, Sarah sat under the blanket on the couch, a movie on her television. She clicked on her email program and scrolled down, trying to find the contents that came into her inbox on the day of the meeting, including the one she couldn't open.

And miracle of miracles, she was able to open it.

It was from Isaac.

Sarah,

I waited to send this email until the last possible minute, I know. I shouldn't have.

But the last thing I wanted to do is raise your expectations or your hopes, especially now that both have become so important for me.

I wanted to tell you that I'm in the middle of a menorah I think I'll be able to finish by the festival. I wanted my plan to be clear before I told anybody, let alone you, in the event I started and the concept didn't work.

My grandmother also knows and she will be delivering the information to the board of trustees tonight.

I hope you like it when you see it,
Isaac.

She'd had trouble sleeping before but she knew it was going to be worse now. Because now she had no idea how to fix what had been broken, what she'd broken. But tomorrow was another day, right?

Right.

BUBBE HAD GUEST rooms and space in her garage, and so once he, Max, Tom, and Liam put the menorah in her garage, leaving Jamie and Oliver to talk, Isaac headed inside.

Of course, *Bubbe* expected him. And his friends. The dinner table was set, latkes were frying on the stove, a Caf and Nosh box on the counter.

"Oy, *tateleh*," his *bubbe* said as he stepped into the room. "I suspect you heard what happened."

He didn't expect very much less than that; Hollowville's gossip chain was at it again, and he'd shoved his *bubbe* in the middle of it...unless she was the gossip chain.

"You know," *Bubbe* continued, "you let down so many people who were counting on you."

"I didn't want to tell anybody," he said. "I just didn't want to make any waves. Didn't want anybody to depend on me. It's why I didn't really say anything because I didn't know whether it would happen."

"Yes, *tateleh*. But once you squeeze the toothpaste out of the tube, you can't put it back. Once people hear you're doing something, you're obligated to follow through."

He nodded. Sighed as his bubbe flipped a few latkes. "I just...the first sign of trouble and she doubts my intentions."

"What makes you think she doubted your intentions, *tateleh*?"

"She didn't tell me they were selling commercial items, which is the reason I didn't want anything to do with the festival at the beginning, and she knew that."

His *bubbe* shook her head and took a few of the latkes out of the pan. "There are two reasons why the committee's doing the merchandise, *tateleh*. First, you said no. They had to do something to give the people, to remember the day, to make a festival for next year and give a little *tzedakah* around Hanukkah. And there's one other thing."

He nodded, taking in his bubbe's words and the lessons she was trying to impart.

"You know that Webster man wants to end the festival. He's close. If there's no menorah tomorrow, even though Fitzgerald won't give a tree, someone will. Someone who doesn't want our festival to exist. And so those pieces, the ones with the logo, they're there to remind people that there was a festival." She sighed, ruffled his hair. "You have to listen when people speak, listen to what they don't say. Webster wanted that menorah to be gone. And he was gleeful all over town when he succeeded."

He swallowed, glad he hadn't taken any of the iced tea his friends were drinking.

"And he rubbed in that there wasn't going to be a menorah. He rubbed in that the committee can't be trusted when they tell people things."

He swallowed again. "Oh God."

"Exactly. Now how can you fix it?"

He had thoughts and he had ideas. And he had a lot to take care of before he'd be able to pull it all together.

Chapter Twenty-Seven

THE NEXT MORNING, the last day before the festival, Sarah was helping Chana, Carol, and Dr. Rodriguez set up the bookselling and reading corner. She figured it was time to explain what had been going on to the trio of older women in her life.

When she'd finished telling the story, Carol was laughing and Dr. Rodriguez was rolling her eyes.

Chana, however, was smiling. "You called him a snob. I can't believe it."

"What?"

"You actually called the sculptor a snob. Not that I blame you, of course."

"Yes, Chana," Carol interjected, rolling her eyes. "I was going to say something if you didn't make it clear you agreed with her."

"I did." Chana shrugged and straightened a bunch of picture books. "If he hadn't followed through on his commitment to bring the menorah, there would be other words for him, but he did, so we're fine."

"Where is that menorah of his anyway?" Dr. Rodriguez

asked. "It's not here."

"Filling up Elsa's garage, of course," Carol said, with the kind of authority in her tone that made it clear she'd spoken with Mrs. Lieberman. Then she turned towards Dr. Rodriguez.

"Speaking of the garage, remind me, Mare, that I need to go in mine and get the rest of my ornaments."

"Wonderful place to be asking that, Carol," Chana said, "But don't worry. By the time you're done with today, the town will remind you, *bubeleh.* Now. Where were we, because," Chana turned her laser-sharp gaze on her, as if she'd thought she'd escaped the reckoning, "we seem to have quiet on the Sarah/Isaac front. So, *nu*, why did you call him a snob? That's why I'm so curious."

"Well," she said thinking about her randomly tossed insult, "to be fair, the first time I met him, he was a snob. And so is his mother."

"Why or how Elsa Lieberman's son married that woman," Carol interjected, "I will never ever know."

Dr. Rodriguez nodded. "I'm not one to gossip," she began as Chana and Carol started to laugh, "but honestly, she's so completely different from Elsa or Elsa's late husband, it's positively unreal."

"And," added Chana, "Elsa is the member of his family he spends the most time with—she's the one he loves most. And she's the person he models himself after."

Chana's words sank into her head, and Sarah found herself thinking of all the time she'd spent with Isaac and the person he was. The love he had for his grandmother, the way he talked about her and how often he was in town to spend time with her. The things he'd said about his parents were like grains of rice you could see on the floor; small snippets of a life you knew existed, but not as substantive as you thought they'd be.

She sighed. "Yes. He does."

"So, what was the problem, really?"

Sarah found herself thinking again about that moment between her and Isaac, when things went awry. "He didn't like the fact that I didn't tell him about the commemorative stuff. He didn't like that we were doing it."

This time, it was Carol who raised her hand. "Sarah, love, I really need to know. What do you think bothered him the most? That the committee was doing the commemorative stuff? Or that he heard that first from Webster and maybe not the only person who could make it make sense to him?"

"A little bit of both," she replied. "Because we wouldn't have done any kind of branded commemorative stuff if we knew from the beginning there was going to be a sculpture."

"So," Dr. Rodriguez said, "seems to me that all of this could have been fixed if all of you could communicate. Or," she smiled. "At least deal with in a way that could have ensured a clearer understanding of how everybody felt."

Make your feelings clearer. Don't hide behind festivals or

romance instead of telling people how you feel. And listen to others when they tried. That she could do. And that would be how she'd fix the trouble she'd done her fair share to help cause.

"WELL," TOM SAID as the guys all sat down to coffee after dinner, "what's the story? How are we going to play this?"

Isaac settled onto the couch, taking his water glass. "So," he said to both Oliver and Jamie. "I understand why you didn't tell me about the merchandise, and I realize that there's a reason for it."

Jamie nodded, squeezing Oliver's hand. "They thought the festival was over," she said. "And you weren't doing anything. There wasn't a reason to tell you until it was too late."

"I'm sorry for not listening to you, either of you." His *bubbe* snorted. "All of you."

"It's a start," Oliver said.

"And I'm going to try to be a better communicator, using email when I think your phones are off."

It was now Max's turn to snort, but for some reason this one made him laugh. "If you stick to it, I'm good with it."

Then, it was time for the next question. "So who do we talk to about the menorah?"

"Well if you haven't dropped and broken it in a fit of

pique," his *bubbe* said, "I'll text Chana and make sure the place that was cleared for it isn't covered by something else."

There was an ominous silence in the room, and Isaac knew it was his fault. "I'm sorry."

"You're cleaning up the mess," his grandmother said. "That's what's important. You fix what you broke and you'll save the day."

Isaac nodded and listened to his friends and his *bubbe* as they continued to make plans. Tomorrow would be a wonderful day for miracles and menorahs, if he had any say in it.

Chapter Twenty-Eight

ON THE DAY of the festival, Sarah got up to powder-sugar snow falling just outside the window, only to discover her alarm hadn't gone off.

She took a quick shower and dressed in most of her Hanukkah armor. Her '*I'm Menorahble*' T-shirt, jeans, and her fuzzy menorah socks were first, followed by a Hanukkah sweater. Then she put on makeup, her favorite pair of menorah earrings, covered her jacket with dreidel pins, and grabbed her brand-new dreidel-shaped messenger bag.

Once the bag was settled, she stepped into a pair of comfy boots and opened the door only to discover her mother there, waiting. With coffee cups.

"I love you," Sarah said.

"This is perfect," her mother said, holding out what Sarah hoped to be a soofi latte.

Despite everything, Sarah had to admit her mother was right. The day itself looked like a snow globe, and, hopefully the festival would run the way it was supposed to. The storyteller, the vendors, the games, the skating—it would run according to plan. Most importantly, at sundown, everybody would go to the center of town to celebrate with the official ribbon cutting and the blessings, even if they didn't have a large enough menorah to light.

But as much as she tried to convince herself otherwise, there was something missing and she didn't know how to fix it. Except take a long drink of her latte, drowning herself in the caffeine and the sugar.

"You ready?"

She wasn't. "Yes," she said, because she needed to at least try to convince herself. "I'm ready. And it will be perfect."

And if it wasn't, she'd fake it until she made it. Or at least she'd try.

ISAAC WAS EXHAUSTED.

But he, Oliver, Liam, Tom, and Max had managed to arrive at the spot the menorah was supposed to go pretty early on the first day of the festival.

Except when they got out of the van to begin the process of unloading and assembling the structure, they found Trustee Webster, standing in the center, holding long, thin boxes.

"What are you doing?" Chana, the committee chair, asked, making it clear she was glaring at Webster.

"We have trees," he said, waving his hand at the boxes. "And we're going to put them up like we should, considering there's no menorah to put here."

"Well," Isaac replied, gesturing in the general direction of the van, "we do have a menorah."

"But don't you need a permit to burn things, you know fire codes and all," Webster said, smirking as if he knew everything. Which was his entire problem.

"Electric lights," Isaac replied, "covered with jars large enough to protect the bulbs."

"Still have to get the menorah out, and there are trees." Petty people like Webster were dangerous, Isaac decided, and as his friends stood trying to figure out how to deal with the problem, there was another voice that joined the crowd.

"What are you doing, Trustee?"

"Mayor Erlichman, hello. I was just putting up some trees, you know, to fill the space the committee wasn't able to."

The gentleman who was the mayor looked at him. "I see, and you, sir?"

"Isaac Lieberman…"

"Yep. Moshe and I were friends in school, all those years ago. Haven't seen him in years, but I see him in you."

Which was the most random thing to say, but again, small towns were like that. "I'll tell my father you asked after him when I see him next. He's on a cruise with my mother right now."

"Nice. I've never been on one," the mayor replied with a grin. "I get seasick."

"Mayor," said both Chana and Trustee Webster at the same time, in what Isaac saw as an attempt to get things back on track.

"Mrs. Levitan, Trustee Webster. I see you both," said the mayor, smiling. "So the way I see the situation right now is that there are trees obstructing the space reserved for the menorah."

"Yes," Chana said. "The trustee obtained the space by fraudulent means and is now attempting to use his own personal desires to obstruct the assembly of the menorah."

"The chairwoman is attempting to illegally influence you, Mayor, as well as establish a menorah in the square where the trees are supposed to go."

The mayor rolled his eyes and turned to Isaac. "So there are trees obstructing the space reserved for the menorah?"

Isaac got the hint and nodded. "Yes, your honor. The space I was told was reserved for the menorah has trees in it."

"Webster, the trees are not welcome in this space or in this town."

"But, Mayor, *you* have a tree, and we all should—"

"Webster," continued the mayor, "my own tree is irrelevant to this conversation. But even more importantly, I also don't take kindly to the way I've heard you've been interfering in this process. We like to have different voices on the board of trustees, but you have to think twice about whether outright sabotage of an event before a decision is made is a good thing for a board member to do. I definitely don't think it's a good example, especially when you are supposedly a member of our church in good standing."

Webster's face went read, and it looked like he was ready to explode. Instead he paused and let out a breath. "I'll take time to think about it, but most likely I'll tender my resignation from the board in the New Year."

The mayor nodded. "I think that might be best."

And as Webster walked away, the committee chair and the mayor smiled at his friends and his *bubbe*. "I think," the mayor said, "we have a menorah to assemble."

Isaac nodded. "We do."

After the menorah was assembled and placed in the designated spot, the library director, Dr. Rodriguez, stared at them.

"What, ma'am?" he asked.

"Can't believe you pulled it off." She shook her head. "Shouldn't have doubted you or Elsa."

"Thank you," he said, smiling. "I appreciate your faith in me."

"Faith in your grandmother," said Carol, the woman who'd gotten him and his friends to organize the library for Dr. Abraham's signing back in October. She held her hands as if she was two steps away from strangling him. Because of course, the other detail he'd managed to forget was that this woman was also the owner of the bookstore, aka Sarah's boss there. "Faith in you depends on how you fix the heart you broke."

Tom and Liam nodded, much to his surprise. "You messed up, dude," Liam said, "and hopefully you're as good at crafting apologies as you are at crafting metal."

He laughed as they covered the menorah with a tarp to hide it from prying eyes.

He just hoped it, and what he had planned, would impress the right person.

THE FIRST FULL day of the festival was simply perfect.

Mostly.

People started to run the dreidel races on the lawn of the high school, others ventured down to the lake to try out the ice skating, and from what Sarah had heard, the brand-new hot chocolate booths were doing a pretty rapid business.

As was the redesigned food area. Some of the restaurants were even reporting that some of the attendees would order food from a booth and then run into the restaurant for more, but in a heated location with a closed door.

The lack of doors didn't discourage the jewelry vendors, especially the ones running specials for people who'd waited until the festival to go last-minute shopping.

But when the sun went down and the stars came out, everybody gathered in the center of town, near a covered item. Sarah had no idea what it was, but she hoped, she wished. She'd tried to enjoy the festival, even with the questions people asked her as a member of the committee, even with her fears she'd messed everything up. But now she stood, listening to the HHC choir sing a beautiful song about the reason the lights in the menorah were bright in the first place.

As they sang, the mayor, Chana, and the rabbi from HHC walked up to the dais.

"Tonight," announced the mayor, "marks the tenth anniversary of the Hollowville Hanukkah festival. The town of Hollowville is proud to host a festival that can serve as a beacon of light in the darkness. We are a town, we are a family, and we are friends. And we have come together to celebrate the first of eight nights of Hanukkah.

"And we would also like to confirm the fact that next year's festival," the mayor continued, "will in fact be a *Hanukkah* festival. Despite everything you may have heard, Hollowville will continue to be a place where people all over the world, and from right here in town, can gather to celebrate the festival of lights."

Chana smiled, and from her spot next to Anna in the crowd, Sarah held her breath.

"Ten years ago, Mayor, you opened the town, you opened the space for a small festival," Chana said. "With help from friends and neighbors, the festival grew. And we grew with it. Our hopes and our hearts are intertwined with the community, and as a thank you…"

Sarah took a deep breath. "Oh my gosh," she whispered.

"I want to invite Mr. Isaac Lieberman to the stage. He's the grandson of Elsa Lieberman, a longtime Hollowville resident. He's also a prominent sculptor. Mr. Lieberman will present a gift from the Hollowville Hebrew Center and the Hollowville Hanukkah festival committee to the town of Hollowville."

The entire crowed cheered, and Sarah couldn't breathe. She grabbed Anna's hand.

Isaac emerged wearing a hat almost identical to the one she wore when they spent the day together walking around Hollowville. Bright blue, fluffy, and tall atop his head. He had never looked more handsome.

"Good evening, everybody—*chag sameach* and happy Hanukkah. I want to thank the entire committee, the town of Hollowville, my beloved grandmother, and my friends for all the help all of you have given me as I embarked on this journey. It wasn't an easy one because in order to complete it, I needed to understand how important Hanukkah is to Hollowville. I needed to learn, like a very wise person told me, that to Hollowville, Hanukkah isn't a time to hide. And like the holiday it celebrates, the Hanukkah festival is a time to share, in a way that lets Hollowville serve as a beacon in the darkness. To give light to those who need it. And it was someone important who taught me all of these lessons."

She held her breath.

"So, it is my deepest honor and with utmost gratitude, to present this beautiful menorah to the town of Hollowville.

May it take all of you from strength to strength."

And as he lifted the cover, she burst into tears.

HE SAW SARAH'S tears from the stage and desperately wanted to dry them, but running down from the dais in the middle of the ceremony, in the middle of a speech, was a horrible idea. So, he forced himself to focus on the menorah, on the hours he'd spent welding and cutting and working the metal.

Then he watched the rabbi lead the blessings and twist the bulbs into place. He held his breath as they said the *shehecheyanu*, the prayer celebrating the chance they had to do something for the first time. He was so lucky he had the chance to be anywhere near Sarah now, to know her. He couldn't wait to tell her.

And when the protective jar went over the last lit bulb, he took a deep breath of relief. It worked.

Then he was free, heading down into the crowd almost immediately, without pausing and a barely polite greeting to those who knew him because his destination was clear. He had to say some important things to someone who mattered the most to him in the world.

To Sarah.

But she found him first; she stopped suddenly in the middle of the aisle before throwing her arms around him. He pulled her close, letting her relax in the safety of his arms.

But words were important. Telling her how he felt was important. And he needed to start the process then if they had a chance, which he desperately hoped they did. "You were right, Sarah. You were absolutely right, and I was an unmitigated snob."

She tensed, then looked up at him, her eyes wide as if she couldn't believe what she was hearing. But then her shoulders released just a fraction, and she looked away from him, swallowed as if she was concerned.

"I didn't listen," she said, sniffing as she looked back up at him. "I didn't listen; I didn't read your email. And I didn't tell you what I was feeling either. I was so scared to break the bubble I thought we had, that I didn't even recognize the possibility of you wanting to make this beautiful menorah. I was scared to even confront it. But *you're here* and you're wearing that gorgeous, funny, ridiculous hat."

"Just to see that smile on your face, I'd jump into a vat of sour cream."

She laughed—oh God, she laughed, and he'd say ridiculous things to make her laugh forever.

"But seriously," he said. "You like the hat?"

She nodded, grinning back at him. "It looks great on you. You know what else looks great on you?"

"What?"

She leaned closer, her breath on his neck. "You," she said. "Everything. The truth is that you're amazing, and I cannot wait to get to see more layers of you, find different facets of you."

He cupped her cheek with his gloved hand. "Just so you know, trains between here and the city run semi regularly, and you know the subway also runs a lot."

"They do." He felt the gloved tips of her fingers as they moved up his neck. "There are also car services of all sorts that cover that distance."

"And," he said as he bent his head down, following the unspoken instructions she'd given him with the whisper touch of her fingers on the back of his head, "my grandmother lives here."

She laughed. "That is true," she said once she recovered. "Maybe I can do some advance scouting in Brooklyn for events. Maybe see your forge?"

"And maybe…we can celebrate more, learn a bit?"

Sarah nodded. "I love this idea. You know what I also love?"

"What?"

She smiled at him. "You." Then, without any further ado, she kissed him.

In the basking glow of the candles, he kissed her back, tasting sweet fried soofganiyot and forever.

The End

If you enjoyed Sarah and Isaac's story, please support the author and leave a review!

Join Tule Publishing's newsletter for more great reads and weekly deals!

Dear Reader,

There were no Hanukkah festivals harmed in the making of this book.

But that's because I've never been to a Hanukkah festival. I've been to small gatherings in a temple, shared moments with friends frying latkes. But nothing ever this big.

My vision of Hollowville's festival was pieced together from many moments and ideas I've seen over the years. A community gathering at the Warner Library and Temple Beth Abraham in the wake of Hurricane Sandy, Temple Beth Abraham's bright and fun Purim Carnival, the various large menorahs displayed in Brooklyn and Manhattan, and all of the Christmas festivals I've seen or witnessed personally.

Which meant that a Hanukkah festival is plausible, and that was the most important thing to me, the vision of light in the darkness as I wrote this story.

Because one of the major themes I've tried to explore is how Hanukkah is a light in the darkness. A beacon for those who need it in difficult times. Especially in a small town like Hollowville.

As Rabbi Danya Ruttenberg wrote in an article that appeared in the *Washington Post* as I was revising this story:

> (A visible menorah in the window) is an invitation to others to find us, and to stand with and for us. To let everyone know that they are not alone, and that we are all in this together.[1]

Like the visible menorahs we Jews place in our windows, the Hollowville Hanukkah festival, and the story of Sarah, Isaac, and the rest of their communities is my beacon to you. May you find love, happiness, and miracles in this book.

Thank you for reading.

Stacey

---

[1] https://www.washingtonpost.com/outlook/2019/12/18/hanukkah-calls-jews-light-darkness-this-year-we-need-it-even-more/

Acknowledgements

This book took a village. From beginning to end, so many people stood with me.

To Lorna Michaels and Alina Adams. You paved the path I walk upon, and I will be always thankful and grateful. I definitely stand on the shoulders of giants. May you always go from strength to strength.

To Megan Hart, Rose Lerner, Zoe Archer. You are inspirations and so very talented. I am so lucky to know all of you, let alone write in the same genre. ♥

Sara Rider, Laura Brown, Miranda Wolfe, Melanie Ting, and Michelle Lawson read tons of this story as I wrote it.

Isabo Kelly helped me figure out the pieces and has listened to me talk about what became the foundation of this story.

Jennifer Gracen and Kim Rocha held my hand as I sent this book out.

Vivi Parish and Jeannie Moon held me upright as I figured out what to do when Jane Porter and Meghan Farrell said they believed in me and this book.

Jessica Sinisheimer, LaQuette, Alexis Daria, JN Welsh, Adriana Herrera, Kwana Jackson, Laura Curtis, Patty Blount, Meara Platt, Wendy LaCapra, Alys Murray and

Falguni Kothari kept me calm and answered questions like the amazing friends they are. I am so lucky to know all of them. ♥

Lynnette Novak took a chance on me and my wild ideas.

Julie Sturgeon and Jenny Silver were the dream team as the book went into production.

Lee Hyat made my cover dreams come true!

Felicia Grossman held my hand as I revised and reminded me why I was writing this book. It's not an understatement to say I don't think I would have finished without her.

To the Schmoozers: I am so glad we have our space to talk about good things and bad, good times and bad, and to just be ourselves. Kol ha Kavod. ♥

Being around Lucy Eden, Joanna Hart, Eliza Luce, Marina Garcia, Lory Wendy, Charlotte Welsh and Rhonda Merewarth inspires me. Looking forward to sharing more words and more moments with all of you.

Lydia SanAndres was always up for a fun adventure and answered more questions about museum curators than I care to admit. Looking forward to more fun adventures and I am so very lucky we're friends.

Tamsen Parker, Zoe York, AJ Cousins, Jane Lee Baird, Kelly Maher, Suleikha Snyder, Olivia Dade, Ruby Lang, Emma Barry, Isabo Kelly *yes I'm thanking you twice* Cassandra Carr, Heather Lire, Laura Hunsaker, KK Hendin, Megan Hart, Jennifer Gracen *yes you also get thanked twice* and anybody else who I've been in an anthology with. One of the reasons I love anthologies so much is the people I've met along the way. I'm so lucky I've gotten to know all of you through this process. ♥

Scott Rosen, Sabrina Schmidt, Devon Wambold and Roxanne Wasliuk listened to me talk about the book at many, many concerts, and helped me broaden my playlists. Looking forward to sharing even more. To Leanna Hieber and Elizabeth Mahon. We've been friends for so long, I'm so very glad get to share this with you too. ♥

Marnie McMahon, Megan Walski: so much has changed since we met, but our friendship has only gotten stronger. I am one of the luckiest people in the world because you two are my friends.

To Russ Agdern, Marisa Harford. The two of you make me think, smile, and so very proud to be your family. You bring light, music and love to my life.

To Elijah. Your smile makes me smile and spending time with you is one of the most amazing things I get to do. Auntie Stacey loves you. ♥

To Jane and Barry Agdern, the most supportive and amazing parents. It is because of you I know the words, the story, and the inspiration. And it is because of you I have a voice.

To everybody else I've met along the way, thank you. Every single word in this story is the result of a journey I've taken. And I'm glad you've come along with me.

About the Author

Stacey Agdern is an award-winning former bookseller who has reviewed romance novels in multiple formats and given talks about various aspects of the romance genre. She incorporates Jewish characters and traditions into her stories so that people who grew up like she did can see themselves take center stage on the page. She's also a member of both LIRW and RWA NYC. She lives in New York, not far from her favorite hockey team's practice facility.

Thank you for reading

Miracles and Menorahs

If you enjoyed this book, you can find more from all our great authors at TulePublishing.com, or from your favorite online retailer.

TULE

PUBLISHING

Made in the USA
Middletown, DE
01 December 2022

16643985R00194